Mediums Guild

Mediums Guild

Lee Fishman

TransMedia Press
Philadelphia, PA

Library of Congress Cataloging-Publication Data on File

ISBN 978-0-9820255-6-7
ebook ISBN 978-0-9820255-7-4

www.leefishman.net

TransMedia Publishing Group
Philadelphia, PA

For Bob and Mary

"Always be the pilot not the passenger."

Dr. Peebles

1

The crowd, boisterous and high spirited, milled around the entrance to Monahan Hall. Though Halloween was still a few days off, anticipation was in the air and the students were keen to get inside. Unfortunately, the Hayden College Psychic Fair was running a little late.

It was ten past seven when Alisha and I hustled our way through. We knocked, waiting while the student manager opened the door a crack. She checked us off the list on her clipboard and we squeezed inside. "Everyone else is here." She said. "You're the last to arrive." Past her shoulder I saw all the other members of the Mediums Guild settled in, ready to work.

"Sorry, we made a wrong turn." I said. Actually it wasn't "we" it was me. I always try to get an early start just in case I get lost. But that fall night the moon rose so full, so orange, so intense it distracted Alisha and me. Off the Expressway exit, I went left instead of right and we ended up in the middle of nowhere.

Alisha waved hello to the three tarot readers, two palm readers and one astrologer already seated along the edges of Monahan Hall's basketball court. Then she made a beeline for the last free table near the bleachers. That meant I was stuck with the table nobody wanted, right under the basketball net. Not ideal. It's already weird enough doing readings in a gym without a hoop dangling overhead.

Across the room, Zara, our astrologer caught my eye. She pointed to the gaudy team pennants and sports memorabilia that hung down from the rafters. Half amused, half resigned, her expression said it all. When I laughed, she shrugged as if to say, "What can you do?"

I'd just set my bag down when a student assistant checked her watch and asked if we were ready. I begged for one more minute. She gave a quick nod and I tossed my brocade cloth over the tabletop, placing crystals here and there. I unwrapped my tarot deck, sorting through in search of the "Death" card with its somber image. The card has many possible meanings. It could symbolize rebirth, liberation transformation, or renewal. Still, college students don't much relate to the concept and they sure don't like the graphic illustration. Over the course of an evening, you can almost count on one young diva to plunk herself down and say, "Please, don't tell me when I'm going to die!" Trust me, I won't. Not that I ever could. Still, to be on the safe side, I slipped the scary card from the deck and put it away, glad for one less thing to worry about.

I lit a thick white candle, sat back, and caught my breath. For the next three hours we would work with just two things certain: Number One, student romance would be the hot topic. Number Two, there would be no tips for readings.

When Alisha let me know she was ready, I waved back, gesturing for her to stand so I could see what she was wearing. She'd had her coat on in the car. Her dress, maroon velvet, was striking and the gold threads holding back her dark hair added sparkle. I looked down at my usual black, hoping the new scarf at my throat, green and glittery with sequins kicked it up a little. People always tell me green is my color. It brings out my eyes.

The student manager cleared her throat. We all looked ready so I gave a "thumbs up" and the doors swung open. For the price of one ticket, undergrads could have their cards or their palms read. For the adventurous with two tickets, Alisha described details of their past lives. Students who purchased three tickets and knew the date and time of their birth might leave with a full natal chart from our astrologer.

Early arrivals, freshman by their look, wandered in and began to circulate. Three giggling girls sauntered by. Drifting from table to table, they dared each other to be the first to see what the future held. Boys in team jackets hung back, lurking near the door, mugging and cracking wise to cover their jitters. Still a wariness around their eyes showed that it wasn't all a joke to them.

The first hour or so I fielded questions about campus hook-ups and speculated on good choices for majors. Once I'd worked through a dozen readings back-to-back, I was ready for a break. I stood and stretched, put my "Back in Five Minutes" sign on the table and made for the door. At Alisha's table, I noticed a tall, thin man with a military haircut. His serious expression told me he wasn't a student. A professor? A dean? Not likely. He seemed seriously out of place. As I strode past, she gestured for him to sit. I'd definitely have to ask her about that one later.

As the evening wore on, upperclassmen arrived. Chattering girls in matching hoodies from Alpha Gamma Alpha sorority surrounded our tables, leaving us no chance to think about anything else. The rest of the evening flew by.

By ten o'clock the crowd thinned and the student manager chased the stragglers from the gym. Tired but happy, we packed our gear, and Alisha and I dragged ourselves out to the parking lot, anxious to get home. It was getting late and we both had regular jobs to go to in the morning.

Alisha brought a baggie stuffed with trail mix. She passed it over and I grabbed a handful and passed it back. We munched in silence for a few minutes to recharge our batteries. Then I remembered something. "Who was that guy, the one that looked like a Boy Scout leader?"

"I don't know where he came from. He just appeared. Looked like a cop, didn't he?"

"What did he want? Wait, don't tell me. Stupid psychic tricks?" That's what Alisha calls it when people come up to her and demand that she tell them what year they were born, how many children they have or how many fingers they're holding up behind their backs.

I started the car, checked the rearview and pulled onto the dark campus street. Figuring no traffic, we had a twenty-five minute drive home to Philadelphia.

"He just moved his family to a new house," Alisha said. "Guess it's an old house really, but they're hearing doors slam, seeing puffs of smoke where there's no fire. The kids said they heard voices. He's worried. The wife is scared. He asked if I would come and check it out."

"What did you tell him? You didn't make plans, did you?"

She shrugged. "Not really. I couldn't spend any more time with him. The girls started lining up at my table. You know how busy it got. I gave him my card, but it's not something I really like to do."

"What if he wants to pay you?"

"Even so, I'm not much for exorcism. Too much negative energy."

It's not so unusual for someone to show up at our events with a request like that. There are things that people want to ask us, questions they might not ask their closest friend. I remembered one night working at a restaurant on Valentine's Day. After her tarot reading, a woman asked if I would meet with her son to see if I could help him get rid of his bad karma. Whatever she meant, it felt way above my pay grade. Still I always try to help out so I gave her the name of a trusted counselor instead. I always wondered how her son made out.

"Earth to Margo!" Alisha's voice broke through my thoughts. "Hello! You missed the turn."

Oh Geez, she was right. "Glad you caught that." I needed to pay attention. A fast u-turn and we veered up the on-ramp.

Alisha peered up through the windshield. "Look at the moon now." High overhead, it glowed silver. "There's a lunar eclipse on Friday," she said.

"Really? What time?"

"Late, but don't worry. I'll be up." She sounded excited. "It's been ages since there was an eclipse in late October. Think about it. Halloween is around the corner, we're moving into Scorpio and we get a full lunar eclipse!"

I told myself to watch the road and just in time. Up ahead a creature's luminous eyes flashed in the headlights. I jerked the wheel, tires squealed, and the animal scampered off. Dear Goddess, I prayed. Just let me get home in one piece.

But Alisha barely noticed. She was still focused on the eclipse. "I hope everybody has their emotional body armor handy. Things are about to get intense."

The next days were a blur of work, family, and more events. My last Halloween party of the season was a Saturday night in the suburbs. Grateful for my new GPS, I congratulated myself on arriving a few minutes early. I parked on the street, got out of the car, and walked up to the house to ring the doorbell.

The host introduced himself as John. "The den's this way," he said. "I have you set up in here."

He led me down half a flight of stairs to a comfortable looking room with a leather sofa and plaid drapes. There was even a little fire in the fireplace. John pointed at a small table in a corner. "This okay?"

"Perfect."

"Would you like something to drink?"

"Just some water, please."

I felt the muscles in my neck loosen. This would be an easy gig, I thought. And it was. That night, I read tarot cards. Looking at the images, telling their story, and watching the faces respond across the table is its own reward. After two hours, I'd read the cards for everyone who was interested. I waited another ten minutes before packing up. I had just wrapped the cards back inside their silk covering when John came back into the den. "I wonder if you could do me a favor. A special reading?"

Why do they always wait until the last minute? "Sure, I'll do my best." I hid my frustration behind a smile. "What would you like?"

He blushed a little. "Not for me. It's a friend. He wasn't interested in the tarot cards, but he wondered if there's anything else."

"I could do a palm reading, if that works." I still hoped for a speedy exit.

"Sounds good. I'll go get him."

I had wanted to be home before my kids' midnight curfew, but there it was. I closed my eyes and cleared my thoughts with a minute of deep breathing. John returned with his friend, a tall, rugged thirty-something guy with a full head of sandy hair and a nice smile. I knew I hadn't seen him before. I would have remembered.

"Hi, I'm Greg Parrish." He held out his hand for me to read.

I shook it instead. "Hey, Greg, I'm Margo Fellshur."

I unwrapped the cards again. "I'll read your palm, but before we start would you select three cards from the deck? It helps me connect with you." A quick shuffle, then I fanned the cards face down on the table.

Greg thought for a moment. One by one he selected, handing over the Hanged Man, the King of Swords, and the Tower. He listened to my explanation, head cocked to one side. "Tell me about that one again." He pointed to the Tower, an image of people toppling from a castle wall to the ground below.

"Don't worry. It can mean the end of the old order and the beginning of the new. Maybe you've had some radical opportunities to rethink your life?"

He laughed.

Now I was ready. I took his hand again. It was warm and somewhat calloused. He's not afraid to get his hands dirty, I thought. Running my fingers over the surface, I waited to pick up some energy. His palm was square, with straight, even fingers and a longish thumb. Often people want to know if they'll live a long life. But Greg stayed quiet. I explored the geography of his hand.

His headline was long. It stretched across the palm from under the index finger past the pinky. But what surprised me was his lifeline. His lifeline broke completely. It started again about a quarter inch later, very strong and deep, something I'd never seen before. I wasn't ready to go there yet. Instead, I concentrated on his love line and commented on a strong line cutting through it, a sign of a romance gone wrong. He agreed that there were actions he regretted and that he had learned to appreciate what he'd had only after it was gone. I pointed out a few of the stars on his palm, signs of a caring nature. "I guess you could say that I feel for people, try to help if I can."

"Would you say you're inclined to think things through?"

He laughed. "No, I count more on my gut to steer me straight."

I couldn't avoid the lifeline any longer. My fingertips brushed it lightly. "It looks like you've been granted a second life." I stared straight into his eyes.

A shadow flickered there and was gone.

"You were in an accident and walked away from something very few people survive."

He nodded and sat back, pulling his hand from mine.

"I've never seen such a break," I said. "This looks like a near-death experience, one that must have changed your life."

"I'm a pilot. Last fall I was out in my Cessna when the engine failed. I had to take her down, but before I could land, the engine caught fire. Just like they say, my life flashed before my eyes. She hit the ground in the middle of a cornfield. By luck, I was thrown free. I came to just in time to see the plane explode. I felt the heat and managed to drag myself away as the cornfield caught fire. I came out of it with just a concussion, a broken arm, and three broken ribs."

John appeared at the door. "Well?" he asked.

"Yep, she nailed it."

Greg stood. He didn't seem to want to say anything more in front of his friend. I took it as my cue that the evening was over. I felt as if I'd passed a test, one that I didn't necessarily want to take. Still I was satisfied that it had come out right.

Once I'd collected the check for the event and a nice tip besides, I was ready to head home. Greg stopped me by the door.

"Thanks for the reading," he said. "I felt a little funny, but John wanted me to do it, to see what you'd come up with. Sorry for putting you on the spot like that."

"No problem, it comes with the territory. I'm glad to hear things turned out OK."

"Oh, I'm feeling great physically. Mentally, I'm not so sure."

He touched my arm then and I felt a jolt. What was it? The lump in my chest told me it was sorrow. He'd kept it hidden. This sadness was not something I'd seen on his face. It felt fresh. Distinct from what we'd just talked about. "Is there something else?"

"I'm sorry. I didn't want to hold you up." The look in his eyes said different.

I got a flash of a brown-haired woman, thirtyish. "Someone close to you. A woman."

"You're right, but not what you think. It's a family issue. My sister, she disappeared a while back. Couple months ago. We haven't heard from her since."

"How awful. What happened?"

"Carla, that's my sister. First of all, let me say she's a real solid citizen. But things got tough when she and her husband broke up. Before, it was always her and the kids together, going places. But after the split she needed to get a job. It was hard on the kids. But things were going okay."

"You say she disappeared?"

"Yeah. But it's not like her to just take off."

I sensed there was more but that he needed some

encouragement to spill it. "And?"

"After the break-up she reconnected with her old boyfriend, Steve."

"Then what?"

"They both disappeared."

"You think they took off together?"

"At first, we thought maybe she did. But she hasn't called. Hasn't used her phone or her credit card since. Nothing."

"And the boyfriend? How about him?"

He shook his head. "Same. No car. No phone. No word."

"I'm so sorry. How are the children? They must be devastated."

"Yeah, it's pretty rough on them. They're little. Brianna is five. Lizzie's only three."

"I wish there was something I could do."

"I wonder. I wanted to ask. Have you ever tried to find somebody who's missing? You know, like on TV?"

"Not really." I had to admit to myself that with one or two exceptions, my intuitive work didn't go much beyond garden variety fortune-telling.

"Could you help?" His eyes searched mine.

Intuition told me to say yes. There was something so appealing about him. "I work with a group of psychics. We call ourselves the Mediums Guild." I fished out one of the cards. "Here's my phone number. Just give me a call."

He took the card and put it in his shirt pocket. "Thanks. You probably need to get going."

We walked to where my car was parked. The full moon peeked from behind the clouds. He smiled but I thought his eyes looked sad even in the moonlight.

The following Saturday, I called an unofficial meeting of the Mediums Guild. Gwen and I had planned to meet for lunch anyway to celebrate her upcoming job. She'd be doing the makeup for a month's worth of "Babes in Toyland" performances.

I met Gwen and Paula at the Rose Café in Center City, a friendly place we like with good food and moderate prices. We shared hummus while we waited for Alisha.

"Thanks for meeting me," I told them. "Between now and New Years we might not have much time for socializing. And congratulations to you Gwen on your new job."

"Thanks, I'll be working my tail off, but the money's good," Gwen said.

"Let's hope," I said. We clinked glasses. "Cheers!"

There was a burst of cool air and vibrant energy. Alisha bustled toward our table. "Sorry, guys. Raven and I were having significant mother-daughter communication about whether she should get a tattoo." She sighed and settled herself into a chair.

Alisha has an ex-husband always behind on his payments and an unruly thirteen-year-old who needs a lot of supervision. Wednesdays she's onstage singing in a band with her boyfriend. It's complicated. I happened to see her driver's license once. Her real name is Marianne.

After she ordered and we caught up for a few minutes, Alisha got serious. "You said you need our help, Margo. I'm here for you."

I shook my head. "Thanks, but it's not for me." I told them about meeting Greg and reading his palm. "But it's not about him, either, not really. It's his sister. She's been missing for several weeks."

"How old?" Alisha asked. "Could she be a runaway?"

"She's not a teenager. She's a young mother with kids. Separated from her husband."

Alisha's face fell.

"The family is beside themselves. He's called me twice. Apparently the police have done whatever they can, but it's gone nowhere. I told him I'd talk to you all. To see if there's a way for us to help."

"What do you have in mind?" Paula asked.

"I thought maybe we could ask him to send us some things of

his sister's, like jewelry, keys, gloves, other things she liked. We could try to pick up something. What do you think?"

"I'm willing to try," Gwen said. "But I have the show coming up." She scrolled through her phone, checking dates. "Any night except Monday is out for me until after Christmas."

"I can do a Monday," Alisha said.

"Me, too," said Paula. "How about you, Margo?"

"Works for me. We can have it at my place. I'll call Greg first and see if he's willing to send some of his sister's things."

"Do we know the missing woman's name?" Gwen asked.

"No, but maybe that's a good thing," I said. "Let's try to stay away from the newspapers and not read anything about it."

We all agreed just as the kabobs arrived.

2

Later I would be asked how the Medium's Guild got its start. I had a stock answer. There was really no magic to it, I'd say with a laugh. Some of us just know how to connect with the intuitive, and we trust ourselves to interpret it a little better than most people. While the Mediums Guild sounds otherworldly, it's basically a kind of talent agency, albeit a cooperative one, booking members as entertainment at parties and social events.

At various stages of our lives, most of us found that we have certain abilities, skills that others find fascinating. We learned to explore them, earning some extra money along the way. It's like anything else. The more readings you do, the better you get. Practicing your craft on demand enables you to take risks unselfconsciously. Once you let your subconscious loose, positive feedback from clients boosts your self-confidence, and faith in your ability grows. It's a virtuous cycle.

Like many of our group, I have a day job. Not too long ago, when the market was good, I was a high-flying real estate agent selling residential property in Philadelphia, so busy I didn't have time to think. Then it all changed. I remember the day in 2009 when Jerry, my boss, asked me, only half-joking, "Margo, couldn't you have warned me that the market was going to tank?" Despite his comment, I convinced him to retain me on a "commission-only" basis, with a small draw, but my sales have been sporadic.

Alisha works as a paralegal in a law office specializing in intellectual property. Gwen is a makeup artist and sometime hairdresser. When times are good she works backstage at local plays and shows and on the occasional movie set. Renee is a registered nurse turned stay-at-home mom. She chases her two pre-schoolers by day and spends evenings and weekends as a palm-reader and healer. Paula, a retired school teacher, keeps us organized. She does the marketing, takes the bookings and schedules our appearance at the clients' events.

Greg agreed to Fed Ex me some of his sister's things, but when the package arrived, I let it stay unopened until the day of our meeting. My kids, Jamie and Charlie knew everyone was coming over. Over dinner—a large pepperoni pizza from Lorenzo's — I gave them a few details of the situation with Greg at the Halloween party. Jamie, my seventeen-year-old, was fascinated. She wanted to know how I thought my group could help. She'd met some of them before, had even done some babysitting for Renee's two kids. She asked if she could watch us.

"There won't be much to see," I explained. "But if anything gets interesting, I'll let you know."

Twelve-year-old Charlie was another story. My young biologist-to-be, member of the school science club, refused to look me in the eye. He frowned and glanced around the room as if he was looking for a place to hide. Was I imagining it? Had he begun to pooh-pooh the idea of anything not detectable in the physical world? There are worse things, I guess.

"Ignore him, Mom," Jamie advised. "Our little scientist hates anything that's not observable in nature."

Charlie swatted at his older sister's ponytail several times, until she grabbed his ear and gave it a hard tweak. Charlie howled. "Mom!"

"OK, you guys! Cool it. I don't need this."

The kids declared a grudging peace and Charlie agreed to be as friendly as he was able. That settled I made him help me move my big round table and some chairs to the center of the living room. Then he stomped off up the stairs. The kids had their space and I had mine. Our drafty old Victorian in a slowly re-gentrifying neighborhood in West Philadelphia was roomy enough for company on the first floor and privacy on the second.

Gwen and Paula arrived first. Renee came soon after in her van. "Is there any place to park around here? The last thing I need is another ticket from the Parking Authority."

I walked her back to the curb and pointed to my favorite side street fifty yards past the traffic light. "Try over there. Meter maids don't seem to go there very often."

As Renee pulled away in search of safe parking, a taxi stopped. I waited long enough for Alisha to pay the driver and scramble out. She was wearing what she called her "fun fur", a faux leopard jacket I would have killed for. "Do you believe how cold it got?"

We agreed that winter was on its way and I shooed her inside, closing the door against a stiff November wind. On cue, Charlie and Jamie appeared at my side. Jamie shook hands with everyone and asked how they were doing. Charlie did his best, but muttered greetings were all my twelve-year-old could manage before his escape. Jamie hung out for a few moments. Renee returned thrilled with finding a free two hours on the meter. Social niceties completed, we were ready to examine the items Greg had sent to me.

A small flannel pouch slid out of the package. Inside were a set of three keys, a gold ring, a fountain pen, a pair of glasses, and a comb. The objects, ordinary in themselves, belonged to a woman who had gone missing under mysterious circumstances. The thought was sobering.

Anxious to begin, Alisha fingered the objects. "I've done

psychometry before, sort of," she told us. "But never anything this important."

We nodded.

"When I was a kid, I watched my grandmother do it," Alisha said. "People would come to the house, sit around the kitchen, and ask her questions. One time a neighbor's daughter got engaged. The girl's mother didn't like the guy, so she brought some strands of the boyfriend's hair on a comb. Just from that, my grandmother said he was trouble. The girl married him anyway. And guess what? He ended up in jail."

It wasn't funny but we laughed anyway.

Alisha held the ring between her thumb and forefinger, rolling it back and forth. "We're sort of making this up as we go along, right? What if we take turns holding the objects and write down our impressions?"

"Good idea, then we won't influence each other," Paula said.

I went to my desk, scooped up a handful of pens and tore sheets from a spiral-bound copybook. Gwen wondered if we should turn down the lights. I hit the dimmer switch and rejoined the group at the table.

"It's kind of like what they did back in the 1900s when séances where all the rage," Paula said. "That's what this reminds me of."

"This isn't a séance." I said. "Then they were trying to connect with the spirit realm. What we're doing is different. We're hoping to tap into her energy, look for information."

"Sounds the same to me," Paula said.

Alisha rolled her eyes. "Shhh, I'm going to start."

She selected the keys. Eyes closed, she held them between both hands for several seconds. Then she separated them on the table in front of her and held each one before passing them to Renee. She reflected a moment longer then scribbled rapidly.

One by one, the objects made their way around the table. Except for the sound of pens on paper, the room was silent as we concentrated on the items and wrote down our impressions.

More than an hour passed before the final item, the comb, returned to Alisha. She put everything back in the pouch.

"Now what?" Paula asked.

"Why don't we read what we've written out loud and see if there are any similarities," I said.

Paula, who'd written on multiple pages, wanted to go first. "I see a woman sitting in front of a window crying. Behind her outside is a black van." She went on to describe the room, the woman, and more details of what she'd seen.

Renee was next. After holding the objects, she had looked into the mirror she'd brought to the table and said she saw calm water, but she wasn't sure how to interpret that.

From the rest of us, there were descriptions of rooms, houses, and children. There were feelings of loneliness, or looking for someone. But to me, it felt like we were picking up the emotions of the grieving family.

We shared what seemed like random impressions, hoping to build a profile. I had a picture of two children—no, three. One was a boy with a round face and with dark hair. The other two were girls with blond hair, one with glasses, and the other with a cast on her arm. The kids seemed lost. I pictured the girls standing as a window looking out.

I, for one, didn't feel as if we had tapped into the missing woman and I wasn't alone. Even as we struggled to find clues to the mystery, we ended up more uncertain than when we started.

Once everyone straggled out, I cleared the cups and turned on the dishwasher. Drained, I headed upstairs for bed. Charlie's room was dark, but Jamie still had her light on, and I stuck my head in the door. She looked up from her computer. "How was your session? Any luck?"

"Not much. We did our best. I'll be sending everything back to her brother. I only wish there was something more substantial."

"You must feel bad."

"More like frustrated," I said.

Jamie turned back to her computer. "Do you know the woman's name?"

Before our group met, I hadn't wanted to know too much about Greg's missing sister, not that I wasn't curious, it just didn't seem like a good idea to influence our perceptions. But no reason to worry about that now, I thought. "It's Carla Gentile."

She typed it into the search engine, and a few links to newspaper articles appeared. Over Jamie's shoulder I peered at a headline from a New Jersey newspaper: "Police Baffled by Missing Couple."

There were two photos. One showed a round-featured woman, her face framed by light, wavy hair. The other showed the missing man, Steve Kovacs, who had piercing eyes, dark straight hair, and a mustache. The faces looked familiar, as if I'd seen them on the news or something. But the date was six months prior. They'd gone missing in April. Now it was November. I pulled the article from the printer.

"Thanks, Sweetie. Now please turn this thing off or you'll never get up on time," I told her. I kissed the top of her head before pulling her door shut. I would be asleep before she was.

According to the article, both Carla Gentile and Steve Kovacs were married to other people but separated, Carla amicably so. Steve Kovacs had a wife in Florida. There were three children between them, Carla with two, Steve with one. How sad for everyone. I set my alarm clock and tried to put everything out of my mind. I was relieved when Jamie's light went out before I nodded off.

The neighbor's dog woke me at six. I slipped out of bed and spied my notebook on the night table. It was open to a page covered in chicken scratch. I peered at it. It was my handwriting, true enough, but I didn't remember writing anything before bed. I stared at the jumble of words and the rough sketch underneath.

Then it came back. I remembered a voice. An image of a woman's face. Numbers on the digital clock—3:34.

A morsel of a dream flashed into my consciousness. Someone was calling my name. There was a woman's face, her eyes wide and intense, communicating something I was meant to know. I heard the word harmony carefully enunciated three times, as if I would understand. Somehow I knew, it was her, the missing woman. I awoke then in a burst of light. I remembered sitting bolt upright and fumbling for my notebook. I scribbled the word harmony and underlined it three times. At the bottom of the page was a rough sketch of something cylinder shaped but I didn't remember drawing that.

One of the kids was moving around. It was time to start the day. For now, the nocturnal mystery would have to wait. Once the kids were out the door, I barely had time to press a blouse and grab a shower. Today's work agenda included a possible meeting with some clients for a second look at a property. There was, fingers crossed, a chance of an offer.

I got to the office before Jerry, and, as if on cue, the phones started ringing, allowing me no time to think about the dream with its nighttime scrawls. At eleven, I went for coffee. I put a call through to Alisha at her office. She listened to my tale of the dream and the note I'd scrawled in the middle of the night. "I'm almost embarrassed by it. It sounds like a message from the New Age and beyond. Peace, love, and harmony."

Alisha snorted a laugh into the phone and said, "Margo, look at it this way. At least you got something. Otherwise, I'd feel bad calling her brother with the little that we have to tell him."

"I don't want to mention the dream. I hate to look like a space case."

"No, you're wrong. You should tell him. Who knows, it may have meaning for the family that we can't fathom. Since you're passing our notes along to Greg, why not just include your page. Let him decide if it makes any sense."

"Okay," I said, not completely convinced. "I'll do it."

❧❦❧❦

3

Greg and I traded messages. He was out of town on business and hoped we could meet as soon as he got back. Meanwhile, events closer to home took center stage.

Charlie, my twelve-year-old, came down with a puzzling rash. One by one, blisters emerged over various parts of his body, and he freaked out over one huge swollen spot at the end of his nose and another under his eyebrow. After a long night spent dabbing him with calamine lotion, he was a mess, and I wasn't much better. In the morning, I got through to the nurse at our HMO, and she told me about the outbreak of chicken pox raging through the schools. She prescribed an antihistamine to quiet the itching, and by midday my son was calm enough to sleep.

Once the severe phase subsided, Charlie was destined for seven days of pajamas, microwave pizza, and video games until he was cleared to go back to school. Running back and forth between work and home so I could look in on him left me too exhausted to think about missing women and mysterious dreams.

My nerves began to fray, and I was not alone. Jamie, usually calm and composed, came home one day, threw her book bag by the door, and kicked Charlie's sneakers out of the way. "Mom, can you please do something about him? The house is a mess."

In response, Charlie jumped off the couch and danced around his sister, making burping sounds and threatening her with eruptions on his elbow. Immune since her own bout with the disease years ago, Jamie swatted him aside. "Mom, make him stop."

"Charlie, that's enough," I yelled, but he ignored me. I grabbed his game controller and disconnected his game of Grand Theft Auto.

"Mom! I was on my way to a new world record."

He swiped the controller from my hand and curled into a sulky ball on the couch. The phone rang. Jamie grabbed it, looked surprised then handed me the phone. It was Greg on the line.

"Hi, Margo, I'm back. Any chance we can meet? I'd be more than happy to stop by."

My inner self groaned. "I'm kind of tied down right now. My son has the chickenpox."

Behind me, the din of Charlie's video game grew. I retreated to the kitchen and closed the door. "Sorry, Greg, I missed that. What were you saying?"

"We're at the end of our rope here. Your message sounded like you might have something you wanted to tell me. Any chance you could give me a few minutes?"

"There's a Starbucks not far from here," I said. "I could meet you there at five–thirty. How's that?"

He agreed, and we ended the call.

Now I had a decision to make. Should I share the dream? Show him the drawing I'd scribbled in the middle of the night? Tell him about the voice?

In search of calm, I boiled water for tea. Looking around, I took comfort from my kitchen. The red walls, the jumble of mismatched china in the cupboard, and the apothecary cabinet with its small drawers full of bits and pieces of family life helped ease my tension. Out of habit, I wiped the countertops clean and swept non-existent crumbs from the floor just to take my mind off reality.

Two hours later, I changed out of my sweats, fluffed my hair, and put on some makeup. I headed for the Starbucks, spotting Greg through the window. The pained look on his face reminded me that our appointment was professional, not personal.

I still had the flannel pouch with Carla's belongings, and I slid it across the table along with the notes we'd made. I watched Greg read them.

"Thanks, I'll keep these. Show them to my mother. Maybe she'll get something from them."

Clearly he had not. I decided against showing him my scribbles. Instead I asked, "Would the word harmony have any meaning for you or for Carla?"

His face went white. "Harmony? You mean Lake Harmony?"

"Not sure. It came to me in a dream. A woman's voice repeated the word as though it had some special meaning."

After that, everything changed.

"Margo, how did it go? Alisha's voice on the other end of the telephone line was hopeful. "Did any of our notes mean anything to him?"

"Not really. I told Greg we'd hoped for more. But I did tell him about the dream. As it turns out, Harmony is a place where the family used to go camping. It has a lake."

"Okay, what else?"

"It's down in the Pines. He and his sister went there as kids."

"So what did he think?"

"He didn't say too much more, but the dream got his attention. He asked if I ever had other dreams that were similar."

"You've had more than one prophetic dream. Remember when that rock star died? What was his name, Jerry Emanuel?"

"Yeah."

How could I forget a dream with rainbows, clouds, music, and a procession with Jerry on a motorcycle? Only later that day did I learn the shocking news that he'd died in the night.

"He wants me to visit the site with him. Should I do it?"

Alisha sighed. "Of course you should do it."

I needed to see a map of New Jersey. Digging through debris in the cluttered room on the second floor known as "my office," I dug out a binder from a realtor's conference. If the map was correct, the location was in the middle of New Jersey's Pine Barrens, some twenty miles from the ocean. But it showed little detail beyond a pale circle of water with the place name Harmony near an intersection of two secondary roads located about forty miles from where I sat in Philadelphia. The computer provided more detail. I printed out that map and compared it to the residential map on my desk. I took the first map from the binder and folded back the edges so that the blue body of water was front and center.

Outside, a pale November sun disappeared behind dark clouds. The smell of rain was in the air. The room had turned dark. Door closed, I stretched out in the ancient recliner that took up the middle of the room and let my eyes close. Map across my chest, I took a deep breath and slowly exhaled.

After a few moments relaxation, I let my thoughts wander slowly over the folded paper. Whispering Carla's name, I hoped for a flicker of response. A quick snapshot of a road at night, headlights reflecting off trees, and a deer caught in the headlights flashed through my mind and quickly faded. Vivid, though the image was, I still wondered if it was the product of an overactive imagination.

Later Greg called to ask if I could spare a few hours on the weekend to visit the campground. A little scared at what we might find, I agreed. Our plan was to meet at a New Jersey mall near his home. He would drive us to the Pines.

Come Saturday morning, I was beat. In addition to caring for the patient at home, it had been a busy week at work. Jerry was out of the office most days, showing a sample house he'd agreed to represent, so I had manned the phones and tried to line up some clients on my own. I would have loved to stay home and get some rest but no matter. Suck it up. It wouldn't be right to cancel on Greg. I'd given my word. That, plus my natural inquisitiveness — and something else I didn't want to admit to — pushed me out the door.

Greg had told me to look for a white Cherokee parked near the Macy's entrance. I found him leaning against the car. He gave a wave, trying his best to smile, but I could feel his nerves. I pulled up alongside and parked, got out and locked my old Toyota. I climbed into the SUV. I could feel my own nerves as well as his. Greg seemed a little shy today.

After some small talk, he handed me a map and pointed out a vacant-looking corner of New Jersey. "I could get there with my eyes closed, but I wanted you to have a look at where we're going."

"The Pine Barrens, right?"

He nodded. "Maybe forty minutes from here. Do you have to be back any special time?"

I looked at my watch. It was 11:22. "Usually my kids would love for me to be gone all day Saturday, but with Charlie recovering from chickenpox, I better be home in time for dinner. Assuming they haven't killed each other by then."

"How old?" he asked.

I supplied genders, names, and ages. I didn't mention that their father and I were separated.

"How about you?" I asked. "Any kids?"

He grinned. "Not yet. I'm not married. But lately I've been spending time with Carla's kids. They're staying with my mom."

I watched his smile fade. "Tell me a little about Carla and her friend. His name is Steve, right?"

"They dated in high school, but after graduation Steve headed to Florida for college. Carla stayed home, went to community, got her RN, and married Matt. Steve liked Florida and stayed. Got married down there and had a boy of his own. Then his marriage broke up."

I tried to keep my eyes off the speedometer, and the needle edging up. We had pulled onto the highway, and I was white-knuckling it.

"After his dad died, Steve wanted to move his family back up here and take over the family business, a body shop. But his wife wouldn't leave Florida. I heard there was more to the story, money problems and other stuff. Bottom line, he left and she stayed. I met with him not long after he came back. He was all excited about this crazy diving venture, and he wanted me to get involved, but, like a lot of people, I was having trouble with finances. I needed to concentrate on keeping my own business going, so I gave it a pass."

My foot pressed an imaginary brake. "Could you slow down a little?" I asked. "I get nervous at high speeds."

He laughed, easing off the gas just enough for the speedometer to drop below 80. "Sorry, I'm just in a hurry for us to get there."

The road unwound in front of us and Greg told me about the night his sister disappeared. "When Carla asked my mom to babysit, she was very upfront about meeting Steve for dinner. Mom warned her to be careful, what with her separation from Matt being so recent. Carla agreed, but it was just to make my mom feel better. A friend of hers told the police that she dropped Carla off at a restaurant in Mount Laurel."

"So Carla and Steve were seen together that night?" I asked.

"They had dinner at the restaurant. The waitress remembered them. Said they had a few drinks, joked around with another couple, took some pictures and left before midnight." As Greg recounted the story, his knuckles gripped the wheel and his jaw set in a rigid line. "Once they stepped outside the door, they vanished. Neither of them was seen again."

Greg fell silent. We stayed on the Expressway, weaving in and out of Saturday traffic, until we exited at Route 72. Moving east, we passed strip centers and fast food joints that had displaced the main streets of New Jersey's small towns. A sign told us the town of Tabernacle was one mile north. We took the exit less than a minute later.

"Welcome to the land that time forgot," Greg joked. On either side of the two-lane blacktop, single-story houses backed up against pine forest. Abandoned stores, empty gas stations, and ancient farm stands increased in number as evidence of human habitation faded away. What would it be like, I wondered, to live so removed from your neighbors in the middle of the Pines.

After several miles, Greg made an abrupt left and turned onto a rutted dirt lane. A faded hand-lettered sign identified our destination as Riker's Harmony Campground. Beneath that, a fading communication read, "For Sale – 10 Wooded Acres."

We bumped along past a partially burned-out cabin. Greg pointed. "Old Man Riker lived there. When it got struck by lightning, he never rebuilt it. Storms get wild out here."

Past a curve in the road, the view opened up to a lake surrounded by forest. An insipid sun reflected off the shallow rust-colored water lapping against cedars at the edge, their roots exposed by the lake's low level. It isn't every day that you see nature untouched in the middle of one of the most heavily populated states in the country.

"Here we are," Greg said. "Camp Harmony."

In my dream, there had been no water, no cabin, only a vague female presence surrounded by light and a voice insisting on harmony.

"When we were kids, this lake was a favorite place to go, not only for us, but for all the kids we went to school with." Greg turned off the ignition and got out. He came around and opened my door. "We spent a lot of time here. But in a million years, it would never have occurred to me to think about looking here. After you told me about your dream, I asked the detectives to send a team to investigate, but from what I've heard, that hasn't happened yet."

"Maybe they didn't take it seriously," I said.

"Could be." He tried to smile. "Worst case scenario, it's a beautiful day for a hike."

I agreed, sorry that I wasn't wearing sturdier shoes. It felt more than a little odd tramping through the Pine Barrens with a man I barely knew. I was used to making small talk with strangers, no big deal. But we were there in search of something sad and tragic. The unspoken truth was that we were looking for his sister's remains. Something I hoped we wouldn't find.

To avoid the obvious, we chatted about how hot and dry the summer had been, how rough it was for the Jersey farmers, who had suffered through a major drought. Now it was November, and we hadn't had a good rain in weeks. Underfoot, the ground felt firm. As we followed a path into the trees, thoughts of poison ivy flickered through my mind, and I checked to make sure my ankles were covered. The cool, dry autumn air was scented with pine fragrance, and I inhaled it deeply. Putting my worries on hold, I tried to open my senses to anything that might present itself.

Not so Greg, he seemed bent on following the path in front of us at full speed, but I placed a hand on his arm to slow him down. "Can we stop for a minute? I'd like to try to connect with the energy here."

"Sorry. I focus on putting one foot in front of the other. My Type-A mindset."

Greg turned away to give me some space, working hard to make himself invisible. I spied a downed log and pressed a palm against it. Satisfied that it was dry, I sat, closed my eyes, and drew in a slow breath. I focused inward for what might have been seconds or minutes. Energy rose to the top of my head and with it an image of a cliff, a rock wall. My eyes blinked open just as a shower of acorns peppered my skull. Overhead a squirrel skittered for cover in the trees.

Greg brushed leaves from my hair and laughed. "Mother Nature always claims her turf!"

"Greg, wait." I wanted to hold on to the moment. "Is there a cliff around here anywhere?"

Now it was his turn to blink. "Cliff? Oh my God! Half mile back out on the other side of the woods. It's off the property, but there's an abandoned limestone quarry."

He took off at a run, and I stumbled behind, no match for his long-legged stride. Several minutes later, wooded terrain gave way to a road overgrown with vegetation but still clear enough for a car to get through. We followed a curved path, the terrain underfoot sprinkled with stones.

A yellow sign on a tree warned Danger. Beyond a clearing, what I'd taken for a cliff was the rock wall of the quarry.

Greg sprinted from view. I heard his yell before I got close enough to see him skidding down a rock-strewn slope toward the edge, arms out-stretched, struggling to keep his balance. Loose stones rolled down the slope, dropping into the quarry below.

Greg dropped onto his back, but he was still sliding, his momentum carrying him toward the edge. He dug his hands into the dirt and one of them found a vine. He grabbed and it held, halting his desperate slide. My attempt to reach out to him did no good. I lost my balance and stepped back from the edge, tripped on a root and went down in the dust.

He lay still for a moment and then turned on his side. A scrape left blood on his forehead. His chest was heaving. "Better slow down," he muttered to himself.

I felt pain in my right leg and looked down. Torn jeans exposed a scraped and bleeding knee. I dabbed at it with a tissue.

Greg sat up, grabbed a scrawny sapling, and hauled himself to his feet. He hobbled back to where I was sitting. "You okay?"

"No worries. I'll survive."

From his jacket, he produced two bottles of water and offered one. I nodded my thanks, drank half the bottle, and used the remainder to clean my wound.

He drained his and put the empty back in his pocket. "We used to drink from a little waterfall somewhere around here. There's an underground spring nearby, and when there was a lot of rain, this quarry would fill up and we'd talk about going swimming here. A few times we even made our way to that ledge down there and managed to jump in. When my parents caught wind of that, they skinned us alive."

Composure regained, we re-evaluated our approach. I walked as close to the quarry's edge as I dared. Greg pointed to a ledge twenty yards to the right that was more level and had some roots to grab onto. "Let's try over there," he said.

"You're not serious, are you?"

A reluctant climber at best, I chose to stay put while Greg scrabbled partway down to a ledge closer to the murky water below.

He pointed. "I see something in the water. Can you see it from up there?"

I squinted, holding a bruised palm over my eyes. A cloud darkened the sky. "I see a shadow out toward the middle, but I can't make out much."

"I think I see something out there, and that's enough for me. I'm calling the state police. They need to send a crew out here today." He whipped out his cell phone and punched numbers.

The police dispatcher promised action, but I sensed a long wait. I looked at my watch. "Greg, I'm sorry, but I have to go. My kids," I offered by way of explanation. "I wasn't planning to make a whole day of it. Can you take me back?"

"Sure, I'm sorry. I didn't mean to be inconsiderate."

I could feel his reluctance to leave the quarry, but we walked quickly to the car, and he drove me back to the mall. I made him promise to call me the moment the police showed up, and I took his number just in case he forgot.

4

I wasn't sure if we'd found much of anything that day, but I felt a twinge of excitement—and sadness, too. On the phone to Alisha, I joked, half embarrassed, that if circumstances had been different, and if I were ten years younger, I might have focused more of my attention on Greg. After all, how often do you get the chance to meet a tall, handsome man, employed, sober and dedicated to his family? Alisha, the spoilsport, pointed out that he had other things on his mind. We laughed at our nonsense, and I rang off.

I had plenty of things on my mind, too. I was still preoccupied with how the kids were dealing with their father moving out. Were they still hoping he and I would move back together? No doubt. Truth be told, a tiny part of me still hoped the same thing. But I came up against a hard truth. Forever never lasts as long as you think.

All the things about Jack that I always loved, his sense of fun, his ability to see the glass half-full, his willingness to take risks, the way he could talk to anybody about anything, all that took a back seat to things I didn't like. Now all I could focus on was his drinking and his inability to hold a job for more than six months at a time. Clearly these were issues he needed to resolve but he didn't seem to think so. OK, now what? Even though we might be heading for divorce, I wasn't ready to imagine myself single and didn't know when I would be.

One thing that I did know was that until Jack was able to get control of his life, I needed to pay the bills. I didn't want to go to court for support. The financial agreement he'd promised to keep was barely four months old, but he was already behind. My bank account took the hit, and the situation threatened to get worse.

Since the end of summer, I had barely scraped enough together to pay for the basics. Now that was about to change, and not for the better. Toward the end of the year, the real estate market turns cold even in good years. People whose houses haven't sold pull their listings and rethink their plans. Until the market rebounds in the spring, my income freezes, too.

I was glad to have the Mediums Guild roster of holiday parties coming up. I reminded myself to check in with Paula right away. My schedule was clear, and I wanted her to book me for as many jobs as she could. Maybe I should call her now, I thought. Then the phone rang. The New Jersey number looked familiar. It had been almost a week since Greg and I had hiked through the woods.

"Margo?" His voice on the other end was shaky.

"Greg? How are you?" I felt his distress.

"They found it, they found Steve's car. They're dredging it up now."

I staggered back, dropping to a chair. "At the quarry? Was it at the quarry?"

"No, miles from there - way on the other side of the state. Found it totally by accident. New Jersey State EPA workers were doing a survey, getting ready to dredge near the Commodore Barry Bridge."

I didn't want to ask. The image of a black car flashed in my mind. Somehow I knew there were no bodies in the car.

"They found it under the bridge, almost submerged. Empty."

"Today?"

"Yesterday. Motor Vehicles checked. They had it listed as missing. We got the call."

"What's next?"

"They're going over it for prints."

"This is really the first solid evidence that the two of them didn't just run away together, isn't it?"

"Who knows? I guess they could have hidden the car, but I don't think so. I wish there was some way you could be here. I'd be interested to see if you could get any impressions from the scene."

"Greg, I appreciate your confidence, but I really doubt the authorities would let me come within a hundred yards of that car."

"Yeah, you're right. I'll send you photos. What's your email?"

I spoke slowly. "It's Margo4321@gmail.com."

"Got it," Greg said. Then I heard him muttering as if he were speaking to himself. "Reporter at the Times? Shoulda called him already."

The line went dead.

Even with the dream communication from Carla, I wanted to convince myself it was still possible the couple might have met with an accident, under some mysterious, unknowable circumstance. In the months since the couple went missing, could the bodies have drifted far down the river?

Emailed photos arrived the next morning. There was a Burlington County Times link to an article headlined, "Divers Search River for Missing Couple."

State police had dragged the river, so far with no result. Still, the authorities were treating the car and its location as a crime scene and giving the investigation renewed emphasis.

The story got picked up by a news service that week. The day after that, Greg texted me a message: Local cops feeling the heat.

I went online. A small blurb confirmed that the New Jersey State Police were involved. There was no word about what, if anything, the local Burlington police were doing.

Another article showed a photo of Carla's husband being

brought in for questioning, but on the night of the disappearance he'd been out of town on business. He could prove beyond doubt that he'd been a couple of hundred miles away. The family was fairly sure he was not involved, since he and Carla had agreed on a separation well before Steve entered the picture. According to Greg, the separation had been amicable. That left Steve's side of the equation.

An article in the Mount Holly Weekly Review titled "Whereabouts of Local Man Remain a Mystery" filled in the gaps. Before his return to the area, Steve spent ten years in Florida. In search of adventure, he drifted south after college. He found what he was looking for and settled in Key West, making a living by taking tourists out on his boat for sport fishing. He reconnected with a high school buddy, and together they expanded Steve's tourist business to include diving and snorkeling in Florida's warm waters. According to Greg, business was unpredictable, and the fortunes of the two partners rose and fell with the economy. In the past couple years it wasn't only their business that was dying, Florida tourism took a big hit and Steve's relationship with his wife soured as well. When they separated, Steve sold his share of the business, sold his boat, gave his wife a good chunk of the money and came home.

A third article in the New Jersey press provided more on the forensics of the case. Police found a few shreds of evidence in the SUV. Once the car was dried out, it was to be expected they'd find strands of hair and fibers that were possible matches with both Steve and Carla. A detective was quoted as saying, "We already know who was in the car that night." But new evidence appeared. Police found mud residue in the rear hatch that didn't match the Commodore Barry location. Rope fibers were found as well. In addition, several bits of stone were extracted from the vehicle's tire treads. I read Greg's quote insisting that these rocks were identical to what was found at the quarry. I thought back to the pebbles under our feet that day in the Pines.

I was sure Greg had done all he could to persuade the

authorities to see it his way. And I wasn't wrong. He called me at home a few days later, his voice hoarse with emotion. "Margo, I'm at the quarry. After what they found in the car, I came here looking to see if I could spot any tire tracks."

"Greg, you've been on my mind so much lately. I knew you wouldn't …" I didn't really know what to say.

"Remember that dark mass in the center of the quarry?

"Yes." I felt like I knew where this was going and it wasn't good.

"It was even more visible than before."

It made sense. We were still in the middle of a drought, so the water level must be even lower now.

"I would have called you, but things got crazy. I was afraid the cops would blow it off as just another wild goose chase. It took some political muscle to get the police to even come out here. This time, though, they showed up with a team and a diver."

"How is your family holding up? Is anyone else there with you?"

"My father's on his way, but Mom's too upset to be here right now."

Someone called his name.

"They're bringing something up now. Looks like an oil drum. That's crazy. Gotta go."

There was yelling in the background. I expected him to disconnect, but he didn't, so I didn't either. Hearing what might be gears grinding, I imagined a giant pulley hauling a dripping mass out of the quarry. More grating noise, I called his name. Then the line went dead.

Staring at nothing, I slumped down on the stairs. When a fire engine shrieked past, the noise roused me. Scrambling upstairs, I dug the dream notebook from the bureau drawer and leafed through it. I squinted at the sketch from that night. Could it be that what I'd taken for a cylinder was really an oil drum? The pale winter sun faded. My sense of desolation grew. I pondered the notebook still in my lap. But there was nothing I could do for Greg now.

Time to turn on the lights, the kids would be home soon, looking for food. A quick inventory of the refrigerator came up short. I went through closets checking coat pockets for change. Three dollars in a suit jacket was a bonanza. Add that to the coins in my wallet and I might have enough for a meal. Better try to get to the market and scrounge up something for dinner.

Greg called back later, a choke in his voice. "I think we've found them. Two bodies stuffed in oil drums. The police took the bodies to be examined. I didn't get too close, but it's them."

A chill ran up my spine. "Greg, I'm so sorry." No point in telling him about the sketch. He had enough to think about.

"Thanks, Margo. We'll know pretty soon."

Roaring in the background drowned out his voice. "What's that noise?" I yelled over it.

"It's the chopper from Channel Six News. They're filming. I hope you don't mind. I gave them your name."

The roar got louder. The phone went dead.

"No, I guess that's okay," I murmured.

I emailed Mediums Guild members to let them know the latest on the case. Later that afternoon Alisha called. She offered to stop by on her way home from work. "You could probably do with a little support."

"Thanks. How did you know?"

When the kids came home, I asked Jamie to print out any articles on the case, starting from the beginning. Charlie sat silently through the conversation until Jamie asked, "What do you think of Mom now?"

He pursed his lips together in a way that reminded me of his father. "Really cool. Now can we change the subject?"

Half an hour later, Jamie bounded downstairs, papers in hand. I took the articles and arranged them in a semblance of order. Before, I'd avoided learning too much about the couple. Now they became real. I could see their faces, hear their voices. My hands started to shake.

The first glass of pinot grigio did little to calm my nerves. Talk therapy was what I needed. "Bless you," I said after Alisha appeared in my kitchen in jeans and sneakers.

"Margo," She said. "I'm so sorry." She came around to where I was sitting and gave me a hug.

Alisha, usually so well dressed, felt the need to apologize. "Pardon my grunge."

"No worries. Is this is the new office casual?"

"We spent the whole damn day reorganizing the file room, I'm beat."

I held up the bottle of pinot grigio, my eyebrows raised in a silent invitation.

She smirked. "Are you kidding?"

I found another juice glass and filled it for her. I topped off my own. "Here, take a look." I pushed the articles across the kitchen table.

"Where'd these come from?"

"Jamie pulled some of them up before, the rest she found today. I didn't read most of them until now. "

Alisha pored over the printouts. She pointed to a brief clip claiming the couple was seen in Florida. "Did you notice this one?"

"That was way off track. They get all these kinds of false sightings, I guess. It happens."

"I'm sorry, Margo, really sorry. It's all so sad. Still, it brings some resolution. And that's because of your help, so feel good about that. How is Greg taking it?"

"I spoke to him just as they brought the drums out of the water."

"Drums?"

"Oil drums. The bodies were found inside two blue drums."

"That's bizarre."

"I feel bad for the kids. But maybe the important thing to come out of what happened today, it puts an end to the not knowing."

We drained our glasses. I offered a second bottle but Alisha shook her head. "Got to get home. Could I ask a favor before I go?"

"What is it?" I asked.

"Could Raven stay here this coming Friday? The band has a gig in Brooklyn. I hate to leave her alone." When she blushed, an unworthy thought crossed my mind. Was this the real reason for the visit?

"Sure." Perhaps the secret crush Charlie had on Raven would sweeten his mood. "Jamie has room. I'll check with her but I'm sure it's okay."

Alisha's taxi arrived. "Thanks for stopping," I said. "You talked me down from the ledge."

I watched the taxi until it turned left at the end of the street. I was ready to switch off the porch lights when a white van glided to the curb, announcing the presence of 6-ABC News in my life.

Another five minutes and I would have been in my bathrobe, hair skinned back and the day's makeup washed away. I watched the young blond reporter get out of the van and approach my door. "Ms. Fellshur?" she asked.

"Yes?"

"Did I pronounce that right? Is it Margo Fel-shur?"

I nodded a second time, butterflies careening into each other in my stomach. "How can I help you?"

"I'm Tara Morrow, of Action News." She held out her hand, confident in her name's recognition factor. Past her shoulder, I saw the driver unpack audio equipment.

The wiser course would have been to say a few words on the doorstep and let them go their way. Instead I invited Tara and her assistant into the living room. Was it the wine talking? I arranged myself in what I hoped was a dignified posture on the sofa.

Tara sat across from me. "We'd like to do a piece on you for the morning news. Do I have your permission to ask a few questions about finding the missing couple?"

My throat tightened. I often wondered why so many people in terrible circumstances agreed to interviews on what was probably the worst day of their lives. Now I got it. It made no sense, but I felt somehow responsible for these events. Maybe if I explained what I knew, that feeling might go away.

Then there was the reporter's absolute certainty of her right to shove a microphone in anyone's face and expect them to perform. All of a sudden it made me mad.

"Before we start, may I ask how you found me?"

A frown flickered across her features. The cameraman hesitated in his set-up. "Greg Parrish was kind enough to give my associate your telephone number, and we were able to find your address. I hope you don't mind. Trust me, we'll keep your information confidential. It's standard procedure, I promise."

5

Watching myself on the news the next morning was cringe inducing. I blamed the pinot grigio. If I was going to spill my guts, why hadn't I simply excused myself for a minute, grabbed a comb, some lipstick, and a fresh shirt before I faced the camera. But no, there I sat, eyes glassy, hair all over the place, spitting out the story of my dream. What is it about a microphone in your face? I held forth about our group's efforts to help find the missing couple and described the events at the quarry.

"Oh, Mom, how could you?" Charlie groaned. "This sucks."

You can always count on your kids to give it to you straight.

"That stuff about you and your friends acting like a bunch of witches after Halloween? It was the worst." Charlie asked, his dismay reflected in his eyes. "Plus, you looked so weird, Mom. All googly-eyed."

"Honey, have a heart! Last night I was not myself. This was a difficult situation. A family was hurting and I tried to help."

"I don't want to go to school today."

Jamie bounded downstairs. "Stop being such a brat. This is not about you, and who cares what your school friends think, nerd boy."

"Yeah? Well, you didn't see it."

"I'll look for it later online. But don't even worry about it. Nobody will see it. Anyway, Mom didn't do this to get on TV. The family came to her, and so did the news, didn't they, Mom?"

"Yes. After they found the bodies, everyone was in shock, including me. Greg gave them my name. He said it was our help that finally solved the mystery."

I prayed for the twenty-four-hour news cycle to move on. Most of all, I didn't want to be reminded of the way I looked the night before. But it must have been a slow news day. Once the kids left for school, I got ready for work and was just backing out the driveway when two vehicles blocked my path. One vehicle bore the name of Fox News. The second, logo-free, brought a reporter from the local paper.

At least I was showered, combed, and dressed. I did two short interviews at the curb, one on camera, the other into a recorder. I tried to low-ball the dramatic aspects of our involvement in finding Carla and Steve. I just wanted to get it all out of the way, in hopes that things would get back to normal. I wanted to be on my way to the office. It was the one place I counted on to be drama-free.

When I finally got there, Jerry was halfway out the door en route to meeting with a potential buyer. I could tell he was in a good mood. "Margo, do me a favor. Consult your crystal ball and let me know when business is likely to pick up." It was going to be long day.

After he left, the phones began their insistent clamor. The first call was from Paula. She was wondering why I hadn't said more about the Mediums Guild. "I did. Paula, I mentioned it by name and talked about what we do and how long we've been in business. Must have been edited out, but I tried."

Next I heard from my mother. "Margo, dear, you must have been tired. Your words were a little slurred."

Alisha and several other members of the Mediums Guild chimed in. The calls were a mix of fibs on how well I looked on TV, tempered with sympathy for Greg and his family. Jerry returned, and the workday continued, only hitting a pause when a client called, asking him if I could predict how much her house would sell for. "Jerry, I swear, I didn't mention your name," I told him. "I don't know how they found out that I work for you."

"You know how things are. Philadelphia's like a small town. Word travels." Jerry's expression was mildly tolerant, but his patience was limited, and who could blame him? He had a business to run.

Charlie slammed his books onto the counter. "That was the worst day of my life. In science class, I tried to work on my project for the fair, but all I heard about was you." He flickered his fingers at me and made a "woo-wee-oo" sound reminiscent of The Twilight Zone reruns he watched. "They started asking me if you could fly."

Jamie chimed in, pissed by a clip about me that someone had sent her. She asked if I wanted to see it. Her tone surprised me.

"Maybe later." My eyes were drawn to blinking lights on the answering machine that now numbered seventeen new messages. I scrolled through caller ID, looking for familiar numbers and decided to leave it for later. Several of the messages were from local radio and TV stations. I walked toward the kitchen in search of a drink even if it wasn't five o'clock.

The phone rang, and Jamie, out of habit, grabbed for it before I could stop her. She held the receiver wordlessly in my direction. "Who is it?" I mouthed. She shrugged.

A smooth male voice identified itself as a producer for Hello Philadelphia, a daily news show. The voice asked if I'd like to appear as a guest two days down the road. I hesitated. "Out of respect for the family, I think I'd like to wait a decent amount of time after the funeral."

The voice was disappointed. "Did I mention there's a fee for the appearance?"

I considered my empty bank account. "Thanks, but ..."

"We can't say for sure whether this offer will still be on the table, but we'll call you back if we can work it out."

I felt a headache coming on, and the urge to hide turned to a desire for escape. Now my sense of guilt extended to my family. Should I try to make amends? There was still one place the kids wouldn't refuse to accompany me.

As a peace offering we went to our favorite Chinese restaurant, confident that we would be invisible, but my new notoriety followed me even there. Jamie rolled her eyes and Charlie winced in discomfort when the owner, Mr. Chen, personally delivered our wonton soup to the table. He shook my hand. "I saw you on TV. Very nice. How you kids like having a famous mother?"

Jamie put down her chopsticks. Even her favorite steamed dumplings hadn't brightened her mood. "I hope it's over fast and things get back to normal," she told him, echoing my own thoughts.

The funerals, held days apart, were private. Carla was buried at her mother's parish church, St. Mary's in Burlington. Steve's final resting place was in Mount Holly near where he grew up. It seemed best for me not to attend, and I let Greg know in an email in which I offered my most sincere sympathies. The day after, the Mediums Guild sent a fruit basket to Carla's parents, I made a donation to the charity requested, and sent a card to Steve's mother.

Stories of Steve and Carla's lives cycled through the evening news. Their bodies had been found, but the mystery remained. Questions loomed. Why were they killed? Who killed them? Was it robbery, or was retaliation or jealousy a motive? One story claimed Steve had borrowed money from Russian loan sharks in Florida and left town without paying it back. It just didn't ring true.

Another shock came from the autopsy. The medical examiner

reported that the Steve died from a gunshot wound to the head. But Carla wasn't shot. Though results were inconclusive, the cause of her death most likely was asphyxiation.

The stories faded from the public eye but my interest did not. Drawn back to a growing collection of articles, I noticed one news story I'd missed early on. It read, "Man Disappears, Trailer Ransacked."

Dated three days after the disappearance, the Mount Holly Examiner carried a brief story with a photo. The picture showed a woman, her face an older version of Steve's robust features, surveying damaged belongings spilling from a trailer outside her home. The article quoted her as saying, "My son brought stuff from his diving business in Florida, asked if he could store it here. Who would even know it was here, let alone break in and wreck it? It doesn't make sense. Right now, though, I don't care about any diving equipment, I'm just worried about my son. I haven't seen or heard from him in days and neither has anybody else. That's just not like him."

During interviews, I always mentioned the Mediums Guild. But our manager, Paula thought I could have done a better job. To pick up the slack, she sent out press releases with media mentions, quotes, and attention-getting highlights. Claiming she was sensitive to the families' feelings, she assured me that her marketing efforts would not be directed to the general public. They were targeted instead to event planners and promoters and I have to say, it seemed to work.

The Mediums Guild website got lots of hits. Business picked up. Paula snagged special bookings for the group and especially for me. Since my advantage might not last beyond the next full moon, I happily agreed to take the extra work. Broke as I was, I negotiated for more than my normal rate.

For events like the mid-December booking that would send us all the way to New York, I insisted on being paid for travel time as well. We were booked as a last-minute attraction at a Mind Body Spirit Expo. The agenda called for Paula to lead off with a talk on the "power of intuition," and I would follow with a demonstration at a luncheon. Then, together, we would lead a break-out session on psychic ability, mediumship, and the role of spirit in everyday life.

Driving to Manhattan, we decided how it would go. "Just for atmosphere, I've brought my collection of tarot cards and some healing crystals and other things, like a scrying mirror," Paula said.

Paula's son Randy was behind the wheel. He was also our computer support. "I made a PowerPoint of the early Italian tarot cards," he said. "People like to see those."

"Maybe we can ask a few likely candidates to pick three cards and we'll use the web cam to project their card spread on the screen," Paula said.

"What do you want me to do?" I asked.

Paula gave it some thought. "Once we have the audience warmed up, I'd like you to go around the room. Read any auras that are clear to you and see if you feel any messages come through. Even if you don't, make something up. This is New York. People here are results oriented."

I decided not to argue, but I was not about to "make up" anything. Ever.

The traffic gods smiled on us, and we arrived at the West Side neighborhood near the 92nd Street Y earlier than expected. Our good luck continued, and Randy found a nearby parking garage that wasn't full. I gasped at the rates, but Paula said not to worry, she had that expense factored into the equation.

We found the location. Inside, people with clipboards directed us to the right room. We were featured speakers at a special pre-conference lunch. Randy set up fast, testing the equipment to make sure there would be no surprises, at least not of a technological sort. As the doors opened we were calm and serene.

The lunch guests wandered in and found seats at a score of round tables. An event organizer told us to give the waitstaff twenty minutes to bring out the food.

I waived away offers of lunch, sipped at a bottle of Perrier, and watched people eat. Once service ended, the host introduced us, providing a brief synopsis of our credentials. Behind the platform, Randy projected the Mediums Guild's new logo, website, and contact information.

Paula cracked a few innocent jokes and talked about how our group got started. Scanning the room, I caught energy shooting up from a rear table. I craned my neck, peering past a woman with a full mane of auburn hair. Near the door, a youngish man with an unruly mop of dark curls seemed to be the source, his aura spiking red and yellow. Glasses slipped from his nose to reveal a dark, pointed gaze. Our eyes locked. He nodded ever so slightly, as though we'd been introduced. Caught off guard, I looked away. A second peek revealed a bookish pallor beneath dark stubble and a Brooks Brothers–style suit in need of a press.

When Paula called my name I moved to the podium. Randy threw news articles up on the screen. Follow-up video from Channel Six News described the car in the Delaware River and the bodies from the quarry. Before I could even get started on our psychic work, a man with slicked-back hair and a corduroy jacket raised a hand. I wondered if he was a reporter.

"Didn't you know from the beginning this was foul play?"

"Not really. In the beginning, people thought the couple might have just decided to disappear together. Then there was always the possibility of an accident. The police really had no clues until the car was found. But forensics on the car helped."

"And, of course, your dream." His posture signaled disbelief.

"Yes, my dream."

Another hand went up. "But what did the police find?"

"The police crime lab went over the car pretty thoroughly. In the end, the clue tying the vehicle to the location of the bodies was literally something very small. It was a pebble, a limestone pebble, imbedded in one of the tires. It was a match with stone found at the Camp Harmony location in my dream. Still, if the weather had been different, if it hadn't been such a dry summer, both the car and the oil drums with the bodies might never have been found."

Paula gave me a nudge. The slide show changed to the Medium's Guild website. It was time to move on. Our contract called for me to spend thirty minutes doing readings with the audience. Pacing the room, I allowed my instincts to take over while avoiding eye contact with the rumpled man in the back. Something about him made me nervous, maybe his pointed stare.

As I passed a well-turned-out young woman, her hair in a glossy ponytail, I was surprised by the sound of a horse neighing. I stopped near her table. Dark streaks in her aura suggested sorrow. "May I speak with you?" I asked.

She looked around, surprised, until she realized I was addressing her. She nodded.

I heard the horse neigh for a second time. "I feel that you have suffered a loss and that you are in mourning."

She looked down.

"Behind you." Not stopping to think if it made any sense, I went on. "There's a horse with a white diamond marking on his head."

She burst into tears. "Oh my God. That's Fiorello, that's my horse. He fell and broke his leg and we had to put him down three months ago. I've been so upset ever since."

I reconnected with the horse and felt a sense of peace. I did my best to translate the emotions into words. "He wants you to know that he's okay. He understands. He's doing fine."

"Oh, thank you." She said. "I needed that."

A few more people raised their hands, wanting a reading and I did my best to communicate psychic impressions until the host called time and announced the end of the session. The guests pushed back from the tables, moving on to scheduled lectures on past life regression, a doctor who described the power of prayer in cancer therapy, or a psychologist whose patients were alien abductees.

Paula whispered, "We need to hustle. They're waiting for us on the second floor." Randy packed up our computer gear and we made ourselves ready to move us to our next location.

Under the watchful eyes of the audience, we found our spot. Randy got the PowerPoint up and running. Colorful images of Delphi and other mystical locations flashed behind us while Paula spoke about the history of divining over the years. Still, I felt the crowd grow restless. I kicked Paula under the table and gave her our "hurry-up" look.

She took the hint and turned to me. "Margo, can we jump ahead to how you might use a few of these tools in your readings and even in everyday life?"

Eye to the clock, I gave a quick version of my first experience with tarot cards. I remembered my first deck, a gift from my brother, Bart when I was only a teenager. Something in the cards unlocked a door in my consciousness. I was astonished at the images they conjured up in my mind. Piecing together their meaning, the cards told a story. If the startled looks on my friends' faces were any indication, what I came up with struck a nerve. Moving beyond my teen years, my adult challenge was to decode what I saw in the cards and explain their meanings in brief messages people could understand.

I asked the audience about their psychic experiences and we listened to folks share stories of their own lives. I was glad for the shift in focus as the audience related to what the speakers had to say. As the time for the one-hour session melted away, I knew Paula would want to finish on a high note. We just hadn't discussed what form it would take. So I wasn't totally surprised when Paula announced that I would do a past-life reading for a lucky volunteer. A few hands rose but before she could call on someone, rumpled man popped up.

He launched himself to the front of the room, slamming into the empty chair across from me. His energy felt intense. This might not be my favorite reading ever, but I'd get through it. Besides, it was time to bring this dog and pony show to a close. For sure, I thought, these New Yorkers with their short attention spans must be ready to move on to their next session.

"I'd like to connect with you." I looked deep into his eyes and fanned the tarot cards on the table. "Please select three cards."

I watched his hand waver over the deck as he pulled cards from the spread. I wasn't surprised to see an Ace of Pentacles, The Tower, and the World, all indicators of new projects, drive, and chaos. Linking the cards into a brief story, I noticed the corners of his lips curve into an amused little smirk. Ready to move on to the past-life reading, I turned my palms face up, in an unspoken invitation. He took the cue and placed his palms downward on mine. As our hands connected, there was a frisson of electricity. Settling into the deep breathing I needed to clear my mind, I concentrated on the darkness in front of my closed eyelids.

Slowly, images materialized. There was a torch, its light flickering against damp stone walls. Steps descended to murky water as a low-slung boat drifted into its mooring. A door into the wall opened, and a woman, richly dressed in the garb of Renaissance Europe, glided down to where the boat was tied. A bony hand protruded from what I recognized as a gondola. Instinct told me we were in Venice, and I began to speak, slowly at first, then gaining confidence as a story began to emerge from what I was seeing. The tale spun itself out as I described details of the life of a wealthy noblewoman as she stepped into the waiting gondola. Once inside she stayed only long enough to receive the small vial of the poison that she hoped would free her, sending her aging husband from this world to the next.

The reading complete, my eyes blinked open and our hands separated. I felt confident in what I had seen. The stunned look on the man's face seemed to confirm recognition on some unconscious level. Paula raised her eyebrows and shot a quick nod to the moderator. Taking the cue, he said a few words of appreciation. We stood as the room broke into applause.

As the audience straggled out, an older man with a shaggy gray mane and a young Asian woman in an expensive designer dress stopped to pick up business cards, chatting Paula up and sharing a variety of intuitive experiences. Rumpled man seemed to have disappeared, and that was fine with me. To avoid further psychic communication, I busied myself packing up the tarot cards and crystals for the journey home. I could tell Paula was a little miffed but decided not to care. Later in the car, she confirmed my impression. "Margo, I know you always want to provide the most accurate reading possible, but you painted a picture of a very unsavory character. Do you realize that?"

"I have to admit, I wasn't feeling the warm fuzzies for the guy. Something about him bothered me, and I just went with my gut, it was my version of the truth. I didn't say he killed anybody, I just said he got hold of some poison. Sorry."

"I respect your abilities, but you know there are many interpretations of what we see."

"Speaking of interpretations, I wasn't expecting to do that past life reading. I would have appreciated a heads-up."

"You know me." She laughed, "Spontaneous to a fault."

"Still, you could have let me know."

Now it was her turn to apologize. "Sorry, I got carried away in the moment."

We picked up our check and found our way back to the car. I burrowed into the back seat, glad that it was Randy and not me negotiating the late afternoon traffic. I sighed and closed my eyes as we went into the tunnel, and when I awoke we were at Exit Five of the New Jersey Turnpike. Almost home.

Half an hour later, Randy pulled to the curb in front of my house. Every light in the place was on, but before I could fret about the electric bill, Jamie charged out to meet us.

"Oh, Mom, thank God you're home." She burst into tears.

"What happened? Where's Charlie?" In a panic, I spied him at the door of the neighbor's house. Jamie gripped my arm.

"Charlie and I rode our bikes to get something to eat. We were gonna put them in the garage, but on our way back, I saw the glass in the back door was broken. We thought someone broke into the house."

"You didn't go in did you?"

"No, Mom. Mrs. McKelvey was just coming home. I told her about the door. She said to come with her and we should call 9-1-1 from her house,"

I silently blessed my next-door neighbor.

"But when we walked around front, I saw Dad's car down the street. The last time he lost his keys, he got in the same way. So I figured maybe it's him. I called his phone."

"I can't believe this."

"It was him. He apologized, said he didn't mean to scare us. He said he just came by to pick up some stuff, some papers."

My emotions shot from fear to anger. "He's not still here is he?"

"No."

When Jack moved out, the agreement was that he would not come to the house without first asking my permission. And he would definitely not be there alone.

"You didn't go in?"

"I didn't want to, but Charlie wanted to get his video games." She sighed.

"What time was this?"

"Around four."

"Then what?"

She came close to my ear. "I think Dad might have had too much to drink. I didn't want to say anything to Mrs. McKelvey. She waited out on the front steps."

My neighbor bustled over, leading Charlie back into the fold. I gave her a hug.

"Jane, thanks for being there for the kids."

"Don't even think about it. I stayed out front while they went in. He left a few minutes later, but I told them to stay with me until you came home. Just in case."

My neighbor didn't have to say it. She'd seen Jack like this before. I thought back to the time a few years before when she'd called me at the office to say that Jack was sitting on the front steps waiting for the kids to get home from school. Another time he'd lost his keys. She didn't say he was drunk, but the way she put it was something like, "Jack doesn't seem to be himself today. I'll meet the kids at the bus, take them around the back way. They can stay with me until you can get home."

"You are the best kind of neighbor."

Paula and Randy were still in the car. They'd been standing by. I approached the car and Paula lowered the window. "False alarm. Jack just forgot his keys and went through the back door caveman style."

"Sure you're okay?" Paula asked.

"Positive." I thanked them for waiting in my best "No problem" tone of voice.

Randy put the car in gear and they drove off.

"Do you want me to come in with you?" Jane asked.

"No, we'll be okay."

I turned my key in the lock. The living room seemed fine. In the dining room one of the drawers in the china cabinet was half open. I told the kids to stay out of the kitchen while I picked broken glass off the floor. I found a piece of cardboard and taped it over the broken pane in the door. Who could I get to put in a pane of glass? I guessed it would be me making the trip to the hardware store.

Aside from a wardrobe bag with a few of Jack's old suits and his golf clubs, nothing seemed to be missing. Upstairs, nothing was out of place.

Once things settled down, I went to my office and closed the door. I could sense Jack's energy in the room. I took a deep breath and called his cell. Of course he didn't pick up. I left a message.

"Goddammit, Jack. You know you are not supposed to be here. You scared the kids, caused a ruckus with the neighbors, and embarrassed me in front of my friends. And what the hell was so important that you couldn't wait? Your old suits?"

The line beeped the end of the message. I called the number again and kept on talking. "You know I don't keep any cash in the house. How could I? Thanks to you, I'm fucking broke. Oh, and one more thing. If you think I'm going to let the kids come to your place for the holidays, even for two seconds, think again."

❧❧❧

6

After the broken window incident, the phrase "restraining order" kept springing to mind—but once my anger cooled I knew I wouldn't go through with it. The kids, though upset, were always willing to forgive. In a string of emails, Jack begged for another chance and promised to go to AA. He claimed he'd been in denial about the possibility of losing his family and that the whole drinking thing was his way of avoiding the pain he felt. He would do better from now on.

What about me? A therapist friend told me Jack needed some tough love. I went back over our lives together, questioning myself for being the naïve person who once believed in Jack, who bought into the dreams, the promises. How had that person been so gullible? For me, she suggested an Al-Anon session, so I tried it. The next week I showed up at a gathering in a nearby church basement. People were nice. There was a lot of coffee drinking, a lot of sharing, but it felt weird. Maybe my feelings were still too bottled up and all the hugging left me cold. I felt numb. Even though other people open up their lives when they ask me for help, I have a hard time sharing my own feelings, even with people close to me. It reminded me of when someone asked, "How can a psychic help someone else if they can't help themselves?"

Alisha, with experience of her own, offered the names of a few divorce attorneys. Even so, I wasn't ready for the lawyers, the haggling, the court appearance, the property settlement. All of it gave me a full on anxiety attack.

Jack must have done a little soul searching of his own. He promised to try harder. He even mentioned us going back to into counseling. He was staying sober, he said. To prove it he messaged me daily about the twelve-step meetings he attended. He was enthusiastic about the buddy system. It was making a big difference, he said. With Christmas close at hand, Jack sent a token support payment of two hundred dollars as a kind of peace offering. We had divvied up the holidays before all this happened. He promised that if I let the kids spend Christmas Eve with him, as previously agreed, I wouldn't be sorry. He'd been looking forward to spending time with them. As long as he stayed sober, which he assured me he would, things would be fine. Christmas Day would be my day with Jamie and Charlie, and we planned to spend it at Mom's house.

I was leery but on Christmas Eve, I swallowed my misgivings and let the kids go. Alone for the evening, I turned on the Christmas lights and sat up with only a glass of eggnog for company. The annual rerun of White Christmas flickered before my eyes until I nodded off. Television noise finally woke me and I made my groggy way to bed.

Next morning, the kids came home looking happy enough. Charlie carried an armful of new video games while Jamie showed off the red Coach bag she'd not so secretly been lusting after. Even if I'd had the money, which I didn't, the price tag seemed over the top for a seventeen-year-old. Jamie seemed surprised by the gift, but she said her father told her it was a combined Christmas and birthday gift, though her birthday, May 16, was months away.

How could Jack even consider such an extravagant gift when he still wasn't making the long-overdue support payments? Did he have a new job?

"So what's new?" I asked. I couldn't help myself. "Tell me about Dad's new place."

My question got the usual short shrift from Charlie. "It was nice."

I didn't press. I would grill Jamie later for the details.

"What did you have for dinner?" I asked.

"We went out to eat," Charlie replied, with a look that told me I'd get nothing more than name, rank, and serial number. I knew that look. Hating it when I bombarded him with questions, Charlie clammed up altogether.

I turned to Jamie. "Where?"

My daughter tore her eyes away from the text message she was reading long enough to say, "The Sheraton."

"What did you have?"

"Shrimp."

"Anything else?"

"Oh, yeah. We met his upstairs neighbor."

"And?"

"Her name's Audra. She's cool."

"That's nice."

"Yeah, she's an artist. Dad showed us one of her paintings."

Christmas dinner at Mom's was off to a quiet start. It was just the four of us. She and I were just getting the food on the table when there was a knock at the door. "Let me go." I said. But Charlie beat me to it. I heard an explosion of laughter and there stood my brother, Bart with his partner Dave right next to him, their arms filled with gift-wrapped packages.

Mom came in to see what the commotion was and almost dropped the salad. There were screams of delight, hugs all around and a flood of excitement and laughter. "Bart, why didn't you let me know you were coming?" She said.

"Sorry Mom. It all happened yesterday and I didn't know if I could pull it off. I got a few extra days off and Dave's off until the first of the year. I got us two seats on the red-eye. Nobody wants to fly on Christmas morning, so we got up at five, and here we are."

Of course, the kids immediately wanted to open the gifts he brought but judging by the look on Mom's face it seemed best to start the meal and save the presents until later. Dave offered to carve the roast and I made the gravy while Mom fretted about whether there was enough food but she needn't have worried. She always cooked like we were a football team, not the family of skimpy eaters that we actually were.

Dinner was over for hours, but we stayed at the table, happy to be together. The adults sat sipping wine, the kids laughing at Bart's stories. Sometime actor, sometime bartender, my brother is always good for a laugh. When he's around, things get lively. The kids beg him for tales of the Hollywood elite at their worst. Happy to oblige, he dishes juicy tidbits on the glitterati both at work on the set and at play in the Beverly Hills watering holes where he serves drinks.

As we traded tales and reminisced about when we were kids, I remembered how much I wish he'd never left. I could tell Mom felt the same. She was as happy as I'd seen her in months. She'd been out to Los Angeles for a visit two summers ago, but she still missed him. Bart was her only son and he was a charmer; handsome, funny, and generous when he could afford to be. After a full season of work on a cable reality show, Bart must have been feeling pretty flush. It was lovely of him to use the extra money to fly the two of them east for the holidays.

Mom looked across at Bart, then back at me. She turned to Dave. "They could almost be twins, don't you think?"

He considered it for a moment. "You're right. I know they're two years apart but if I didn't know better I could almost believe they were twins except for the fact that Bart's got curly blond hair and Margo, your hair is straight and dark."

"Oh, and one more thing, he's five-eleven and I'm only five-four." I said. "No fair. In my next life I plan to be at least six feet tall."

Jamie weighed in. "Don't listen to them, Gram, they look just like you. Dave, let me show you. " She ran into her grandmother's bedroom and came back with my mother's high school graduation picture.

I always loved that picture. Her hair was swirled up on top of her head in a brown, wavy twist. Her eyes were as green as glass and just as clear. Bart and I shared her eyes, her nose and the same pale complexion.

One time, Mom told us the story of how a photographer came up to her on the street and asked her to pose for him. She never did it but I always thought she was beautiful.

"Gram, you looked like a model in this photo." Jamie said

"I agree." Dave said.

"Well, my hair is lighter now. But I guess we all do look quite a bit alike."

"What year was that taken?" Dave asked.

"I graduated in 1967. Uh-oh, I'm giving away my age."

Dave laughed. "You grew up in the Sixties? Cool. A real hippie chick."

"No not really. My sister, Ruby, she was the hippie."

Charlie rolled his eyes. All of a sudden, I realized how much he reminded me of my father. But I kept it to myself.

When Dave and Bart offered to do the dishes, Jamie got up to help. As she stood, Bart did a double take. "Look at you! If you ever wanted to try your hand at acting, I'd be happy to take you to the talent agency that I work with."

Jamie blushed, "Oh stop it, Uncle Bart."

"No, seriously. You are a knock out, kiddo. Isn't she Dave?"

"She looks gorgeous. A lot of girls would kill for that hair."

Jamie, looking pleased, ran her fingers through her thick auburn hair.

"You're right." Bart said. "Last time I saw you, your hair was a lot shorter and you were still in braces."

"I got those horrible things off at the end of 9th grade. That's when I let my hair grow out. Haven't I seen you since then?"

"I don't think so. Yikes, that's close to three years. Shame on me for not getting home before now."

Later, I overheard Jamie telling her uncle about her plans to go to school in California. Until then I thought of it as a pipe dream, a fantasy, but now I could tell that she was serious. I tried to give Bart the high sign before it was too late but he didn't get it. He continued to entice her, spinning tales of the good life in California until I kicked him under the table.

Charlie was a little shy. Bart lived with us for six months or so before he went to L.A., but Charlie was still a pre-schooler then and he didn't have the emotional connection to his uncle that Jamie did. But Charlie had brought his X-Box, and once the dishes were done, he, Bart, and Dave were engrossed in a game of Grand Theft Auto. It was a good Christmas.

Things are different now, but years ago, when Bart first came out to Dad and Mom, it was tough. It wasn't a great shock to Mom. She always paid close attention to the comings and goings of my brother and me. Bart dated in high school but he never was serious about it. No matter how Bart might have tried to cover up his real feelings, Mom didn't miss much.

Dad was a different story. My father and Bart were never really close. But with Dad that wasn't surprising. He was a little like the locks that he worked with. With my father you had to really try hard to gain his attention. I worked at it, struggling at finding a way into my father's notice. With Bart it was just the opposite. He wanted to fly below the radar. Except for tennis, he avoided most sports, played an instrument in the band and stayed out of Dad's way. Once high school was over, Bart seemed to make up his mind. He became more confident, less willing to hide who he was. I had moved out by the time he came out to the parents but from what he told me, it wasn't pretty. But maybe my father mellowed some with age. Dad asked for his son's forgiveness before he passed away and Bart gave it willingly

The day after Christmas, Bart and Dave came for brunch on their way back to the airport. I made French toast, and Bart, Dave and I downed a bottle of Spanish sparkling wine. Once the kids cleared the room, Bart turned to me. "What's happening with you and Jack?"

"I've probably given you the short version in my emails."

"Yes, but Dave hasn't heard most of it." Bart said.

"OK, in July, Jack came home one day and announced that he'd quit his job. The boss pissed him off and that was it. This was maybe job number ten in the last five years. After that the fighting got so bad. I just couldn't take it any more. He found an apartment, moved out and that was it. Then early this month, he came to the house when I was out, after he'd agreed not to. And he was drinking. Now he's going to a twelve step program and staying sober but I don't really know what's going on."

At that, I surprised myself by bursting into tears. I never like anybody to see me cry. But sitting there with the two of them, I went through half a box of tissues. My tale of poverty struck a nerve. Though he and Jack had always been friendly, Bart was on my side. He advised legal action and even offered to help me out with a loan for legal fees if that's what I needed. Then it was time for kisses and hugs at the door. I was so sorry to see them go but Bart and Dave made me promise to call if I needed anything, no matter what.

The first week of January found the status quo unchanged. School was back in session, and I was looking for a way to pay the bills. It's the worst time of the year for home sales. No one wants to think about buying or selling a house in the winter. Jerry was cutting down on his overhead at the office. And who could blame him. With Jerry needing to reduce my hours, he and I circled around each other over whether I should even bother coming in to work for the month of January.

"I've got houses to show but no serious lookers," he said. "Your draw is maxed out, but if you just want to come in and do a little prospecting on your own, I could, maybe, cover the gas."

I promised to call him back later.

The landline rang, and three minutes after I answered it, I was hyperventilating, wondering if I'd just been the victim of a prank. I thought I would burst. And there was no one to tell. I called Alisha, but she didn't pick up. My mother's phone went to voicemail. Paula was on vacation in California. I tried several others, with no success.

Desperate, I called Jamie's cell. She picked up. I heard chaos in the background. She was at lunch in the school cafeteria. "Mom, are you okay?"

"Jamie, you won't believe this. Channel 27 just offered me money to come on their morning show once a week for the last two weeks in January and the first two weeks of February, before Valentine's Day. Ten-minute spots with me as the resident psychic. Isn't that amazing?"

"Awesome, Mom. But what'll you wear?"

That brought me up short. I mentally scanned my wardrobe. The vibes were bad. "Good question," I said. "You'll have to go shopping with me."

She hesitated a moment. "Only if you agree to go to Bloomingdale's instead of Target."

I pictured her rolling her eyes. "Okay, I promise. No bargain shopping."

"Gotta go, Mom." A buzzer sounded through the din. "There's the bell."

Come Saturday, our shopping destination was the suburban mall with the high-end stores. It was cold but sunny. I felt light-hearted enough to ignore the heavy traffic. Crawling along the Expressway gave me a chance to savor the time Jamie and I still had together before she left for college.

My daughter snuggled against the headrest. Tired but satisfied by her efforts, Jamie had just mailed off her final college application. What a kid! I read her college essay written with no help from me, her father, or anyone else, and it was brilliant!

Thinking about her college applications sparked another, less pleasant thought. "I guess the financial aid applications will be due soon."

Jamie pushed a button on her phone and told me the date.

I looked to my daughter for inspiration. I told myself if she could do it, I could do it. The online version of the FAFSA college financial aid form gave me the willies. At eight pages, it was more than a little intimidating. There were questions about bank accounts, taxes and everything else financial. I needed to have my 1099 from Jerry and another one from the Mediums Guild before I could fill those forms out. And I needed the same from Jack. My chief assets were the house and whatever I had in my checking account. There were some bonds, too. Did I have to report them? I should check on that. I thought about the coins. I didn't think I would have to list them. Weren't they off the books? An accountant would know all this stuff, but I didn't have one.

My thoughts focused on the college fund that was stashed away at the bank. After Jamie was born, my father began a family tradition, one that continued with the arrival of his grandson, Charlie. My dad, a locksmith by occupation, was a very practical man. Instead of buying toys for birthdays or holidays, he socked away money for the kids' education. His investment choices were old-fashioned, but he stuck by them. His contributions, in the form of government savings bonds and gold coins were added to the stash on a regular basis.

The bonds matured, and their value grew. The gold did even better—it tripled and he held on to it. These gifts became lore, something the kids knew about but never actually saw. But Dad loved keeping track, and there was nothing he loved more than sharing the totals from time to time. When the kids blew out the candles on their birthday cake, he'd ask them, "How much is your fund worth this week?"

The kids loved to guess. Whoever came closest, even if they were way off the mark, won a silver dollar.

As much as I tried, there was no way I could convince my father to convert the nest egg into more modern investments. He loved to remind us that when the markets fell, as they sometimes did, his savings stayed strong. When he passed away three years ago, Mom turned over the keys to the safety deposit box. I couldn't bring myself to keep up with the values in the box the way he did, but my last estimate made it close to twenty three thousand dollars.

I congratulated myself. No matter how bad things got, I had always resisted the temptation to touch the college fund. With the skyrocketing cost of tuition, the fund wouldn't provide as much of a cushion as we'd hoped, but it was our only savings, and I treasured it. We all did. Its presence had sustained me through many a sleepless night.

I found a parking spot close to the mall entrance, always a good sign. As we walked into the glitzy mall, I gave Jamie a hug. "You deserve a reward."

What with the prospect of fresh currency coming into the household from my television appearances, I put my worries aside, and we settled into a little celebratory shopping. Bloomingdale's was having its winter clearance, and I found one outfit on sale. Next we hit the shoe department, where my daughter suggested boots to go with it.

When the saleswoman brought me out a couple of pairs, Jamie nodded approval at the ones she liked best "The black ones really make it pop," She said.

"Now I get it," I teased. "More the affluent Bohemian looks instead of the loopy psychic look?" She blushed as if I'd read her mind, and we both laughed.

After a few acquisitions for her, we were circling back for a tea break when I felt a tap on my shoulder. The touch sent a chill down my spine. When I turned, there was rumpled man, his dark eyes level with my own. I gave an involuntary jump and dropped the bag.

"Sorry, didn't mean to startle you."

"You didn't," I lied.

"Remember me? We met, kind of, at the lecture in Manhattan last month. You did a past-life reading. I took your card."

"Yes, I remember now. How are you? I didn't catch your name."

"Josh Bruckner."

We shook. "Margo Fellshur. This is my daughter, Jamie."

"I hate to say it, but I've been stalking you."

I felt another chill. "Why?"

Jamie's elbow hit me in the ribs.

"Your friend Paula wasn't willing to put me in contact with you, so I tracked you with a little detective work, because I—that is, we ..."

He took a breath and pulled himself together. "I'm a partner in a consulting firm. We'd like to talk to you and perhaps some of your colleagues about doing work for us. Are you interested?"

Things were getting crazy. First Channel 27, and now this.

"I'd love to talk, but we're really in the middle of something. Can I get your number? I'll give you a call tomorrow."

Jamie took the hint. "Mom, we've got to pick up Charlie. We're late already."

Bruckner gave me a card that read Future Technologies. It listed a number with a New Jersey area code and a PO Box in Princeton.

"Thanks, Mr. Bruckner. I'll give you a call."

Jamie tugged my arm. Our shopping spree was over. We fled to the parking lot.

Jamie grabbed the card. "Mom, are you really going to call him?"

"No, I don't think so." But I wasn't sure. Some part of me was intrigued, and I wanted to check with Alisha and get her take on this.

That night after dinner, Jamie came into my room, fanning sheets of paper. "You should take a look at these."

I scanned several articles with mentions of Bruckner, and his boss, a former Army major who was once part of a top-secret intelligence unit. When the unit disbanded, its members all left the military and sold their stories to the media. Later they started various consulting enterprises. One was Future Technologies. Josh was recruited right out of Princeton.

As soon as I was finished with the articles Jamie had showed me, I thought of Jerry. I trusted his business sense, and I needed it now. I gave him a call. "I've been offered some work with a consulting firm. I just wondered if you could help me out with a little background." Then I told him about the articles.

Jerry agreed to help. "If you want, I can check the company out on the D&B database; see what their background looks like."

At the office next day, we sifted through the basic facts about Josh's company, Future Technologies. The data sheet listed the name, address, telephone and fax numbers, and a grand total of nine employees. Three principals were identified, Don McPeak, managing partner; Arnold Lawrence, CFO; and Josh Bruckner, vice president of marketing. They paid their bills timely enough to receive a credit rating of Good. The company had no debts outstanding.

I thanked Jerry profusely and offered to pay for the report. I knew it cost him thirty bucks.

"It's on the house," he said.

I shared my good news about the TV gigs. Jerry looked relieved at the way things worked out. We exchanged hugs and promised to stay in touch while we waited for the housing market to emerge from its winter doldrums. He didn't have to feel guilty about not being able to pay me, and I didn't have to feel guilty about running off to chase fast money and another career.

When the car arrived a little past seven in the morning, I was ready, with my outfit in a garment bag. Two doors down, a neighbor, eyes riveted on the limo at my curb, stopped loading her car long enough to take in the scene. As the driver held the door open for me, I couldn't resist an airy wave in her direction.

With two hours to airtime, I sat through hair, make-up, and minor wardrobe assistance from a stylist. Then a production manager prepped me on my spot. "Just follow Melissa's lead. Talk to her as you would to a friend. Try not to worry about the camera. You'll be fine. Just remember the one with the red light is the one that's shooting."

Sitting backstage, strangely nerve-free, I heard the host, Melissa Garfield, say my name as she recapped the mystery of the missing couple, my dream, and the grim discovery in the quarry. I hoped she would mention our group, the Mediums Guild, but she didn't. She cut to commercial, came back, and when the assistant gave me the slightest of taps, I walked onto the set. It was smaller than I expected. I took a quick peek at the audience. There were maybe fifty adults perched on three rows of bleachers.

Melissa and I shook hands. She pointed me to the other comfy chair, and I balanced on the edge of it while we chatted briefly about various psychic experiences. The audience felt primed. After the next commercial break, she told them I would do a reading for one lucky person.

Before the show, the assistant had gone out into the audience and chosen the volunteer. She was waiting backstage now. With little fanfare, they brought out a fortyish red-haired woman who Melissa introduced as Ronda. Melissa gave Ronda a pat on the shoulder. Without saying what it was, Melissa told us she had suffered a recent loss. She hoped to connect with that person.

I gulped. My specialty was reading tarot cards, palms, tea leaves, and sometimes past lives. I'd connected with spirits a few times, but not by a conscious effort. It just happened. In fact, not counting Carla's appearance in my dream and a few other occasions, I'd rarely connected with the beyond at all. But if I wanted to come back again, I had to perform, and fast. I imagined the producers backstage checking their read-outs. I could almost hear them saying, "We don't have all day."

The look in Melissa's eyes was one of expectation. No time for the tarot reading that helped me form a bond with my subject. Shutting out the audience, the producers, the cameras with their red lights took some doing. I took several deep breaths. Behind closed eyelids, I visualized myself sitting in a quiet garden. There was a sense of being in two places at once. As I sat, a presence approached from my left. There was a definite male energy. There was a light radiating from him and I was drawn to it. The entity motioned for me to follow. We connected silently as I told him I was with Ronda.

Next to me, Ronda's expectation was palpable. The energy was intense but I forced myself to concentrate. That part of me in the studio willed my voice to narrate what I was seeing in a very different place.

The entity led me through a doorway to the center hallway of a house. I could make out his person more clearly. His smile grew. "Is there something you'd like me to tell Ronda?" I asked.

His arms opened wide in a gesture that took in his surroundings. I spied a lovely staircase ascending into a haze. He smiled. "Tell her not to worry. I'm keeping busy here." The light grew brighter and then he faded.

I opened my eyes, straining to articulate the details I'd seen. I repeated his message a second time. As Ronda took in my words, she burst into tears and grasped my hand.

Melissa handed her a tissue.

"Oh, thank you," she blurted. "That's my Ed. And the house you described, with the center hallway? That was our dream house. We planned to build it next year."

Her face took on a look of wonder, and her lips curved up in a tearful smile. "I miss him so much. He passed six months ago, in a car accident. Ed's greatest fear was not keeping busy. He was always on the go, making plans, drawing up blueprints, building. A whirlwind of activity. I'm so glad he's okay. Thank you. Thank you. I feel more at peace now."

The audience applauded, and a tearful Ronda was returned to her seat. Melissa and I chatted for another minute or so. Before she cut to commercial, Melissa asked the audience if she should have me back on the show the following week. Thankfully, they all clapped. I took that for a "yes." The assistant producer led me backstage, and I rode home in my suit, still excited and relieved.

The next day, Paula invited all Mediums Guild members to dinner. We rarely have the chance to meet face to face without the pressure of reading our clients and being "on-stage" at a bar mitzvah, birthday, or charity event. It would be a good opportunity to catch up.

I ordered takeout for the kids and drove to Paula's. It felt great to relax a little. Sipping a glass of chardonnay and nibbling on a stuffed mushroom, I gave half an ear, listening to Gwen talk about how the planetary alignments were wreaking havoc on her love life.

Paula reminded us about the upcoming Heart Strings Ball, a charity event on Valentine's Day. Our most upscale event, it was held at a luxury hotel near Rittenhouse Square in downtown Philadelphia. If all went well, there would be plenty of press coverage, fashionable well-heeled guests, and good pay. She did a head count on who would be available.

Living from paycheck to paycheck, we were all happy for any extra income. Knowing this, Paula was thrilled to report that she'd negotiated an extra twenty dollars per hour per person as an incentive. We all agreed to clear our calendars, wear our best, and arrive early. With the evening's business out of the way, talk of romances, careers, spouses, and children continued, our laughter grew in proportion to the number of empty wine bottles.

When I shuttled to the kitchen in search of more cheese dip, Paula followed. She let the door swing shut behind her. "Margo, the event planner made a request for you to do something a little extra. They'd like to use your photo and mention your appearance on Channel 27. Would that would be okay with you?"

The inflection in her voice told me that she expected the answer to be yes. I decided to push it a little. "Paula, I'm always happy to explore new opportunities, but before you answer on my behalf, you should ask me first. I can do it for an extra three hundred dollars."

Paula gasped. I stood firm, sure that the fee she'd negotiated would cover what I asked and still leave some extra profit to share with the group. More to the point, with a stack of unpaid bills, I needed the money. Paula agreed to my deal.

The big occasion arrived and we converged on the Warwick Hotel in plenty of time for the event planner to move us to our spots. There was a table for me in an alcove with an easel that displayed my photo over the words "As seen on Hello Philadelphia." I settled in and set up my crystals, candles, and glitter. Alisha waved to me from another corner of the room. We were far enough from the dance floor and the music to be able to speak without having to scream above the d-jay.

I had burned through a dozen readings when a familiar face peeked around the corner.

"Hi, Margo." Greg moved into the chair across from mine.

His presence washed over me like a warm bath. "Greg!" I tried to keep the excitement out of my voice. "What are you doing here?"

"Trying to expand my social awareness, I guess." He chuckled at his own joke.

"How are you doing?" I asked. "You never did call me."

"Yes, I did. I left a message on your phone."

I thought back to the high phone traffic of late November. "Sorry, I must have missed it. Things got crazy. But it's great to see you here."

"To be honest, this isn't my type of event, but a friend twisted my arm, and I bought a whole table for my company. I keep reminding myself the tickets are tax deductible." He laughed.

"It is a good cause," I said.

"Anyway, a couple of people didn't show up, which means there will be three servings of filet mignon in danger of going to waste. Can I count on you to help us out with one?"

"Greg, I'd love to, but I can't leave my spot. But tell me where your table is, and I'll stop by on my break."

"We're near the stage. Look for the palm tree decorated with the twinkling hearts."

There was a discreet cough from behind. Greg looked over his shoulder. "Looks like you have a customer." He made way for a woman in black silk and pearls. "Don't forget to stop by."

After another hour of readings, dinner was called. Hungry guests went in search of their entrees. It seemed like a good time for a break, My new sign read, "Gone to consult the stars. Back in fifteen minutes." I put it on the table next to my crystals and went to find a restroom.

On the way back, I spotted Greg beneath twinkling lights and slipped into the empty seat next to him. He smiled and motioned to a passing waiter to bring me the first course, shrimp cocktail.

I thanked the waiter but waved him on. "It's better for me to keep an empty stomach while I'm working. But please, keep eating. Don't let me stop you."

"Everybody, this is Margo."

I counted five others at the table. The three men and two women waved or murmured greetings of welcome. A placard in the middle of the table read, "Havens Aviation."

"This is my team at Havens. Tina and Cheryl are my office crew. Mack's a pilot, like me and Gordy, Mr. Bow Tie here is our mechanic." He hit the man next to him in the ribs with his elbow. Gordy nodded, continuing to gobble shrimp. I sipped a glass of water in front of me and ignored the urge to grab a roll from the breadbasket. Greg dipped a shrimp in cocktail sauce and devoured it.

Break time was over but before I went back to work Greg convinced me to meet him for a cup of coffee afterwards. He'd said he wasn't married and I guessed if there was a significant other, she would've been sitting there with him. I still wore my wedding ring, but tonight I'd slipped it off before my shower and hadn't thought to put it back on.

When the event ended I found Greg nursing a beer at the hotel bar. I ordered club soda. He asked if I was hungry. Truth be told, I was starved so the BLT on the menu got my vote. Greg sipped a second beer while we caught up and got reacquainted. He even knew about my recent television career.

I asked about his job. "Winter's our down time. Things start to pick up when the weather warms up." It seemed like he was keeping it light and that was more than fine with me. But when Greg thanked me for sending the fruit basket it opened up a door into his world just a crack. I felt safe enough to ask him how Carla's kids were. "The girls are spending more time with their father. He's changed jobs so he doesn't travel like he used to. My brother-in-law is a good man. He's doing his best. We all are."

Maybe enough time had passed for Greg to talk about what happened. He gave me more details about his sister. Her belongings were mainly intact. Her watch and ring were on her body when it was found, and the same was true for Steve. But one thing had been missing - a necklace Steve gave her. She had considered it almost a pre-engagement gift, or so she told her mother.

"Are you sure she was wearing it that night?" I asked.

"They had their picture taken at the restaurant. A copy turned up later. She was wearing it, for sure."

I wanted to know more than the little he'd shared at the party about his near-death experience. He admitted to having done some reading on near death experience since we'd met at Halloween.

"It was a year ago last fall, near my birthday."

I made a mental note to find out if that made him a Virgo or a Libra.

"We had a job taking some aerial photos for a land use company. My partner Jeff was with me, manning the camera set-up. The day was clear, good visibility. We were still low, maybe only five hundred feet up. A flock of geese flying south appeared in front of us. They veered off to the east, but the last one on the end fell behind. Before I could pull up, the bird flew into the engine. It stalled and we dropped like a lead weight."

"Thank God you weren't alone," I said.

"I wish I were. Coming down we hit an electrical tower on Jeff's side. His face turned gray before my eyes. I took a lot of volts myself, but I managed to stay conscious long enough to land in an open field. I passed out, and when I came to, the Doylestown Fire Company had already pulled Jeff from the wreckage. He was in an ambulance on his way to the hospital. They pulled me out next. I made it. Jeff didn't."

"I'm so sorry." My sandwich turned to dust in my mouth.

"It's been a long process. I feel guilty about Jeff. Why did I make it and he didn't? And now these strange experiences are adding to my feelings of guilt."

"Maybe they're a gift, not a punishment."

"Doesn't feel that way."

I put my hand over his and felt a little electric tingle.

Greg looked into my eyes. "I was planning to call you again anyway, so this is a nice coincidence, don't you think?"

I raised my glass. "To coincidence."

Is there such a thing as an ethical code for psychics? Well, of course, the answer is yes. Does it extend to the realm of romance? I wondered. Was it ethical to date a client, even if he was a non-paying ex-client? I gave it some consideration and decided I could date Greg without fear of cosmic retribution. But I had other questions. It sounds crazy, but even though I blithely advise others on their love life, I'm clueless about my own.

What does a date consist of anymore? It had been over twenty years since the word date was in my vocabulary. My nineteenth wedding anniversary had come and gone without comment, but even before that, I hadn't been in a relationship with anyone except Jack since right after college.

Greg was younger than I was. I mentioned this to Alisha and she got hysterical. "Get over yourself. This is today. Madonna's boyfriend is twenty years younger than she is, Jennifer Lopez's boyfriend almost that much. And you're worrying about what? Five years?"

Alisha is my lifeline to the world of single adulthood. "Well, we haven't actually gone out. We met for a drink after the event last night."

"A drink? How did you leave it?" she asked.

"He said we should hang out some time. That means what, exactly?"

"And he has your number, you have his. You've emailed back and forth. You know the details of his life. He knows some of yours. What he's saying is that he feels comfortable with you."

I liked the sound of that.

"You could even call him."

"No, I don't think so."

7

My agreement with Hello Philadelphia called for three appearances. With Valentine's Day on the calendar, the second and third shows had been devoted to romance. I did a reading for one couple who'd just gotten engaged and afterwards members of the audience wanted to know which zodiac signs were the best matches for romance. With one more appearance to go, the producer changed it up. When I arrived for the last appearance, he let me know he wanted something a little different for number four. I'd be sharing on-air time with two other psychics, as a sort of panel. We'd be taking questions from the audience.

"Sounds like fun. I'm game." I said.

After a few minutes in make-up, I found the "green room". Jen and Kim De Mateo, two sisters from New Jersey, were thrilled at the opportunity to be on Philadelphia TV. And the producers were thrilled to have them. They were show-biz naturals, full of personality and media magic. The audience loved them I and could see why. As we shared on-camera face time, the sisters explained that they had started small by doing psychic readings at their kitchen table. Word spread. People were drawn to them, so they began to make house calls, visiting troubled addresses in need of spiritual cleansing. They traveled around New Jersey taming unruly spirits and removing meddlesome entities that refused to acknowledge it was time for them to leave the physical world.

This was their main source of income, and the whole family was involved in the enterprise. One sister's husband was the driver, a son took care of the audio-visual equipment, and a daughter did sound recording and photography. Born promoters, they were already planning how to put the clip from the Hello Philadelphia show on YouTube. Paula could take a lesson from them, I thought, but maybe not. No videos on the Internet for me.

Afterwards Kim, the more outspoken of the pair pulled me aside. "Margo, I didn't want to say anything while we were on the air, but I saw an older man standing behind you. He was trying to give me a message for you."

Now I felt really foolish. How is it that I could have communication for other people and not for myself? "What?" I asked.

"He showed me a key. Does that mean anything to you?"

"Well, my father was a lock smith. So it makes sense that he might have a key."

"OK. That must have been it. I just thought you should know."

I felt unsettled and wasn't sure why. If Dad wanted to tell me something, why didn't he do more than show them a key - but that was my father for you. Communication wasn't his strong suit in life and apparently that hadn't changed now that he'd moved on to a higher plane. I kept their card for future reference.

An official-looking letter from California addressed to Jamie, arrived from Palo Alto, with the seal of Stanford University to be more precise. Feeling a mixture of joy and dread, I stuck it up on the kitchen cabinet with a magnet. It would be waiting for her after school. Right on schedule, Jamie arrived home and made her usual beeline for the refrigerator. I counted to ten. From the kitchen there was a strangled cry followed by a shout of joy.

"Mom, did you see this?" She waved the letter in my face. "Why didn't you tell me?"

"Wasn't it better finding it yourself?"

"You're right." She gave me a big hug. For the rest of the day, Jamie was as excited as I'd ever seen her. Over the moon, jumping out of her skin excited! I was happy for her, but my heart sank at the thought of the price tag.

Why Stanford? Some years ago, a video about the treatment of farm animals made animal rights one of my daughter's causes. After the video, her biology teacher took them on a field trip to the agriculture school of a local university. From then on it was settled. Jamie wanted to be a vet. It was an interesting choice for a city girl who, except for goldfish, never had a pet in her life, not that she didn't try. She often brought home strays, she just never got to keep them. It wasn't her fault that she had a father who disliked animals, but that didn't stop her. She joined the Four-H Club and spent summer week-ends for a couple of years working in a stable out in the suburbs.

Early on, I'd learned that once Jamie set her heart on something, it did no good to try to dissuade her. Somewhere, somehow, Jamie got wind of a special group at Stanford that helped students get accepted into veterinary school. Once she learned of Stanford's society for pre-vet students, her course was set.

I kept silent, but I thought back to last fall when I had begged, "Be careful what schools you apply to. Add a few state schools just in case. We're not rich." Those words fell on deaf ears.

The next day I was forced to remind her that unless Stanford came through with a huge amount of financial aid, like 99.9 percent, California was out of the question.

"Jamie, we're barely scraping by. California's so far away."

Her tears welled up. "Mom, I've talked about being a vet since I was in middle school."

"Yes, dear. I know that. But there are many ways of making that happen besides an undergrad degree from Stanford."

"But they have that special program."

The discussion went on and on. It wasn't that I wanted my daughter to settle for the local community college, but plunking down huge chunks of cash I didn't have was beyond the realm of possibility.

"What about Grandpa's college fund?"

Following my father's passing three years ago, I became custodian of what was lovingly known as "Grandpa's fund." The government bonds and solid gold coins he presented to his grandchildren for birthdays, Christmas, and everything in between stayed safe and growing in value. For me, it was a source of comfort.

For Jack, it was pure temptation. When the stock market was riding high, he wanted to cash out and transfer the money into some "can't miss" technology start-ups. I resisted. The fund stayed in the safety deposit box where my father put it, and when the stocks crashed I bit my tongue and resisted the urge to tell Jack, "I told you so."

"We're lucky to have it, but things have changed," I said to Jamie. "Tuitions keep going up."

"What about Dad?"

Yes, what about him? I bit my tongue. Why even bring it up? He was already behind on the promised support checks. I knew better than to expect his help paying tuition.

"I hate to say it, but he has yet to send the financials we need for the FAFSA application. Things are pretty much on me, and I'm winging it. We need to come up with a Plan B, okay?"

I reconsidered my financial options. My choices were limited. The check from Hello Philadelphia cleared the bank and disappeared as I paid bills long overdue. My boss, Jerry, would take me back any time I was willing to work in the real estate office for commissions only.

"Welcome back," Jerry said when I showed up at the office the next morning. He sounded like he was genuinely glad to see me. "This place has been way too quiet. It's hard being here on my own."

I gave him a hug. It felt good to be back in the world of bricks and mortar. For the next week, my energies were focused on real estate. Concentrating on the few prospective clients who were looking to buy, I set about helping them find a house they could afford. There was a sweet two bedroom, one and a half bath in a good neighborhood in South Philadelphia. It was priced to sell, and I showed it to three potential buyers before deciding to arrange an open house for the following weekend. Sunday's weather cooperated, and we had quite a few lookers. I arrived home from the open house, tired but exhilarated. A couple who came by with their own agent seemed particularly interested. With a little more work, I might have a sale.

My joy was short-lived. As I pulled into my driveway, there he was again—Josh, the guy with the black hair.

"Margo, I hope you remember me." I ignored his outstretched hand. "Josh Bruckner?"

"Yes, of course. I'm just wondering why you're here."

"Strictly business. Please don't take my presence as anything but cordial. I was hoping you'd call back. And even though you didn't, we're still interested. I'd like to make you an offer. We want to hire you."

I played dumb. "Who is we?"

"Did I mention that I represent a consulting firm, Future Technologies? We're located in Princeton."

A cold wind was whipping up, threatening rain. But I was determined not to invite him in. "When I didn't call you back, that was my answer."

"Do you think we could go inside?"

I shook my head. "There's a Starbucks around the corner. Why don't we talk there?"

We walked quickly, pushed along by a gust of wind. Inside the café, I ordered green tea, and Bruckner made do with bottled water. We found a seat near the window. "Okay, now that we're inside, please continue."

"Our firm is unique. We have experience that few others have. I'd like to explain it to you." He took off his rimless glasses and gave them a quick swipe. Without the glasses, his eyes looked strangely exposed, I thought.

I sipped tea and waited.

"Some years back, the U.S. government, not unlike other nations, got involved in what I'll call psychic warfare. Certain capabilities were explored in the name of national defense. At the tail end of the Cold War, it was above top secret. A group in military intelligence worked on a little known project called Starfire."

Starfire? Oh, please.

"But things changed. Once they disbanded the group, word leaked."

Wasn't Josh Bruckner too young for that? A little mental arithmetic told me he would have been barely a teenager when the Cold War ended.

"Most people in the project left the military. My partners were part of that group. Now we, that is, our firm, make use of those skills for other purposes."

"Is that legal?"

"Why not? We just approach problem solving in a slightly different way. I'm sure it's something you do all the time without even thinking about it. For example, if someone wanted you to help them find something that was lost, what might you do?"

He had a point.

"I'd try to visualize it."

"Correct! That's exactly what we do."

"Okay, so what do you need me for?"

"We're looking to expand. We want to explore new ways of approaching what we do—we want some different techniques. I can tell you we're well-funded. Trust me. Are you interested?"

My current cash squeeze had changed my outlook. I had to

admit that a tiny part of me was definitely interested.

"Am I correct in remembering that your colleague, Paula, mentioned you work together with a group of psychics? What's the name?"

"The Mediums Guild.

"Yes. We'd like to see how this kind of group might be able to function as a team, working on some projects."

"What kind of projects?"

"You've heard of Uri Geller, right?"

"Of course, who hasn't?"

"Here's one thing you might not know about him. He became a multimillionaire helping companies locate gold and diamond deposits."

"I don't know that I'd have the skill for that kind of thing. Besides, if I could do that I might just walk around on my own with a metal detector."

He smiled politely.

This conversation felt like it was going in circles. "So what's the bottom line? Why me?"

"I already told you. I read an article about you and saw you in New York. We were intrigued. You seem to have the skills we need."

I registered his words. Would they translate into dollars?

"The other question is, would your colleagues be willing to work as a group?"

I thought back on our attempt to help find information about Carla when she was still the unknown missing woman. Our group results were less than stellar, but I wasn't about to share that bit of information.

"Obviously that would be an individual decision by each member of the group, but I'll check with them and get back to you. Of course, they would expect compensation for their time." I looked at him and waited for the answer.

"Of course. Once they've had the training. This is a business venture and will be conducted as such. We have clients of means."

"May I have your card?"

A glossy card revealed only the company name, Future Technologies, and a website address. This time I would keep it. "Do you have a phone number? I asked.

"This is my cell." He wrote an 856 area code number on the back of the card and handed it back. "Just leave me a message when you're ready. Our office in Princeton isn't far. I'll be back in touch."

I tried not to think too much more about Mr. Bruckner and his office in New Jersey, although truth be told, I tried to do a little casual "remote viewing" of my own. When that didn't work, I went to a map of the area and ran my hand over the street intersections. I felt a certain amount of warmth but no images aside from traffic. I went to the Internet next and pulled up a few news stories from some New Jersey papers. One of them, a press release dating from the firm's opening, provided an address. Using it, I found the location's latitude and longitude and wrote it down.

I went into my "study" and plopped into what I call my meditation chair. Inhaling deeply and exhaling slowly to clear my mind, I felt myself going within. After several minutes, I picked up the sheet where I'd written the Princeton address, skimming the paper with my fingertips. Nothing. I went back to the computer and pulled up Google Earth. The image showed a strip mall along a highway. I found articles, even a book that described the group and their past. There was nothing about their present.

My research came to an end when a door slammed and a familiar voice pulled me back to the here and now. "Mom, where did you put my skateboard?" Charlie bawled.

I took a moment to ground myself. "In the closet, if you can believe it."

The sarcasm lost on him, he mumbled, "Thanks," and banged outside again.

Next day, February 25th, was Charlie's birthday, and Jamie begged me to let Jack come to dinner with us. He'd spent many weeks on the twelve step plan since the incident when he'd been in the house without permission. His emails promised that he was moving forward, getting his life back together. I wasn't sure if I bought it. Still, I knew Jamie wanted to embrace her father's attempt at transformation, and I wanted to send the right message as well. I left it up to Charlie, the birthday boy. He agreed to Jack joining us as long as we celebrated with pizza at his favorite Italian restaurant.

I'd been urging Jack to send me his income statements and bank accounts for the year just past so I could complete Jamie's financial aid application. Jack had never been forthcoming about his finances, and now it was even worse. There were only bits and pieces of his finances to work with. But there were deadlines to meet, so I crossed my fingers and made up the rest, hoping I wouldn't be accused of fraud if I used what he gave me.

My intentions were to keep the birthday dinner light and cordial. But the sight of Jack waiting for us at a table for four was a surprise. The twelve-step program he joined was working a miracle. I wanted to say that sobriety was agreeing with him but held my tongue. He looked about twenty years younger than the last time I'd seen him. His skin glowed, his hair was stylishly cut, and his lavender button-down shirt sported a familiar logo on the pocket. He and Charlie gave each other a fist-bump and Jamie gave him a hug.

The kids seemed more than willing to forgive and forget. Part of me still wanted to give him a chance, and I knew Charlie and Jamie—especially Jamie—hoped we'd get back together. With Jack behind on support payments to the tune of several thousand, I wasn't so sure.

I was more than content to let the kids chatter on about school, music, their desire for smart phones, and everything else that had gone on in their lives for the last couple of months. Jamie hoped for a medal in her upcoming gymnastics meet. Charlie was proud of the signs he'd just finished for his Science Fair project, due the next day. In times gone by, I would have poured my heart out to him, too, dissecting this or that situation, merging my intuitive sense with his salesman's prodigious ability to read human foibles. But the old Jack was gone and I wasn't sure he would ever return.

For the table, we decided on a favorite chopped salad layered with bits of pancetta and avocado. Jack and the kids stuck with pizza, and I kept it simple with chicken in lemon sauce. When Alphonse, the owner, took our order for entrées, he asked if we wanted to see the wine list. I noticed the surprised look when Jack demurred, saying, "We'll have a bottle of Pellegrino and the kids will have Cokes."

Dinner passed, pleasant enough. Jamie shared her good news about the college acceptance, and Jack claimed to be thrilled, but I noticed a weird look in his eye when the word tuition came up. I reminded him that he'd given me last year's income estimates but I needed his actual tax forms now so I could complete the financial aid application. He blanched and changed the subject.

I hadn't thought about who was going to be paying for tonight's restaurant tab, but I guessed that Jack wouldn't fight me for the check. While Charlie and Jamie argued over who would get the last piece of chocolate cheesecake, Jack turned his blue eyes on me. It was a look I knew well. He didn't need to ask. I felt the measure of his desire squarely in the middle of my chest. He didn't say a word, but I heard the question in my head. I knew it was only for tonight, just as I knew that the moment would pass. Still, part of me wanted to say "yes," but with a shake of the head, I mouthed the word, "No."

Dinner quickly ended when Jack remembered an important call he needed to make. I reminded everyone it was a school night and called for the check. We separated in the parking lot with repeated "Happy Birthday" wishes followed by more hugs and fist bumps and Jack's solemn promise to come to Charlie's Science Fair three days later.

The drive home was silent. Without much prodding, the kids settled into their bedrooms for homework. Minutes later, I turned off the downstairs lights and climbed to my bedroom with a feeling something like regret.

I was proud of Charlie, my seventh grader. His after-school activity with the science club was time well spent. He'd kept the science project pretty much to himself, but I knew his topic was seed germination. What little I knew came by accident. Weeks ago, I caught him rummaging in the kitchen cupboards looking for some dried beans. When we came up empty, I'd given him a few dollars to buy a bag at the supermarket.

Now I could see the results. Charlie's experiment demonstrated how identical seeds planted at the same time will grow at different rates after rinsing them in different chemicals before planting. While the concept wasn't advanced, his graphics and illustrations next to pots of sprouting seedlings carried the day.

My mother came along to cheer on her grandson and by the time we arrived, Charlie's project was already graced with a ribbon and an honorable mention for presentation and general interest. Charlie was beaming. I gave him a big hug, and his grandmother promised to treat him to the ice cream sundae of his choosing. For the next half hour, Charlie continued smiling, but I could see his eyes dart around the room only to return to the door. He was waiting for Jack.

Another hour passed. Parents began to leave. Soon the maintenance man came in to sweep up. I called Jack's cell phone and left a message the gist of which was, "How dare you."

With Jack a no-show, Charlie's face said it all. The pleasure in his accomplishment faded. He decided to leave his project where it was. And no amount of coaxing could make him change his mind. He swept the project into a trash can where it landed with a clunk. "At least take the ribbon with you." I dug out the red garland, but he waved it away. I put it in my bag. And we headed to the door.

The next day I drove by Jack's new digs. I'd never been there but I had the address. It was time to confront him about how he'd broken faith with his son. As I drove by, I spied an "apartments for rent" sign on the window. I parked the car. I marched up the steps. I mashed the buzzer under Jack's name. There was no answer.

A woman moved past with her shopping. She looked up at me. "Are you here to see the apartment?"

"No. I'm looking for Jack. He lives on the second floor."

"Jack? I'm looking for him too. But we're both too late. He moved out yesterday."

"Are you sure?"

"I guess I am." She drew herself up. "I'm the owner."

"Sorry. I'm just shocked is all. Did he say where he was going?"

"I don't know for sure. I thought I heard them talking about going out west."

"Them?"

"Yes, Jack and the other tenant, Audra. I wasn't home. Went to visit my grandchildren for the week-end and when I came back they were both gone. Broke their leases and left me with two vacancies. His apartment is a studio on the second floor. She had the one-bedroom on the third. Both furnished if you want to see them."

Part of me wanted to scream and throw things, but I needed any facts I could wring from the tight-lipped woman in front of me. "Did he leave a forwarding address?"

"Why? Does he owe you money too?"

Shamefaced, I admitted we were married.

She shook her head. "He didn't leave a forwarding address. If he had, I'd be giving it to my lawyer. I did overhear them talking one time, it might have been California."

Thunderstruck, I stood on the stoop. Then it hit me. I ran to the car and drove to the First Federal Savings and Loan as fast as I could.

Except for our wedding album and a second copy of the mortgage, the safety deposit box was empty. The money was gone. Our nest egg, Grandpa's fund, was missing. The savings bonds and the gold coins hoarded since the kids were born were gone. Was his name was still on the signature card for the safety deposit box? According to the bank officer, it was. How had I forgotten to take care of that? I knew he didn't have a key. But I knew wrong. The clerk who let him into the vault said that he did.

How did he get it? Then it came to me. Was that why he was there at the house that day? Had he found the spare key, the one I'd kept hidden in my old jewelry box? And how would he know it was there? What about the police? Should I report the theft?

I called the police. An officer met me at the savings and loan. He took a statement from the clerk and the bank officer and I filled out a form. He gave me a copy along with his card. Teary-eyed I drove myself home.

Back home I threw Jack's photo in the fireplace. The glass shattered. In need of more violence, I kicked at his chair. That felt good but I wanted more. So I bashed it against the kitchen floor, until the leg splintered. Feeling satisfied, I hauled it to the trash. Good thing the kids were in school. I didn't want them to see my tears. It took some time, but I took deep breaths and waited. When I could count on my voice not to break, I dug out Josh Bruckner's card and dialed the number

8

The following Wednesday, I gathered the Mediums Guild members at my house. Once everyone was seated, they were ready for me to tell them why they were here. Beginning in the middle, I described the trip Paula and I took to New York. Was it only a few months back? Paula remembered the man with dark curly hair who had volunteered for the past life reading. She'd heard from him since.

"He took my card," she said. "He called a few days later asking how to reach you. You know I would never give out that kind of information."

"Thanks, but he found me anyway." I tried for a dry chuckle. Focusing on what was important, I cut to the reason for the meeting.

"Josh's consulting firm, Future Technologies, has plans for an experimental project. He wants to develop a group with intuitive powers who can be called on as part of what he calls a "cohort of perception." I winced at his terminology. "He wants a group with capabilities to predict lottery numbers and foretell winners of horse races and other events. When the outcomes could be predicted with a measure of accuracy, it could be profitable."

"Prophecy on demand?" Alisha asked. A few others chuckled.

"Something like that. Their theory is that lottery numbers, stock market movements, even looking for a lost diamond mine might be something that could be predicted with the right techniques."

In short, would it be possible to draw on the techniques we use to give information to individuals about their love life to help companies increase their profits? The "consultants," as I referred to them, also offered opportunities for training in new techniques. These were nontraditional methods that moved beyond the intuitive, techniques that might be at the edge of the psychic frontier.

"What kind of techniques?" Gwen wanted to know.

"He mentioned remote viewing and something he called future progression."

Alisha scrunched up her nose like she smelled something funny. "Remote viewing I've read about. But I don't see how that involves us. That's not something we do."

"They're going on the theory that we're already remote viewers. We're familiar with intuitive experience, we're comfortable with it. We have our own ways of doing things. They want to teach us the newest techniques. Then they want to test us and see how we adapt to it."

I related the Uri Geller story, telling them about his road to wealth and the fees he'd charged over the years, helping others find hidden resources. Could it be possible that we might actually benefit from the use of our own abilities? I reminded the group that other people benefited from our intuitive information, and then I asked them to recall even one time we'd increased our own fortunes with it. We all drew a blank on that one.

"I'd be willing to try," Renee said. "Anybody else?"

Around the room, I could see the wheels turning. For Paula, ever the entrepreneur, I could see this was something to consider.

Gwen had a different perspective. "It feels like such a sell-out. I like to think I use my abilities to help people."

"You do," I said. "This would be helping in a different kind of way." I felt a little ashamed saying that, but I'd agreed to this sales job as part of the pact I'd made with Josh.

"Just think about it. In our group, it's always the cobbler's son who has no shoes. We help other people, but rarely do we benefit from our own abilities."

My words were met with silence until I sensed an "aha" moment across the room—Alisha. Always in debt, the idea of extra cash obviously intrigued her. Most of the Mediums Guild members present that night opted out right away. Gwen had a job lined up to do hair and make-up for a touring Jersey Boys production. Zara couldn't take off time from her school guidance counselor job until summer vacation. Paula wondered aloud how our business would manage to stay afloat if she left. That left Alisha, Renee, and me.

Alisha and Renee stayed behind for a second glass of wine. Alisha brought us up to date on the trials of supporting a daughter with a huge cell phone habit and a taste for high-end jeans. Renee wanted to finance her own business and dreamed of setting up a spa, fantasizing that money from this venture would help her do it. With my kids moving toward college and our family savings in the wind, I had a pressing need for cash. The three of us had big dreams about how the money would bring security—maybe even some comfort—to our lives.

We traded tales about how we'd gotten to this point in our intuitive journey. Though I'd heard it before, I listened as Alisha described her Italian grandmother teaching her to read tea leaves when she was six. Renee's story was just the opposite. She learned to hide her gift from devoutly Christian parents who called it a sign of the devil. By the time she turned seventeen, things had gotten so bad that she went away to nursing school and rarely returned home.

With less drama I recalled the tarot cards I'd received as a holiday joke gift from my brother. With teenage skepticism, I'd laughed at them initially. Barely knowing the meaning of the individual cards, I knew the emotions they evoked were real. Only later did I lose sleep over the images the cards brought to mind when I did my first-ever reading for a family friend. A reading that later proved to be true.

We talked shop a little longer, marveling over the divergent paths we'd taken to get to this point and wondering where they would lead from here. Without the participation of the full group, would Josh and company still be interested? Would he be satisfied with just the few of us? If so, this venture might well involve some travel. I promised to make the call next day, the call that would set it all in motion.

Before they left we decided to use a psychic's technique that Alisha's grandmother taught her. To my mind it had always looked and sounded a little like the cauldron scene from Macbeth, but Alisha found it comforting. I moved a small round table into the middle of the room, placed a candle on top, and lit it. Renee, Alisha, and I joined hands around the table.

"Wait," Alisha said. "Something doesn't feel right." She flipped off the light. "That's better."

Now the room was bathed in shadow. We joined hands again. We closed our eyes and slowly began circling the table. Alisha began the chant. "We are many, yet we are one." Renee picked it up, and I went last. After that, we continued in unison three times until a feeling of power filled the room. Still clasping hands, we stood for several seconds until the feeling faded.

With a promise to sleep on the idea, Renee and Alisha left. I stared at the candle for what may have been minutes or hours, returned the table to its former space, and went to bed.

I wasn't sure about the two of them, but I was committed. There would be no turning back. The check was cut. Still, my internal dialog went something like, "Okay, you don't much like Josh. Okay, you don't much trust Josh. But look at Uri Geller. Okay, you are not Uri Geller. But you need the money. Jerry told you to ask Josh for a contract. Have you done that yet? No. Take his advice. You had better put it out there before this partnership goes any further.

❧❧❧

9

A raw wind whipped specks of snow across the gray March sky. I stood at the door waiting for Josh. According to a signed contract, my ten days of "intuitive training" at the Perception Studies Institute would begin the next day. Not wanting to go it alone, I had tried to recruit Alisha double hard, but she couldn't get the time off from work and Renee bowed out at the last minute when her kids got sick.

A silver SUV pulled to the curb. This was it. I grabbed my bag and headed out. Josh was at the wheel. "One stop to make in Jersey," he said. "Picking up another passenger at the Newark airport, then we'll cut over to New York and head up the Hudson."

I tried for lighthearted. "Should I have brought my skis?"

"There might be snow up there, but I don't think you'll have time. We got a pretty full agenda."

At Exit 14 we pulled off the New Jersey Turnpike for the airport. Josh left me in short-term parking while he ducked inside the International Terminal. Sooner than expected, he reappeared steering a thirty-something traveler. He introduced her as Nina Pritchett and then threw her bags in the trunk. As

Nina crawled into the rear, she pushed long dark hair off her forehead and took off her sunglasses. Her smile was meant to communicate warmth, but her eyes stayed cool.

From behind, I heard teeth chattering. "Damn bloody cold."

Josh heard it too. "Sorry about the weather, let me turn up the heat. I guess it's summer where you're coming from." He turned to me. "Nina's just in from New Zealand."

"It was seventy-three degrees when we took off from Auckland, whenever the hell that was," Nina said. "Almost twenty hours on that freaking airplane. I lost track of how many time zones we crossed."

We drove northwest, bypassing Manhattan, and crossed into New York State. Traffic diminished. After another hour, we made a coffee stop in Kingston, an old industrial town on the Hudson enjoying new status as a tourist destination. Nina wasn't charmed. She pulled her coat around her, finding relief from the New York weather by dozing for the remainder of the trip.

On the way, Josh seemed less intense than I had remembered. He'd switched gears, exchanging his Brooks Brothers suit for corduroys and a sweatshirt. Was he shedding his uptight demeanor? Chatting away about the history of the Hudson River and the surrounding area, he sounded almost human. Maybe I had misjudged him. Time would tell.

Past Saratoga Springs we turned west, off the highway onto a local two-lane. On either side, towering pines and power lines were the main features. I peeked at the GPS, hoping to pinpoint a town or the name of a landmark along the route. Before I'd agreed to the bargain, the one thing I had insisted on knowing was where I was headed. I had seen the location designated as Perception Studies Institute, or PSI, when I signed the contract, but I had been unable to find it on Google Maps, MapQuest, or any other locator. And I was good at finding addresses. We moved further from civilization. There were no signs to guide us, but Josh seemed to know where we were going. At the crest of a hill, he announced, "Here we are."

Past a weathered wooden gate, Perception Studies Institute spread out before us. The property consisted of three one-story buildings, a faded red barn, and a large two-story lodge fashioned from logs. Later we learned the property had once been a New Age spa and retreat.

Sun broke through the clouds as we pulled up the drive. I wasn't sure what I'd been expecting, but a lodge of hewn logs Catskill-style and a faded red barn wasn't it. From the porch, a tall man with a salt-and-pepper beard and a paunch came out to greet us.

Josh stepped up to greet him. "Dr. Salazar, meet Margo Fellshur."

"Greetings! Welcome to Perception. I'm Victor Salazar." He grasped my hand between his two warm paws and shook hard. The folksy demeanor, complete with vest, flannel shirt, and jeans seemed at odds with the look in his eye, like that of a hungry eagle.

Josh filled me in. "Dr. Salazar is our resident physician-slash-scientist. He's the director of PSI."

I remembered seeing his name on the contract. I could have kicked myself for not digging further, doing a computer search or asking Jamie to look him up for me. I watched him closely as his focus shifted to Nina.

"Welcome, welcome, Nina." He patted her shoulder. "It's great to see you again."

Nina's disposition improved a little. She even smiled.

Salazar checked his watch. "You must all be exhausted."

He was right. I wasn't sure why, but I was beat.

"Dinner's at six. We can talk then. In the meantime, take these few hours to rest up. Come tomorrow, time will be precious."

A dark-haired woman waited nearby. "Maria, can you show these lovely ladies to their rooms?"

"One thing I must tell you," Salazar said before we went with Maria to find our rooms. "Unfortunately, our cell phone coverage is bad here. You know how it is with these carriers in the hinterlands." He pointed to a telephone on the wall. "But you are more than welcome to use the house phone whenever you need to."

Nina and I followed Maria through the common room where a long oak table was set for a meal. I counted eight plates. Up one flight, my bags already waited in the corridor outside a smallish room. It came with a bed, dresser, chair, and a bath across the hall.

Tension circled my temples. I longed to flop down and pull the covers over my head, but relaxation was impossible. There were too many questions. I peered into the silent hallway but there was no one to ask.

I dialed my cell. It felt like a small victory when the call went through. My mother's voice on the other end was reassuring. "Margo, sweetie. How was your trip?"

"It was fine." I decided not to tell her that I was at the end of forever. "We're way further north than you guys. And it's more than a little colder."

"Thank goodness it's warming up here," she said.

"Mom, I really appreciate your staying with the kids. I know you think what I'm doing is crazy, and you may be right, but it's a chance to bank some money for tuition. It's worth the risk."

As we spoke, I thought of the $5,000 deposit I had already received from Josh Bruckner. Once we completed training, there would be a similar cash payment followed by incremental fees whenever I would be asked to "consult" on any of their projects.

"How are the kids?"

"Charlie ran in after school, grabbed his skateboard and ran out. Am I correct in assuming he'll be home for dinner when he gets hungry enough? Jamie's up in her room. She seems a little quiet."

"Maybe I should talk to her."

"Yes, Margo, I wish you would."

Jamie picked up, her voice sounding flat. "Mom, do you remember how we circled that date on the calendar before you left?"

I wanted to block it but it came back to me. The date for the down payment on the tuition. The thousand dollars. "Yes, I remember."

"And you told me not to worry."

"What makes you so sure I didn't do it?" I bit my tongue. I hadn't sent it in.

"Well, did you?"

"No, but with good reason. We still haven't heard about financial aid. Don't you remember when you sent in your applications we agreed that the school that provided the most money would be it. That's where you would go. We haven't heard, and we don't know which school that is yet, do we?"

"This is just your way of keeping me here, isn't it? You just want me to live at home and go to community college, don't you?"

"No, honey, that's so not true."

I heard tears on the other end. The conversation was over. "Please put Gram back on the line."

At dinner, I shared one side of the table with Salazar and Nina. Across from us sat Josh and two associates, two guys with military haircuts who didn't say much. Their knife-creased duds and spit-shined shoes spoke for them.

Before we finished the main course, a newcomer livened things up. Harlan Trebold, with vivid red hair and a Southern drawl, dropped his bags at the door. He spotted food, found a seat, and made himself comfortable.

As though picking up a conversation they'd just left off, Salazar pressed Harlan for stories about his family traditions and what he'd learned at the knees of the older generation. Harlan obliged us with how he came to be the last in a long line of dowsers.

We learned of his grandfather, famous in Mississippi, not only for finding water but also for locating minerals. He passed a wallet photo of his famous relative, dowsing rods in hand. "Granddaddy made more than a couple people rich finding the oil on their property. Shame he couldn't find none on ours."

Salazar and Josh exchanged glances. Harlan's chatter wound down, but we stayed at the table, listening as Salazar held forth on his own history, first as an undergrad, starting college at age fifteen and then as a fellow at Massachusetts Research Institute where he worked with scientists to develop standard procedures for remote viewing. "Our work was based on the theory that remote viewing and other psychic phenomena could be carried out at will and used to gather intelligence for national security. The CIA wanted to build better spies." He laughed. "They figured if the Russians were doing it, we should be doing it, too."

A perennial student, he didn't stop there. Salazar's next degree was an M.D. How he found the time and energy I have yet to fathom. Then he'd worked with pharmaceutical firms on the curative properties of native plants in the rain forests of Central and South America. "Native peoples of the Americas were and are head and shoulders above us in their understanding of these substances," Salazar said.

Finding their spiritual practices not only fascinating but also useful, he now hoped to combine a career in the sciences with the intuitive and the extrasensory. "Exploring boundaries" was the way he put it. "I always say that no work we do is ever wasted."

Josh's seatmates exchanged looks. Were they on board?

Salazar turned to all of us. "I hope you can share my passion. The days ahead will be an exciting time for this project. You are here at the beginning of a new era of discovery."

And a new era of money? I hoped so.

Salazar stood, the evening suddenly over. "All of that aside, time to turn in. You should all be rested for tomorrow."

Sleep that night was hard to come by. The chatter in my head wouldn't quit. Something told me to grab my bag and run, but I was stuck here. I counted sheep, but they turned to dollar signs. Is it always about the money? My thoughts fell back on themselves, back to October. Meeting Greg, the way he'd reached out for help to find his sister. It had been the start of a strange time but that connection felt real. The whole experience seemed organic, almost like watching a plant send out shoots in several directions. Opportunities sprouted from there. And given my situation, I needed to meet anything that came my way head on. What choice did I have? The kids were getting older. They'd be on their own in a few years and so would I.

My mind jumped from one question to another. Where was the money for this project coming from? What was the purpose? I'd wondered about Josh, remembered what he's said about Uri Geller. Was he a middleman? Who was running the show? What were the boundaries? Where would they lead? Right before drifting off, a thought popped into my head. Somewhere I remembered hearing that no energy is ever wasted. Where did that come from? In any event, it made sense at the moment and I hoped it was true.

That first morning, we assembled at dawn for two hours of meditation and yoga. Nina and I knew most of the poses, but I felt sorry for Harlan trying to arrange his bulky frame in warrior, downward dog, plank, and child's pose. After breakfast, Josh lectured us on remote viewing techniques. He went on about the status it once had within the intelligence community and how, as the Cold War ended, remote viewing lost favor. Of course, that didn't stop a believer like Salazar.

"We're talking back in the Cold War era," Josh said. "This was strange stuff for our military, as you can imagine. But once the generals heard the Russians were setting up their own units using extrasensory perception and remote viewing, they had to do the same."

Harlan leaned toward me and whispered, "Like they said, building a better spy."

By afternoon, Nina, Harlan, and I were well acquainted with sets of numbers Josh called remote viewing coordinates. Early on, the CIA used actual latitude and longitude as a way of identifying a location to be viewed. Later they found that any string of numbers, randomly generated, would work just as well. The codes were the only information given to us "viewers." It didn't seem like much to go on. When Josh called out the target, would my subconscious collect real impressions of a specific place? Or would it be my imagination?

We sat in meditation pose, opening our senses with deep breathing. I worked at making my mind a blank. Josh read out the numbers, and we did our best. On paper we scribbled fast, recording whatever we saw or felt - anything that popped into our heads. At the end of each session, it was time to report. Almost like kids calling out to the teacher, we described what we'd written. The payoff came when he showed us a photo. If we matched the target, we felt like winners. If not, there was always the next one.

Most of this wasn't new for me. I had read about it, attended a lecture or two, and even tried my own version of the technique. But I was being paid to be here, so I put on an interested face and took it all in. Finally, we broke for individual viewing sessions, each of us with our own debriefer. Josh was mine, and I told myself I could handle that. Over the last few days, I'd spent time and energy working to calm my gut reaction to Josh, telling myself he was like certain bosses I'd known. You didn't have to like them—you just had to work with them.

Josh took me through fifteen minutes of relaxation. That done, he held up a manila envelope. "A photo of the target is inside. I'll read out the coordinates. You write them down. Use the techniques we covered. We'll see what you come up with."

I settled into the chair. The only sound was the buzz of fluorescent lights overhead. I tuned it out. He read out the string of numbers. I wrote them on the tablet in front of me. Eyes closed, I rubbed my fingertips lightly over what I'd written. For several seconds there was only darkness. Then clouds parted. There was bright sunlight streaming down on a solid edifice rising below.

"Make full use of smell, taste, hearing, and tactile sensations." Josh said.

My eyelids stayed closed as I held tight to the image until Josh called time. Then I scribbled furiously and kept going until the buzzer sounded. Pen down, I looked at my drawing, a pyramid shape with straight lines above the apex. Below that, I'd scrawled a few phrases. My descriptive words were "warm, "crumbling," "stone," and "dust".

He showed me the photo. "It looks like a Mayan pyramid," I said.

Josh kept a straight face but his tone was upbeat. "Have you ever seen photos of this site before?"

"Yes, believe it nor not, I think I was there once. On my honeymoon. It's in Mexico, right?"

"Right. The site is Palenque."

Josh walked over to where I sitting. What did he want me to do? I wasn't sure. But he put up his palm and smiled. We high-fived. "Good job!" he said.

Day Two began with more meditation and yoga. After a short tea break, we were herded into a windowless room on the ground floor. There were three recliners and a chair.

"More remote viewing, I guess," Harlan said.

Nina shook her head.

Before she could say anything more, Salazar appeared, looking well rested and ready to go. "Let's try something different today." He turned to Harlan and me. "Any experience with hypnosis?" he asked.

"A little," I said. "In a past life regression class."

"Not me," said Harlan.

No problem! The three of us were slated for a group hypnosis session then and there. Salazar started a metronome ticking softly. We got comfortable on our individual recliners. Salazar settled into his chair in the corner. He asked us to relax and pay attention to our breathing. I closed my eyes. His voice took on a disembodied quality, and I seemed to float away on his words. After several minutes, Nina, Harlan, and I were invited to return to points in our pasts.

We went back from the present in five-year blocks of time. At the first increment, I was a married real estate saleswoman selling houses during an economic boom. The sense of satisfaction I felt made me smile. Ten years back, I was a harried young mother chasing a two-year-old Charlie around the playground. Back fifteen years, Jamie was scooting around on her tricycle. I was not aware of what my two companions were feeling, but I continued back in time until I regressed through infancy and beyond. I awoke from a deep trance unsure of where I was. Nina was rubbing her eyes. Over in the corner, Harlan snored peacefully, and we had to tap him on the shoulder to wake him up and tell him it was time for lunch.

That afternoon, the sessions were one-on-one. There was a recorder next to the recliner where I sat. I went under quickly, and when Salazar brought me back to full consciousness, we reviewed the session.

Salazar's prompts took me to a place he called pre-birth. My voice, slow and groggy to my ears, described sensations of contentment as I floated in a sea of warmth, listening to sounds and voices as though underwater. Salazar's next request was more expected. "Go to a part of your consciousness where you can access past lives."

Deeper still, I heard myself describe a long corridor with many doors. Salazar asked me to choose a door that my subconscious would draw me toward. I did and was immediately plunged into a horrific scene. On the playback my voice sounded like a wounded animal.

I heard Salazar asking, "What do you hear?"

"Noise. Lots of noise. I'm scared."

"What kind of noise?"

"Shooting, bombs, explosions." My voice grew shrill with strain.

When Salazar prompted me to look down at my hands, I saw the large grimy hands of a man. "What are you wearing?" he asked.

"Boots, muddy boots. Water is leaking in, my feet are cold. My pants are brown, like a uniform." I saw other men similarly dressed running toward a barn. From behind, bombs exploded as an airplane strafed us overhead. I was relieved when Salazar pulled me out of it and ended the session. "Margo, you did well. We'll see you at dinner."

Time for a break. Outdoors it was quiet. The only sound was the scraping of branches overhead as the wind blew through the pines. I gulped in the cold clean air. Off in the distance a dog barked. I walked around a little, made a snow ball and threw it at a fencepost. I made another one and threw it in Harlan's direction as he walked out of the barn.

"How did your sessions go?" He asked.

"I've been hypnotized before but only went back maybe a few years. This time I went all the way back and kept going. It's kind of weird," I said. "These pictures just pop into your mind. I was a soldier caught in the middle of battle, running for my life. The emotions felt real. All I could think about was staying alive. How about you?"

"I didn't get back much further than the age of fifteen." He sounded disappointed. "One thing did tickle me," he said. "When they played back the recording, my voice sounded young, like I really was fifteen. I'd swear my voice kind of cracked."

Nina usually kept to herself, shying away from our sharing sessions, so we were surprised when she sauntered over. For once, she seemed eager to join the conversation. In a rare moment of candor, Nina talked about her experiences going back to a previous life. "I was a slave woman trapped on a cane plantation in the tropics. We worked from dawn until dark. My body was racked with pain." I felt sad when Nina told us her greatest wish was for death.

Later Nina came tapping on my door. She asked if I had a needle and thread. I didn't, but she came in anyway and we hung out in my room for a little while. Once the barriers slipped a little, she wasn't so bad and we found ourselves sharing some personal information. After all, she and I were the only two women in this thing. I told her we needed to stick together, so why not get to know each other a little better. Sharing didn't seem to be her style, so I went first. I showed her photos of Charlie and Jamie and described my life as a single mom with financial troubles. She did her best to reciprocate, but her eyes narrowed when I asked how long she'd known Salazar. She changed the subject and told me about her family in New Zealand and her ex, an engineer who was originally from Canada. That was progress. Not much, I thought, but it was a start.

On Day 3, our new technique involved the use of sound waves to transport us into altered states. These were more free form, and we didn't know what to expect. Initially, we lay on cots wearing headphones and listening to a variety of sound patterns. I fell asleep during the first session and was embarrassed when I didn't do much better on the next.

Harlan not only stayed awake through the long sound-wave sessions but also described an intense encounter with a being surrounded by light. His face was a mixture of wonder and doubt as he talked about an "entity" inside his head. "I'm not one for religion," he said. "But I felt like somebody was telling me something I was meant to know."

During a long conversation, the being told Harlan he had been sent to Earth to learn life's difficult lessons. He urged Harlan to look for answers in the environment. But what did that mean? Was it a dream or reality?

Harlan and I compared notes at the end of the day. Feeling like outsiders, he and I had connected from the first. His mix of down-home smarts and dry country humor was a refreshing break from the intensely serious vibe that Salazar brought to the proceedings. We took our afternoon breaks together, swapping gossip on what we'd seen and heard around "campus." With not much else to occupy our minds during down time, we had ample opportunity to play detective. Encouraged by one another's revelations, we became skilled eavesdroppers, determined to know the purpose of our training at PSI.

While I was skeptical of what we were doing, Harlan, was having the time of his life. With his sheer physical enthusiasm, he was attached to the three-dimensional world. Harlan liked nothing more than a relaxing soak. During a leisurely bath in an old-fashioned claw-foot tub, he'd heard snippets of conversation from the floor above. Ear to the laundry chute, he tuned in to the voices of Salazar and Josh. Salazar's voice was low, more difficult to hear, but Josh's voice, he said, came through pretty clear.

From these conversations, Harlan learned that Josh was depending on Salazar to come up with some funds. More than once Harlan heard Josh ask, "Can you get the investors to buy into it?" I remembered the story Josh had told me about Uri Geller and how he became a millionaire. Did their plans include cornering the market on commodities?

Once we realized the value of our find, we spent our sparse down time lurking nearby, waiting for these meetings in hopes they would clarify what was really going on. In one of these conversations, we weren't surprised to learn how closely our progress was tracked. Each of us was monitored to see which techniques were most successful. Nina scored well on hypnosis. She was able to slip into a trance within seconds and move easily from one phase to another. Her scores on events such as predicting news headlines, lottery numbers, and horse races using future progression were the highest. With a wink, Harlan noted that Dr. Salazar insisted on handling her sessions individually.

We heard that I was best at remote viewing. Josh sounded pretty pleased about the times when I'd zeroed in on the target. Harlan responded to sound patterns that sent him into an altered state in which he received information from unknown sources. Maybe they hoped Harlan would become their own "Uri Geller" and find the mother lode of whatever it was they were looking for.

One afternoon, I overheard Salazar telling Josh he'd moved Nina into the immediate future and asked her to look at a newspaper. She read a headline about the increasing jobless rate in the United States. Next, he quizzed her on economic data. She read out a string of numbers from the front page. They discussed how that would affect the stock market and how they could best profit from what they learned.

Salazar progressed her further, all the way past 2020. When Nina reported that newspapers no longer existed in print form, he asked her to look at a calendar. There were no print calendars either. Instead Nina looked at an electronic device on her wrist, reporting the date was November 9, 2021. At her next session, Salazar progressed Nina further into the future and asked her to report any economic information she was able to identify. She reported that the date was 2024. The New York Stock Exchange had been moved to Hawaii. She had moved from New Zealand to Australia and she reported, sadly, that her bank account was empty.

Dr. Salazar didn't like this information. Josh, too, was skeptical. They tried another approach. "We need somebody to corroborate what Nina tells us. We can't make a move based on one person's predictions. Let's test it out with a lottery number."

The next day, they gave it a whirl. We were all progressed one day into the future to see if we could provide any other numbers. We were prompted to scan the environment for markers. We looked for stock quotes, for lottery tickets and horse races. We looked for draft picks, oil prices, and other commodities. Once Salazar had tested us and recorded the answers, they were sealed until the next day when they could be checked for accuracy.

After the first five days, we got a breather. The sun was out. Snow was melting. Thanks to global warming, it almost felt like spring. Harlan made friends with two swaybacked mares sheltered in the barn. Harlan trusted these gentle souls, inherited from the previous owner, to carry us for a short ride. I'd been on horseback only a few times in my life, but I was willing to try it. Harlan begged and Salazar agreed. Salazar assured us there was no danger of getting lost since the horses knew the way home. Like kids on an outing, we'd pack lunch and ride into the surrounding hills.

We gave the horses their lead and sat back as they carried us, good-naturedly meandering along the path. With food and water in our saddlebags, we could go at least a couple of hours. But Harlan wasn't much of a horseman and I sure wasn't either. Soon we were ready to give our backsides a rest. We unpacked sandwiches and fruit and spread a tarp over a flat rock.

"What do you think this is all about?" I asked, falling back to our usual conversation.

Harlan pulled a face. "Money, don't you think? That's what my gut is telling me. But I can tell you what it's not."

"What's that?" I asked.

"For sure, it ain't about expanding human potential like that speech Salazar made that first night at dinner."

"I'm getting the sense, especially from Salazar, that they're not quite sure where this is going. But Josh is pushing for something. What do you think?"

"For right now, I'm not sure I care. I'm having fun and getting paid." Harlan removed his baseball cap and scratched his forehead. "I get to spend time hanging out. Best of all, I'm not sitting in the cab of a truck all day long, so I'm a happy camper."

We ate in silence after that, alone with our thoughts. The horses nosed clumps of sodden leaves, searching for lunch of their own. Harlan stood and stretched. Fishing in his pack, he pulled out a knife that would have made Jim Bowie proud. He cut an apple in two, and offered it to the horses. The horses waited patiently to see if their benefactor had any more food and I gave them my apple.

Harlan walked to the edge of the woods and squinted at a bare oak. He sawed away at a tree branch overhead. "Let me see if I can make this thing work out here." He stood silently for a moment, his meaty fists grasping the two ends of the Y-shaped branch he had just cut. Slowly the rod began to tremble and then to propel him forward. I trailed him up hills and around rocks. We stopped at the top of a ridge. I gazed back down the way we had come at the horses still tethered below.

The branch jerked downward hard. "Whoa, whoa, here she goes," Harlan said. "We're getting somewhere."

Harlan followed the lead, stopping at the base of a wall of rock. There seemed to be no place else for him to go. He used the knife to dig into the earth at the foot of the rock cliff, sending soggy leaves, roots, and pebbles flying. After two minutes, water gushed up into a muddy little hole at our feet. Harlan had found water. "It's a little easier to do this back home, but I just wanted to test it here," he said. He grinned. "Mission accomplished."

We made our way back down to the horses. But just as we were ready to mount up and head back, Harlan got an itch. "Margo, do you want to try?"

"No, I'm not feeling lucky today."

"Well, let me give it one more shot."

He moved away from the horses, holding the branch. It began to vibrate. He walked a short distance and stopped. He looked down and began digging with his knife. There was a clang as metal struck metal. He started to laugh and pulled the head of an old hatchet from the ground. "Bingo." He rinsed it in the stream. "Looks handmade, iron maybe. Probably a hundred years old." He looked pleased. "Looks like I still got it," he said.

Nina talked about her afternoon in Saratoga Springs, occasionally substituting "we" for "I" as she prattled on. Salazar was uncharacteristically silent as Nina handed around a drawing she had bought from a sidewalk artist and enthused over her—their lunch at the Saratoga Hotel. I felt Harlan tap my foot under the table when Nina complained about limiting " ourselves" to only two mimosas apiece.

"Think it's about winning the Powerball?" Harlan joked later. He pointed to a headline that described a lottery windfall of eighty million dollars waiting for the lucky person who could win the Pick 6.

"Where did you get the paper?" I asked.

Salazar's insistence on a news blackout meant that from Day 1, we'd been advised not to read the news, watch TV, or listen to the radio. Or, God forbid, go on the Internet.

"Found it in the barn."

Later we heard Salazar tell Josh he'd bought a lottery ticket based on numbers Nina read out to him. They were waiting for the winner to be announced on the seven o'clock news.

We checked the time. At six thirty, I went into the lounge and pretended to read. Salazar and Josh huddled in the corner. Harlan played solitaire on the coffee table. I thought it was odd that Nina was nowhere to be seen. We sat through the local news. The air was thick with anticipation. Then it was time. We didn't really know which numbers Nina had picked. All we had to go by was the expression on Salazar's face. The first four balls fell into place. Josh wrote them down. Things seemed to be going well - very well, that is until they weren't. It all crashed and burned after that.

After that Salazar and Josh didn't seem to care about keeping it quiet. They went back and forth, wondering what went wrong. The last three numbers were each off by one digit. Instead of a 17, there was a 13 and instead of a 42, it was a 47. The last one, a 9 should have been 28. By my guess, the ticket was still worth some money, it just wasn't the big score.

Dinner was a pretty somber affair. Nina appeared, folding herself silently into her chair to the right of Josh. Her eyes asked a question but Josh just shook his head. There was no discussion of the lottery. Voices, so animated less than an hour before, went muted.

Once, Dr Salazar informed us that we would be doing what he called targeted exercises he pushed back his chair and left the table. We would work separately using a variety of techniques, all with the same goal. I would do remote viewing, Harlan would be dowsing on a map out in the barn, and Nina would be progressed hypnotically.

Were we getting any closer to where this project was headed? That night Harlan and I huddled for more speculation on what the next day might bring. Our intuition clued us in that the stakes were increasing.

10

Breakfast arrived on a tray early next morning. I made quick work of sliced fruit, plain yogurt, and a cup of green tea. It was healthy, for sure, but I wished there were more of it. Waiting for what might come next, I kissed my wallet-size photos of Charlie and Jamie. I'd been able to get a call through the night before. Everyone was fine and my mother reassured me that if there were any problems, she would not waste a second before she called.

Two raps on the door broke my reverie. "Margo, you decent?"

Josh stood in the corridor. "I'm your escort for the dance," he joked, a first for our relationship.

We went to our usual workroom. Down the hall, a low buzz of voices signaled group activity but Josh had his maneuvers planned. I would be isolated until the target sessions were over. It felt like a test but I was up for it. After fifteen minutes of meditation, Josh turned off the light. It was time to prepare.

He waved the brown manila envelope. "Ready?"

I got the message. I would do my best. With intense focus, I listened as he read the target co-ordinates. The familiar fluorescent buzz and my pen scratching numbers broke the silence.

I sat back, closed my eyes, and let my mind soar. Immediately,

I moved to a location of water. At the horizon, bright sky met a murky sea. The sun radiated warmth. But there were no identifying landmarks. "There's nothing to see."

"Go down a level." Previously he'd used this phrase when he wanted me to go deeper into the experience. I followed his prompt, and the horizon expanded. Instead of deeper, I went higher. I could see a coastline to my left. To my right, two barges steamed toward an oil rig. I went higher still and felt a pull to the left, in the opposite direction

A coastline came into view, flat with little vegetation. Perhaps, a mile out I could see what looked like a flat beach fronting a chain of barrier islands. I began to speculate on location. But no, best not to speculate on what I was seeing. Like a bird that spots its prey, I stopped dead above the water, stretching wide in all directions. I felt this was my target, but there was nothing else visible.

"Go deeper," Josh said.

This time I took him at his word. Fighting the urge to hold my nose, I forced myself to plunge below the water's surface. Water became a substance through which I struggled. At the lower depths, the light was murky and dim. Then I saw something, a dark shape rested in a canyon of water. "It's big, massive, coated with something."

"What kind of dimensions are you looking at? The length, the width?"

I did my best to translate impressions into feet or inches. "Maybe eighty feet long, thirty feet wide."

"How deep are you?"

"Deep, but I can't tell how far down."

Outside the window, a bird flew by, screeching. My mind followed it. "I'm starting to lose the signal."

He brought me up, ended the session, and shoved a tablet and a pencil into my hands. "Draw it now."

Desperate to keep hold of what I'd seen, I started sketching before the lights came on. A bulky shape emerged, cylindrical in outline, seen from different angles.

Josh looked pleased. He provided me with the photo for confirmation. I could see the bottom of a ship turned on its side, vestiges of a prow almost visible below a thick coating of seaweed.

At lunch, it was just Harlan and me. Salazar was off somewhere and Josh disappeared too. Nina took her soup and went into another room. We were fine with that. We compared notes. He'd spent a chilly morning in the barn with a runny nose to prove it. "They kept me out there three hours straight. Goddamn freezing, too."

Working on a fifteen-by-fifteen wooden platform with a giant topographic map tacked to it, Harlan had dowsed, using L-shaped metal rods instead of yesterday's tree branch. Under Salazar's direction, he actually stood on the map and let the rods lead him, waiting as they wobbled first one way and then the other. They came to rest on what he described as a cluster of blue swirls off a coastline.

"After Salazar marked the spot, I took a break," Harlan said. "When they called me back in, they had a fresh map tacked to the platform."

Harlan had taken up his rods again and repeated the exercise. Salazar marked the spot and sent Harlan out for a cup of coffee. By the fifth or sixth go-round, Harlan was tired but the rods stayed strong. He stood firm on the spot where they pointed down, and Salazar marked the map for the last time.

"After a couple of hours, my energy starts to drop. The arm gets wobbly. After something to eat and a rest, I can go again. But them three hours? By the end I was done in." He declared.

"Ouch."

Afterwards he said Salazar clapped him on the back. "If I was a dog, I guess he would have given me a chewy toy. But the thing is, the longer I work, the weaker it gets."

"It?"

"You know. It's the energy, the signal. Whatever it is that keeps me going."

"Can you tell the difference in what the rods pick up?"

"Yeah, Water feels different, oil feels different. Granddad said he could feel the difference between gold and silver."

I began to look forward to the end of the training. Only a few more days of the testing then we'd be ready to go home. Who knew I would even miss my kids constant bickering, or Charlie's need to be reminded not to drop all his gear in a pile at the front door but I did. It's a funny thing that happens. Like when you go on vacation. Once you leave town, home starts to look better and better.

Later that afternoon, I heard a scratch at my door. Harlan, red-faced from the bath, slipped into my room. "I just heard something that blew my mind. This thing is crazier than a squirrel in a nut shop."

"Whoa, back up. Tell me."

"I was dozing off in the tub. You know me, trying to relax and get the kinks out. I start hearing our two buddies up above. Salazar comes in and he's all excited. He's saying he got it."

"Got what?"

"He said, 'I got it. I got the map.'"

Harlan looked pleased. "Since I been doin' nothing but staring at maps all day, something tells me I need to hear this. So I ease out of the tub, wrap myself in a towel, tiptoe over to the laundry chute, and open her up."

"What was it? What was the map?"

"Josh gets all wound up. They start to argue about something. Josh wants to stick with future predictions with the stock market, horse races, and lottery numbers for a while. But not Dr. Salazar. He wasn't going along with that. I could hear that they were going back and forth but I couldn't hear the rest of it until Salazar gets loud. He reminds Josh that the money is coming from him. Then their voices got low. Does it make any sense?"

"God, I wish we could get hold of that map. Maybe they'll have you dowse it."

"Maybe."

At dinner, any traces of Salazar's earlier excitement were undetectable. Josh, equally calm told us to get a good night's sleep. "We have a full day planned for tomorrow. And don't forget to dress for a hike."

Taking mental inventory of my suitcase contents, I realized my sneakers might not be up to the task, and I told him so. "Josh, I'm a city girl. I'm more likely to have boots with three inch heels in my wardrobe than hiking gear for the great outdoors."

"Don't worry about it." More of the mysterious smile. "You'll be fine."

Harlan reassured me. "I'm betting you'll have boots tomorrow."

"You must be psychic." We laughed, as much to blow off tension as anything else.

It turned out Harlan was right. By the time we were ready to leave the next morning, several pairs of hiking boots in appropriate sizes, along with pairs of thick thermal socks, were waiting for all of us.

I looked at my phone. The date was March 20th, the vernal equinox. I asked if that might have anything to do with our destination. Josh smiled, continuing to play up the mystery of where we were going. Mr. Big Deal! He loved keeping secrets. It was just another way for him to flex. Once Harlan, Nina, Josh, and I were geared up, we waited in the cold air at the front of the main house, clapping our gloved hands for warmth. It was March, still winter in upstate New York. The high that day was forecast to be near thirty.

Salazar appeared, driving a van with three rows of seats. He pulled to a stop with a flourish of dust and climbed out. "Ladies and gentlemen, your chariot awaits." With an inviting air, he opened the doors wide. "We're heading out to Ringing Rocks, and I think you'll enjoy it."

Josh got in the van and fiddled with the GPS, but Salazar told him not to bother. "I know this place by heart."

We climbed in, jockeying for window seats. Less than five minutes out, the bumpy road and lack of cushioning had my posterior aching. I wasn't alone. In the row in front of me, Harlan shifted uncomfortably from side to side. "Josh, where'd you rent this rig? Backaches R Us? This seat's like a rock."

Salazar ignored the complaints and kept driving. "Now you'll see what first brought me to this area."

A few minutes later we pulled over and parked. We were on a ridge. Down below, irregular walls of ancient stone were interspersed with tall triangular standing stones.

Salazar pointed to a ring of stone monoliths. "See those stones?"

"What the hell is this place?" Harlan asked. His voice was hoarse with excitement.

"My friend, these stones are fairly accurate predictors of astronomical sightings. They've been studied by the Astronomy Department at SUNY. Found to be aligned to predict prominent astral events."

Harlan grew animated. What was he picking up? "It's a vortex. I can feel it." He muttered, already rummaging for his dowsing rods.

"What did you say?" Josh asked.

"I'm getting hungry. Wondered if you brought any food?"

We unpacked our gear and followed Harlan and Josh down the slope. "It's a miracle these stones are still standing," Salazar told us over his shoulder. "Fifty, sixty years ago, farmers in the area just called it Mystery Valley because they didn't know what to make of it."

Harlan leaned toward me and whispered, "I bet I know why we're here. They think a vortex will increase the psychic powers. They think they can boost Nina's predictions. Kick it up a notch."

"They originally thought it had been erected by one of the Algonquin tribes that lived in the area. That proved to be wrong but there are several other theories." Salazar continued. "When I was an undergrad, I worked here summers as part of a research project. The university bought it from the last family who owned it, the Norris brothers. They sold off the stone slabs for spare change. Locals hauled away tons of it before the university came in, bought up the property, and stopped them from using it for a quarry."

At the center of the complex, a T-shaped chamber anchored several other smaller rooms around it. Harlan produced a flashlight and peered inside. There was an interior bench. Above the bench, a hole about three inches in diameter ascended to the exterior surface.

Salazar pointed to where the opening ascended to the surface. "You might have seen other configurations like this," he said. "It's similar to an oracle chamber I've seen in Europe."

"This is all fascinating," Nina said. "But why we are here?"

Harlan whispered, "When it's cold, she gets nasty, doesn't she?"

"It's not a coincidence," said Salazar, tapping the date on his watch. "The vernal equinox."

A sudden noise stopped the lecture. A truck rattled to a stop at the top of the hill.

"Not only that, we're expecting guests," Salazar said. "Every year, members from the local reservation come here to honor their ancestors. This is considered a day of prophecy."

Two ancient-looking men and one younger woman emerged from the vehicle. The men carried round cases that I took to be drums. Salazar climbed back up to join them on the ridge. From where I stood, I watched Salazar pump the hand of one of the men and greet them in a language I couldn't understand. They made their way toward us. Salazar introduced the new arrivals as John Smallbear, Amos Roche, and Sarah Davis. We nodded greetings to one another.

Sarah stepped away from her comrades. She was tall and thin with long dark hair streaked with red. "Hi, I'm Sarah. Sorry, I didn't catch your name."

"I'm Margo." Harlan and Nina were already headed back to the van.

"Margo, by any chance would you have any tissues? Usually I don't forget but...well you know. We're roughing it out there." She laughed.

I dug in my bag for some tissues. "Here's a few for starters. I'm sure there's more in the van."

"Thanks, I'll be back."

"Good, we brought lunch."

Josh went to the van and brought out a folding table, some chairs, and several coolers. Harlan and Josh set up the table and chairs. Eager to keep warm, I pitched in and we covered the table with a healthy spread that Maria had packed. A large thermos of soup and another of hot coffee cut some of the chill of the damp day. The visitors ate heartily.

Salazar kept the conversation going sometimes in English and sometimes he and the guests spoke in what I later learned was the Oneida language. Sarah translated a sentence or two into English for us but soon she began to yawn. "I don't mean to be rude but I didn't get all that much sleep. My sister's kid was up crying all night with an earache. But since the good Dr. Salazar already paid us to be here, I just hauled myself up and got dressed. But we've got a few more hours so if you'll excuse me, I'm going to go catch a nap in the truck." She finished her coffee and stood.

I trailed her with a question. "What's going on?" I asked. "What are we waiting for?"

"Waiting for dark." Sarah said.

By my watch, we had more than a few hours to kill. I asked Harlan if he wanted to explore while there was still daylight. Salazar and Nina were off to the side, talking. I could hear Salazar's cajoling tone as he worked to convince Nina to follow him down the hill. Salazar, Nina, and Josh went down the em- bankment, while Harlan and I broke down the lunch things and stowed the table and chairs back inside the van. Save for the sounds of the wind whipping through the trees, all was quiet. After several minutes, a high-pitched scream pierced the air. Nina, eyes wide, charged back in our direction.

"Nina, you okay? What happened? What's the matter?" I asked.

"Snakes, the place is full of snakes."

Salazar lumbered back up. "A snake slid over Nina's foot. It was just a little black snake."

"There's no such thing as a little snake." Nina's face was stretched and pale. "It was a snake, and it was ugly and disgusting."

For someone who claimed to have grown up on a farm, Nina's relationship with nature was lukewarm at best. When she refused to go back, Salazar stayed to placate her. Josh sat in the van and played games on his phone. As far as Harlan was concerned the coast was clear, so he and I made our excuses and climbed down to the site.

"Where are we going?" I asked as I followed him to the center of the array of stones.

Harlan took the dowsing rods from his backpack.

"You see how these stones are positioned?" Harlan pointed the rods first one way and then another. "I've seen this before. There could be a vortex here."

"What does that mean?"

"It means that at certain times, like today, earth energies are stronger."

"Is that why we're here?"

"Like I said, it could be. Maybe we're part of an experiment. I bet they want to see if our abilities can be boosted by the energies that come with the vortex."

Harlan followed the rods toward the center of the stones to a small structure. He dared me to peek inside the chamber room.

"I will if you will."

Harlan grinned. "I'll go first, make sure there's no snakes."

He played his flashlight around the edges and turned over a few rocks. He waved me in. "All clear."

"It's a little cramped for two people, isn't it?" I said.

Harlan left to explore, but I stayed. Something about the space held me. I began to feel something taking over, as though a veil covered my face. For what may have been seconds or minutes, the world went dark. When I awoke, Harlan was beside me. "Margo, Margo. Wake up."

"I think I went into the vortex," I joked.

He pulled me to my feet. "Was that you?" he asked.

"Was what me?"

"I heard a strange voice. A female voice, but different. It went like, 'Nina, watch out. Be careful.'"

"I don't think I said anything. Maybe I just yelled 'ouch.' Even if I did say something, it wouldn't be about Nina. That doesn't make sense. Promise me something."

"Sure. What?"

"Don't say anything about this to Salazar. He'll get on my case, and, who knows, he might want me to spend the night out here."

Harlan promised.

"Now excuse me," I said as I dug in my pocket for tissues and went in search of a place to pee.

Back up on the ridge, Salazar wondered what we thought of the site. Harlan offered to go back down and explore the vortex. I pled a headache and went in search of warmth inside the van. Salazar kept trying to persuade Nina to go back down to the site with him. Finally, he and Harlan led the way back down, Josh and Nina trailing behind. But before long, Nina came back alone, tight-lipped, and sat with me in the truck. She didn't say a word.

When the other three returned, we all sat in the van and amused ourselves with a game of poker. "I should go ask our friends in the truck to join us." I said. I got out the thermos of tea and walked to the red truck. I knocked on the window. Sarah was asleep. I asked John and Amos if they were interested in a friendly game of poker. John shook his head. He held up his reader. The glow reflected on his face, "Catching up on my reading." He said. "But thanks."

"Here, I'll leave the tea with you, just in case you want some."

Back in our van, Josh kept trying to make the game "interesting." First he insisted on calling out "red" or "black" for each card before it was turned until Nina and I begged him to stop. Then he wanted to play for matchsticks. I won like crazy. It was a shame we weren't playing for cash. Maybe it was the vortex, but whatever it was I knew each card before it was even dealt.

It was dark by close to seven, putting an end to the poker game. I got out of the van and looked up, amazed by the night sky. I realized then why the ancients were so intrigued by the stars. Away from civilization, without lights to dull their luminosity, it was possible to see constellations. For the first time ever, I saw the Milky Way.

Harlan gathered dry branches and started a fire in a circle of stones. The embers burned low until a lick of wind surged, sending a shower of sparks into the night sky. As if on signal, our guests arrived and arranged themselves in a ceremonial circle. In the distance, a creature howled. Then the drumming began. John and Amos beat their drums in unison, building a solid wall of sound. Sarah began a slow chant. Amos joined her. Finally John took up the song, keening an ancient prayer.

Part of me wanted to open myself to the beauty of the experience, while the more practical side was aware of my cold toes. Drawn into the fire, merging into the experience, I waited to see where it would take us. The chanting continued unabated for an hour. I was amazed by their strength. Then, just as wordlessly as they had begun, the drummers fell silent even as the vibrations of their drums lingered, echoing against the rocks. They bowed to the four corners.

Mesmerized, we followed as they climbed back up the ridge. John waited as the Amos returned the drums to the truck bed and climbed in. Salazar shook their hands. From his perch in the rear of the cab, Amos waved. "Na ki wah. Good bye."

Sarah climbed into the cab behind him. "Nice meeting you." She called out. "Na ki wah."

A moment later, the truck began a return to their world. Shortly after, we were back in the van for a return trip of our own. The ride back was quiet. The warmth was soothing, but there was something emanating from Salazar. Was it a sense of disappointment? Perhaps.

When we got back, Maria gave me a message to call home. I'd

tried to get a call through early that morning but with no luck. It was late, after ten o'clock, but I thought my mother would still be awake. Even if she wasn't, surely one of the kids would be staying up and destroying their minds with TV or the Internet. My mother answered right away, her voice sounding a little tight.

"Mom, how are you? Is everything okay?"

"Well, Margo, I don't want to upset you, and I'm sure it's nothing, but the police called for you. They want to talk to you as soon as you get back."

"The police? Did they mention Jack's name?"

Was it possible they found Jack? Had the bank followed up with their insurance company? Mine claimed the loss wasn't covered by my homeowner's policy. But maybe?

"Nothing about Jack. They didn't say what it was about."

"Give me the number, I'll call right now."

She read it back to me.

"Damn it, Mom, that's a New Jersey area code."

"Margo, I'm just the messenger. Don't blame me."

"I'm sorry, Mom." The only thing I could think of was an unpaid speeding ticket I'd gotten near the Cherry Hill Mall. But that was over a year ago. "Did they say anything about a ticket?"

"No, honey, he just said he had to talk to you. He mentioned something about New Jersey jurisdiction. Did I give you the name of the detective?"

"No. Mom, don't worry. I'm sure this is not about me."

"Honey, of course it's not. I just felt like I should call."

"You did the right thing, Mom. And I'm sorry if I'm sounding cranky. It's just that I've been so busy here. Really earning my money, if you know what I mean. At the end of the day, it's all I can do to brush my teeth before I fall asleep."

"Well, don't worry about us. The kids are fine. I'm fine. When will you be back?"

"Is this Day 7 or Day 8? I'm brain dead, but the end is in sight. I'll be home soon. I'll call you tomorrow. Love you."

"Love you, too, honey."

It was too late that night to call the New Jersey police number but I called first thing when I woke up next morning. I got switched around quite a bit. The person Mom talked to, a Detective Flynn wasn't available. I spoke to another officer and left my name and number just to be on the record. After that I tried to put it all out of my head.

I checked the calendar, glad there were eight days already crossed off. Tomorrow would be Day Nine and then just one more day to go. At breakfast, I was surprised when Josh said he'd be driving Harlan and me to New York City the following day. With a flourish, he produced train tickets, one for Harlan and one for me. I was booked for six o'clock on Amtrak from Penn Station to Philadelphia's Thirtieth Street Station. If all went well, I would be home by nine o'clock at the latest.

Harlan was taking the Silver Crescent to Birmingham, Alabama. He'd be getting in very early the next morning. It was another fifty miles to his home in Mississippi, but he didn't care. He just wanted to get to a phone to let his wife know when to pick him up. After he put the call through, he said she liked the idea so much that she was making plans for them to stay over at a hotel, go out to eat in a fancy restaurant, and do some shopping.

"I did my best to sound excited," he said, but he hoped she wouldn't want to stay too long. He couldn't wait to get home.

Later I quizzed Josh. "I don't mind the train to Philly, but that's a long ride down South. Why didn't you get him a plane ticket?"

"He didn't tell you?

"Tell me what?"

"He doesn't fly."

"He didn't mention it."

11

Day Ten dawned bright and cold. My spirits were up. It felt like the last day of a very tough year at school. Only one more run-through—Salazar's last chance to squeeze whatever was left out of my poor brain. I knew better than to rush. According to my contract, there was still the final payment to be made, and I didn't want to screw that up.

I kept my mind blank and wrote the coordinates as directed. I allowed my subconscious to be open to wherever it might go. For a brief second, it felt like I was flying. I looked down on a spit of land nearly covered by water, a coastline visible off to the left with a rising tubular structure. I heard squawking, saw motion as though birds circled through the air. I strained to summon precise descriptors, recorded my most detailed impressions, and then the session was over.

My descriptors were a rocky cliff-like geography, salt air, rough water, and a sense of motion as though the tide was coming in.

It was time for the reveal. He showed me the photo.

Not bad, I thought. It was a lighthouse situated on a rocky shoreline with birds circling around.

"Good job," Salazar said.

High praise from him, I thought. And with that we were done. The pressure to perform was over.

Later that day, I was packed and ready to leave. The sun was warming things up, I even thought I saw a pale crocus sticking up out of melting snow. Nina wandered the grounds with no particular sense of urgency. I wondered if she was returning with us. Something in her manner told me not to ask. So it was just Harlan and me hauling our bags into the rear of the van while Josh waited up front in the driver's seat. Once Salazar shook my hand and I waved to Maria, we were off.

Happiness was Perception Studies Institute in the rearview mirror. It was over. The contract was fulfilled and the money was in my account. That much was confirmed. Was this something I wanted to continue? If I signed on for more, I promised myself that I would be a more savvy negotiator.

As we passed the front gate, I felt my shoulders relax. Had they been up around my ears most of the time here? We took the same route to New York City, but somehow the ride back to civilization seemed to go a little faster. Harlan and I chattered away until he fell asleep. I was wide-awake, looking forward to hugging the kids. When we arrived in Manhattan, rush hour was hitting full tilt. Dwindling sunlight threw shadows across the concrete canyons. Harlan was captivated by what he saw. It was his first time in the city. His face was pressed against the window, neck craned skyward in an attempt to catch sight of the tops of the buildings. As we crawled toward Penn Station, his amazement grew.

"Never seen the like." He poked me in the ribs and pointed to a towering transvestite in hot pants, tights and full make-up. "Damn, and as cold as it is, wearing short shorts."

"They call them hot pants," I said. That got a laugh.

Josh waved us out at Penn Station with a promise to talk soon. Inside I pointed Harlan to a listing for his train on the information screen. He had plenty of time until his 7:25 departure.

"Just don't get so busy staring at people that you forget your train," I told him.

He laughed. "I won't."

"Remember, New Yorkers don't like to be gawked at."

We gave each other a quick hug. I went in search of my train on Track 3.

My train was a commuter. That meant extra stops in New Jersey, but I spent the time dozing. Even though I was in the quiet car, something told me to check in at home, and I sneaked a quick call to let my mother know I was on my way.

"Everything okay?" I asked.

"Margo honey, it's nothing to worry about."

"What's nothing to worry about, Mom?"

"Nobody got hurt. Thank God."

Now I was worried. The kids' faces flashed though my mind. "What happened?"

"It's the car. Jamie wanted to drive to the gymnastics meet. It seemed okay. I know you don't want her to drive on the Expressway. She promised to take a back road home and she did. She hit a huge pothole, what with the weather and all. The axle cracked."

"Is she OK? Did anyone get hurt?"

"Now Margo, calm down. God bless her. Our Jamie kept her wits about her. It could have been so much worse. She lost control and they collided with a parked car. They weren't going fast. The worst was a bump on the head, and her friend in the front got a little cut, but most of the damage was to the car. They had to tow it to the shop."

"Where is it?"

"It's the one Jamie said you go to in South Philadelphia. I talked to the mechanic. They'll wait to hear from you."

"Put Jamie on. Let me talk to her."

"Give yourself a little while to calm down. I think she's in the shower anyway. Just come home and give her a hug. That's the best medicine."

A freezing rain was my welcome back to Philadelphia, but I didn't care. I grabbed a taxi and told him my address. At the door, I breathed in the familiar smells of home, a mix of coffee, eucalyptus and teen-age angst. My mother met me with the offer of a drink. "The weather is awful but officially its spring so I'm having my first gin and tonic of the season. Would you like one?"

I shook my head but immediately changed my mind. "On second thought, make that a yes."

She fixed me a drink. I grabbed it and plopped myself in my favorite chair. "Okay, I'm ready now. Tell me everything."

"Now, Margo, just remember what's important here. No one was hurt."

She was right. It was only a car. I repeated that mantra over and over in my head.

Jamie came downstairs, still in shock by the look of her. Poor kid. Only hours before, she'd had to call the police, call road service, and take a trip in a police car to the emergency room so that she and her passenger could get themselves checked out. That was a lot for anyone, let alone my teenager with only six months behind the wheel. When I saw the look on her face, any irritation I might have felt took a back seat. I did my best to comfort her with a hug and a tissue.

"I bet you won't ever let me drive again will you?"

"Who said any thing about that? It doesn't sound like it was your fault."

"Well, my friend Lisa told me that after she had an accident, her father took her license and told her she couldn't have it back for a year."

"I'm not Lisa's father and I don't think it's fair to compare the two of you when we don't know the circumstances. Let me make you a cup of mint tea. You can tell me what happened and then go to bed. OK?"

We sat at the kitchen table, just the two of us and between sobs, she spilled it out. I had to agree, it really wasn't her fault and I told her so. "I'm proud of you for being so brave and so responsible."

Jamie nodded with relief. "Thanks, Mom." She took her mug of tea and two aspirin and went to bed.

The house was quiet. I sat at the kitchen table and stared at the clock. Everyone was in bed. For distraction, I sorted through the unopened mail, bills mostly, if you didn't count an invitation to a ladies-only tea to discuss how to build wealth for retirement. Fat chance, I thought. It hit the recycle bin with a resounding thunk.

After being out in the hinterlands for more than a week, I was still feeling a little cut off from the human race. Even though it was late and I was exhausted, I checked email and messages. One message from Jerry, my boss, said he'd call me when he had something for me to do. A message from my cell phone provider told me my coverage could be extended if I wanted to go on an automatic payment system.

Next morning, Mom was packed and ready to go. She would be glad to get back to her suburban townhouse where her plants and the next meeting of her book club awaited. Who could blame her? We walked out to the car and I thanked her for the tenth time.

"Margo, it would be lovely if you and the kids come out for Easter dinner. It will be nice to see you under more relaxing cir-cumstances." We hugged.

Jamie declined my suggestion to stay home from school. I didn't push it. She looked okay and claimed to feel fine. A morning French test she didn't want to make up cinched the deal in her mind. Charlie, who had been asleep when I came in, grabbed his lunch from the counter and gave me a kiss. Then they were gone.

Once the house was empty, I took a few breaths, easing into the quiet. Then I called the garage, ready to hear about the dam-age before my second call to the insurance adjuster.

I was in luck. He was already in the neighborhood. We confirmed a time to meet. I showered, dressed, and checked the weather. Thankful that sun was predicted, I took the subway to its final stop and then changed to a bus that dropped me close to the garage. By the time I got there, the mechanic already had the car up on the lift. I usually feel out of my element in this setting, but I decided to play it out for all I could.

The adjuster's flashlight swept over the damage. He frowned, took a few notes and promised to call me with the verdict. A few days later I heard from him. "It's totaled. Cost you three thousand to fix it."

It was hard to argue with that. "What do you think?" I asked.

"Not sure. Let me see if I can get you two."

Moving down my "to-do" list, there was the phone call to make to the New Jersey State Police. I had a number and a name, Detective Flynn. No clue what it was about.

"Flynn, here."

"Detective, this is Margo Fellshur returning your call. You called me a few days back."

"Yes. Thanks, appreciate your getting back in touch. There's a few things we'd like to go over with you. When could we meet?"

That seemed odd. "Can you tell me a little more? Is it something we could handle on the phone?"

"It's about Carla Gentile and Steve Kovacs. Best if we meet in person. Would you mind coming here? I can send a car."

I thanked him for the offer but shrank at the thought of the police at my door. "Why don't I take the train across the bridge? Perhaps the car could meet me at the station."

Later, I gave Greg a call to see if he had any idea why they'd want to talk to me. When I did, he sounded pleased. "Margo, how have you been? I've been meaning to get in touch."

"Busy." I wasn't about to go into details. It was too complicated. "You?"

"Same, business is starting to pick up."

We chatted for a few minutes. Picturing his face on the other end helped my mood. Despite the reason for the call, my spirits lifted "I got a call from a Detective Flynn. Do you know him?

"Yeah, I do."

"What does he want to talk to me about?"

"They're scrambling to get somewhere with this case. It's been a year now. Everything has gone cold. There were a few articles in the local news asking where the investigation was going. The answer was nowhere. So they got a little heat from the press. Now they're going back over everything to try to come up with some kind of lead."

"But why me?"

"My guess is that they're desperate. First it was Carla's husband. Then Russian loan sharks. They looked at Steve's ex as a possibility. Then there's that break-in at Steve's trailer and the theft of the diving equipment. Every little thing is on the table. They're going through the motions again, checking things off the list. Don't take it personally. Probably got down to your name and just want to cross you off."

"Okay. I'll let you know if anything new comes up."

"Margo, I'm going out of town, but I'd love to get together when I get back. What do you think?"

"Sounds good. Call me." Hmmmm.

The patrol car waited for me outside the train station. White with blue lettering, it looked like others that often lurked near the Atlantic City Expressway to discourage speeders. The officer in the driver's seat was polite but quiet. He must have called me Ma'am about twenty times during the course of the ride. Once we arrived at the New Jersey State Police barracks, he escorted me down a long beige-tiled corridor. The desk officer called Flynn and invited me to have a seat. The only chair looked hard and cold. I decided to stand. Luckily, it wasn't for long.

"Ms. Fellshur, I'm Detective Flynn. Thanks for coming in."

"Nice to meet you," I lied, holding eye contact.

Short, wiry, and muscular, he steered me into a windowless room. The room could have used some air freshener, as could Flynn, his breath a mix of cigarettes and coffee. With a glancing attempt at hospitality, he offered me a seat, then some water.

Once the niceties were out of the way, he went straight to the point—how I'd heard of Carla's disappearance.

I talked about meeting Greg at a Halloween party and reading his palm. I downplayed the "woo-woo" aspects of the Mediums Guild group session during which we tried to uncover information about the missing couple or their whereabouts.

I gave him the names of the other group members and described our poor results, which had produced little about Carla and Steve. He was curious about how I came up with Camp Harmony and asked what I knew about the place.

"I didn't know a thing about it, didn't even know it existed," I told him.

When I described the dream, his eyes broke from mine for the first time.

A twinge grabbed me in the mid-section. I looked around. Were we being filmed? Something told me we were. Maybe I'd seen too many reality cop shows. But this was not a place I'd ever expected to be.

"Would you be willing to take a polygraph test?" he asked.

I was stunned. "I wasn't expecting that. May I ask why?"

"Process of elimination. We're taking a look at everything. It's just routine. Since you're already here, we could do it now."

If he suspected me, he was really scrambling. Still, he made it sound so matter of fact that it might seem suspicious if I declined. I thought I would do it just to show him. Would it make good cocktail party conversation? Probably not, but more out of curiosity than anything else, I found myself agreeing. "Just to help out," I said.

He left the room. After that, my nerves took over. I felt like one of those poor bastards on TV. I had to keep myself from pacing the room. In two more seconds, I thought, I'll be pounding on the door, calling for the warden, claiming innocence and begging to speak to my lawyer.

After forever, Flynn reappeared. "Ms. Pearlmutter is ready for you," he said.

I almost told him to forget about it, but I figured I'd get it over with and leave. I followed him into the next room.

I sat across from the polygraph technician, a forty-something woman with dark hair tucked behind her ears. She tried to be chatty and smiled at me as she explained how everything worked. The old technology that used pens to record responses on a moving strip of paper had been replaced with computer technology. Now everything was digitized.

Once the preliminaries were out of the way, she attached electrodes to my fingertips, a pressure cuff to my arm and a bib of wires over my chest and middle. After a pre-test interview of routine questions like my name, my age, and where I lived, we got to it. I sat across from her feeling a little disoriented but still curious about the electronic patterns my answers might form. My eyes grazed a mirror across the room until I realized it might be two-way glass.

One by one, the technician read a list of names—Steve, Carla, Carla's husband Matt, Steve's wife, his business partner Bo something—asking if I knew or had ever met any of them. I could honestly answer that I had never had any personal contact with any person on the list. She watched my responses on the screen of her laptop. She would have made a good actor, her expression and her eyes unreadable behind the glasses. Later, on the train, I wrote as many of the names as I could remember. I wanted to share the list with Greg. The examiner echoed Flynn, asking if I was familiar with Camp Harmony.

I thought back to the dream, a female voice uttering one word, harmony. It seemed innocuous then. "No I was not," I said. "I thought it was just a word. I didn't know it was a place." It hit me then. The name Harmony became anything but. It would be forever fixed in my thoughts as an ominous place where the bodies of Carla and Steve were found.

After a few more questions, the test concluded. On cue, Flynn returned to lead me back to the interrogation room. He asked if I wanted anything. I asked for water. Should I feel insulted, aggrieved? Would there be a record of this, something that might hurt me if I ever needed to have a background check run? It had been dumb not to ask. I should have been more cautious, I thought. If I ever needed clearance for a job, would this work against me? Even though I didn't have one, maybe I should have talked to a lawyer first.

Flynn returned with the water and apologized for taking up so much of my time. He thanked me for my cooperation and escorted me back to the front desk. "Officer Keenan will take you to the High Speed Line. Thanks for coming. We'll be in touch if we have any more questions.

12

It had been over a week since my polygraph and still no word from Greg. "Should I call him?" I asked Alisha, my go-to person for help with "lifestyles of the suddenly single."

"You might as well," she said. "You know you want to."

"But I haven't made that kind of phone call since college."

"OK, then email him. Make a plan to meet him for coffee. That's pretty safe."

"What would be my reason?" I felt like a five-year-old.

"Start out small. Ask if there's anything new with the case. Then tell him what you've been doing since you saw him at that event. That's, what—a couple months? Tell him about Perception. Didn't you say he'd been experiencing some things of his own?"

"The last time we talked was before my visit to the New Jersey State Police. I could tell him about that, about my polygraph." I ticked off the possibilities.

"Sure. You've got the perfect reason to call."

I waited another day. Then I called. Greg's voice made me tingle. I felt the emotions of a high school kid. "How was your trip?" I asked him.

"For work, not bad. Went to Texas for an aerial surveying job.

Fun, but like I said, work. What have you been up to?"

"Well, I had what I hope was my first and last polygraph."

"Oh, no! Not Flynn? I can't believe it. He must be flipping out."

"Maybe. I agreed to it just to show him. But then afterwards I was sorry I did."

"I feel responsible. I got you into this mess. Let me at least buy you a drink. I know that won't even begin to make up for what you've been through, but I was hoping we could get together."

There it was. All of a sudden, everything changed.

"That would be great."

"How about tomorrow? You free?"

"I'm free." I wasn't ready to bring anyone to the house. "Where do you want to meet?"

"How about Devil's Alley at 5:30? Ever been there? Good bar food."

I mumbled agreement and hung up.

Now what? This would be my first real date in close to twenty years, and I was clueless. Even the word date had changed. The Love Guru radio show featured a psychologist whose shtick was something called "Ten Dating Tips for the Newly Divorced." I tried writing them down but didn't get past Number 3. At the bookstore the next day, I spent hours browsing, first in the magazines, then in the self-help section. There's texting and sexting and TTYL, all of it scary. And what about those ads on TV? Meet your soul mate via the Internet? My head was spinning. After 24 hours of stressing over it, I went shopping.

That night it took me over an hour to decide what to wear. Once I had the outfit down, I stared in the mirror long and hard. Then I whipped out the new Chanel makeup I'd just bought. The saleswoman promised it would provide good coverage and reflect the light. Was that her way of saying I needed something to brighten me up?

The restaurant was fun, and on a Tuesday night, it was quiet enough to have a decent conversation. Our drink lasted two hours. I nursed a couple of vodka cranberries. Greg went for a couple of micro-brews. We shared a pizza. Afterwards he walked me to my car. It was still early. Not even eight o'clock, streets still full of commuters hustling for home.

Our lips met. A good-bye peck became a hot, passionate embrace. I looked around. Thankful for the dark, I extricated myself. "I have to go," I said. "The kids." I hoped we would see each other again. I unlocked my door.

He leaned in. "You're gorgeous."

"Thanks," I mumbled. Did he really mean that?

"Next time, I'll make you dinner at my place," he said.

Could he see me blush?

After my time with Greg, I was in the zone, in a space I hadn't inhabited since high school. That night, I sat in the car for several minutes until I could trust myself to be casual without my face giving me away.

Next day I barely registered my surroundings. If not for Charlie's traditional switch of salt and sugar in the sugar bowl, I would never have noticed it was April 1. I spooned white granules into my tea, took a sip, and sprayed salty liquid across the kitchen table, to the delight of my son, who yelled, "April Fool!" I felt like one, too.

I looked at the calendar. April meant a certain moment of truth was drawing closer. I told myself to wake up. I soon would have to face reality. And I was not the only one. Whether we liked it or not, Jamie and I would be facing it together. Early in the school year, I begged Jamie to let me help her with the college applications, but she said she didn't need me. There was plenty of help at school, and I was grateful for that.

Though her high school, Hamilton Academy, was housed in an old relic of a building, it still claimed high marks educationally. Class sizes were small and the curriculum was rigorous and fast-paced. It lacked the polished facilities of a private school, but city kids were used to making the most of things. While that might mean no manicured playing fields or glossy chem labs, there was excellent instruction in math, science, music, and the arts. Tough admissions standards meant the students' test scores ranked high, and there was plenty of competition for openings. Teachers, attracted by the brightness of the student body, were first-rate. I was always proud that both my kids were getting the best education they could in a public school.

Sometimes, though, the counselors got out of hand. Representing the highest-ranked public school in the state, their agenda demanded that, after graduation, the students attend prestige colleges. I remembered the discussion at the annual college night for parents. The message to seniors was "aim high." Go for it and maybe keep only one school for the safety net. It was easy to understand how the kids bought into the competitive atmosphere. Why not? Many of their parents did, too. But we had to keep it real.

When Jamie and her friends drew up lists of their first-tier, second-tier, and safety net schools, I prayed for a way to find the cash. Despite my pleas for a backup plan, our practical girl got carried away by "the dream." All the schools she applied to were "top tier." And while she didn't refuse my help outright, she insisted that she could do the applications by herself. One part of me thought this should be an exercise in learning how the real world works. I should have realized we were courting disaster. Like every other parent at her school, I wanted the best for my daughter, but my pleas for schools that were closer to what we could afford got drowned out.

The previous fall, as I pored over college reference books and scrolled through online catalogs, sticker shock set in. I asked myself how many of her classmates had families who would find the forty thousand plus dollars these schools charge. Why had I written checks for application fees to schools we could never afford?

All over America, parents were facing up to the grim economic realities of life in the twenty-first century. The financial disasters

I read about in the newspaper were reminders of what I faced on a much smaller level. For the last ten years, the real estate bubble had fueled our lives. My commissions on the sales I made brought us a nice income. I never considered that there would be an expiration date to those paychecks. But that money tree shriveled and died. Just when Jamie needed financial stability, it wasn't there.

The one piece she needed me and her father for was the place where we came up short. With Jack in the breeze, I had crossed my fingers and filled out the FAFSA forms on my own. Things were touchy enough between my daughter and me, and I didn't want to make it worse by telling her that her father had taken off with the money. For all I knew, Jack had left the state, maybe even left the country. I had gone to the police with a complaint, given them his photo, his Social Security number, the car registration, anything I could think of. But this wasn't a case for Homeland Security. It was just another domestic dispute, and Jack was just another deadbeat dad. They referred me back to the savings and loan. If the bank had lost my money, I could have put in an insurance claim. If Jack's name hadn't still been on the account, it would have been theft, pure and simple. The manager at the savings and loan suggested a skip trace, but short of hiring someone to track him down, the options were few.

When Jamie and I sat down for what I came to think of as "the talk," I was more than a little afraid of what her reaction might be. Jamie was so smart and so mature that I hoped she would see where I was coming from.

Even if Stanford were to provide scholarship money, there was still room and board to be paid, not to mention transportation. Jamie would be attending school three thousand miles from home. That meant a minimum of two round-trip airfares a year. While she was there, she'd be paying high California prices for all her other needs. It was a fantasy I couldn't afford to keep going. We had to talk.

I waited for a time when things were calm. Charlie was off with a friend. The house was quiet. I called her into the kitchen, poured us each a cup of mint tea. I decided to start with the positives. "We are so lucky to be living where we do."

Jamie sipped her tea, searching my face.

"Do you know there are over eighty colleges within driving distance of this house?"

"Where is this going, Mom?"

"What I'm trying to say is that we have options."

"What options? You don't want me to go to Stanford, is that it?"

Her voice was as harsh as I'd ever heard it. Oh, God.

"More than anything I would love for you to be able to go to Stanford, but if things don't turn out, there are other very good schools right here in our backyard."

She brushed back angry tears.

"This has been a difficult year for all of us. You know I would do anything in the world for you and Charlie. It's just that things are tough right now."

Her face tightened. "But, Mom, what about my college fund?"

"The money in your own account is fine." The small account where Jamie banked her money from summer jobs and babysitting was intact. "But it's the other fund, Grandpa's fund."

"Mom, what are you saying?"

"This is hard for me." Now I was crying. Why hadn't I told her sooner? I was ashamed, hurt, humiliated by what Jack had done, and pride had made me hold my tongue. "I wish I could say that it was still there, honey. But it's gone. Your father took it. I've tried to get in touch with him. I don't know where he is."

The painful information played across her face. When I reached out to comfort her, she shrank from my touch. She turned away. Her back heaved with sobs. I slid the box of tissues in her direction. There was nothing to do but wait for the storm to subside.

Finally she was able to speak. "OK, so what you're saying is that I should go to Penn State or Temple or some community college?"

"No, I'm not saying that, but lots of people do. And it's not the worst thing in the world. They go to community college for the first two years, then transfer to a university for the last two. Jane McKelvey's daughter did it." I reminded Jamie of a neighbor's success story. "And look at her now—she's in medical school."

"Great! So you want me to go to community college. And what? Live at home?"

"I wasn't focusing on that part of it, but if you don't want to live at home, you could always get an apartment with some friends. That's what I did in my sophomore year. You know my parents weren't rich either. I was pretty glad I was able to get a job to help out with the rent. Sometimes it was hard but it worked out OK."

Jamie stood. I could see that she was biting her lip to keep from saying what was on her mind. We'd promised so much more than we were able to deliver right now. I should have told her sooner. Maybe I'd been hoping for a miracle. Whatever I'd been hoping for, this conversation ended worse than I had expected.

Alone with my laptop, I scanned real estate databases searching for "Sale by Owner" opportunities. It was spring. Might that be a good time to snag do-it-yourself sellers ready to switch to an agent? Next, I searched offerings of online employment boards, looking for sales jobs. Suddenly my phone burped up a text message. "Call me. Josh"

During the time in New York, I'd become more relaxed around Josh, but not what you would call comfortable. Still, I reminded myself who it was that needed the money and who was writing the checks in this equation. I dialed.

On the other end, Josh surprised me by asking how I was. He even listened to me grouse for a few seconds before he cut me off. "OK, don't worry about it. Do you know the Rosenbach Museum?"

"Near the University of Pennsylvania? Pine Street?"

"That's it. Can you be there by three? There's someone I want you to meet."

I agreed to the meeting and tried to find out who it was with. When I sensed Josh falling back on his "need to know" protocol, I knew further communication would not be forthcoming.

By the time I grabbed a shower and made myself presentable, it was close to two o'clock. The weather was inviting. It was a good day to be outside. I cinched my beige trench at the waist, locked the front door, and set off. It was a brisk fifteen-minute walk but I took my time.

It was warm for early April, one of those spring days that teases the senses and plays tricks on the cherry trees. Blossoms had burst forth, tempting winter to come back at them with the next frost.

Nearer to the university, sidewalks were alive with students enjoying the sunshine. I turned onto Pine Street. Pacing mid-block, I spied Josh moving in my direction, hustling to keep up with the long strides of his companion, a tall, thin, bespectacled young man. Josh waved me forward.

"Margo, I want you to meet Albert Seiber. Actually, he's Dr. Seiber now. Just finished his dissertation at Princeton."

"Congratulations." I smiled at the young scholar, who blushed to the roots of his straight dark hair.

Albert led us up the steps of a Victorian townhouse. Next to double glass doors, a small brass plate identified the Rosenbach Foundation. The four-story brick structure had been converted to a rare-book library and museum. Seiber rang the bell.

The young woman who answered seemed to be expecting him. After brief introductions, she led us into a center hall with oriental carpets and richly polished wood. We climbed a grand staircase to a room lined with glassed-in bookcases. Two shelves of bound manuscripts lined a wall. In the hushed atmosphere, I almost ex-pected a guard to appear warning us not to touch.

The staffer unlocked a side door, and we entered a workroom. "We're set up in here with the map collection," Seiber told Josh.

Map collection?

Albert made himself at home. Ancient maps and charts lined

the walls, their locales boldly labeled.

Josh settled in at an oak table. I perched next to him on the edge of a stool. My curiosity was piqued, but knowing Josh, he would take his time, even though he most likely had a plan fully devised and ready to execute.

The young woman disappeared. At the sound of heels descending the stairs, Josh informed me that Dr. Seiber's dissertation was titled "Privateers on the Atlantic Coast."

Laughter bubbled up in my throat but I held it in. "How did you get involved in the subject?" I asked. My actual thought was, I guess just about anything can be the subject of a dissertation these days.

It's quite a tale," Josh said. He sat back with a smile, gesturing for Seiber to begin.

"As a kid, I spent summers with my grandparents on Long Island. One day, I think I was about seven, my grandfather asked me if I wanted to see something very special. He unlocked a drawer and showed me a book, an old journal bound in leather. It was cracked at the edges. The pages were thick and stiff with age. Grandfather turned over the top leaf very carefully. You could only make out first few lines. They read, 'Peter Prosser, his book.' Even with a magnifying glass, my grandfather couldn't make out much of the rest."

Seiber explained that the journal, handed down from generation to generation, was the diary of a young man's life at sea. Seiber's grandfather hired a local historian to do a genealogy. Eventually, they learned that Prosser, the restless son of a blacksmith, went to sea as a boy of fifteen.

Seiber was hooked. He became obsessed, and when his grandfather died, he inherited the journal. Anxious to read the story but unable to work out more than a few words of the fading manuscript, Seiber spent the next twenty years finding a way to decipher the words of his ancestor. His desire to know led to a life of scholarship. Technology made the pursuit easier. Scanners and new digitization allowed him to photograph the pages, enhancing and transcribing as he went. Along the way, he became a mariner historian. Now the document's painstakingly reconstructed pages were in his briefcase, transcribed into his laptop.

"I first heard about Dr Seiber's research from a professor up in Princeton who helped him with the technology," Josh said.

"And the privateers in your dissertation?"

"For centuries, men have told and retold tales of privateers and pirates who hid the riches they plundered. Most of them were just that—tales," Seiber said.

I nodded, remembering my son Charlie going through a pirate phase in grade school, but I kept it to myself.

"Until the journal was transcribed, no one realized the riddles it held," Josh said. "Prosser sailed with a captain whose name was a legend—William Kidd."

It sounded kind of familiar.

"Kidd was a legitimate sea captain, a respected member of colonial New York society," Seiber continued. "He was hired to protect English ships from pirates. The bulk of any loot he seized was to be turned over to his employers."

Seiber explained that the bargain was harsher than Kidd expected. Eventually, his crew demanded pay, but there was nothing to share out. The threat of mutiny loomed. Finally, after hard years at sea, Kidd returned to the New World with two ships loaded with treasure. But a political struggle between the governor of New York and the English crown made Kidd a scapegoat. He heard himself condemned for piracy by the very men who had hired him. According to Prosser's diary, Kidd's enemies were waiting for him at New York seaport. To elude them, he hid the loot before he returned to New York.

Josh's color was rising. "There have been a million stories about Kidd and his treasure. This one is different."

Seiber had searched for answers. Consumed with old maps and sea charts, he shuffled endlessly between libraries and museums, teasing out the facts behind the diary. After a winter in Princeton, the next summer might find him in London at the

Archives of the Admiralty. He compared his findings with Prosser's descriptions and with the old British, Dutch, and Swedish charts collected at the museum where we now sat.

"From blacksmith's son to pirate," I said. "That's quite a story."

Josh looked at me with a challenge in his eyes.

"Are we talking about a search for Kidd's treasure?" I asked.

Josh put a finger to his lips. I looked around. There wasn't anyone in the room but us, and the heavy wooden door was closed.

"Why am I here?" I whispered.

Seiber shrugged. "Josh asked if I would meet with you, but nothing is set."

"Just exploring possibilities," Josh said.

Seiber stood up. "Perhaps we should leave it at that for now."

"I'll just walk Margo out and be right back," Josh said. He steered me out into the hall and back to the first floor, where the smiling staffer let us out.

Back on the street, Josh stopped in front of a shiny black Prius and unlocked the doors. He motioned me into the front seat. "Margo, here's the deal. Salazar wants us to do this project, but first we have to convince Seiber to give us the transcript of the journal and the map. That's where you come in."

"Me?"

"Yes. I want you to send him a message telepathically."

"Oh, God, Josh. I don't know."

"I want you to direct your thoughts to him."

"What thoughts?"

"Working with Josh Bruckner and Victor Salazar will be good thing. The treasure hunt, I'll do it. Something like that."

"You want me to manipulate him."

"It's just a different type of negotiation. Humor me. Try it."

Eventually he wore me down and I agreed.

"You stay here," Josh said. "I'll be right back, with Seiber."

When Josh didn't come right back, I tried to focus my thoughts on Seiber anyway but soon gave it up. Josh would have to do the convincing without my help. I closed my eyes and dozed.

Josh came back to the car an hour later, without Seiber.

"Good job, Margo, it worked. He agreed."

I just stared at him.

"Salazar's in New York right now putting some money together. He's got foreign backers who are ready to run with it."

"Run where?"

"Most of the time we'll be on the Eastern seaboard. It's off the Jersey coast."

"If you knew all this was going on, why didn't you tell me sooner?"

"We have information from other sources, but we didn't want to go ahead without Seiber's buy-in. His journal is crucial."

"When?"

"Late spring to early summer. Before the tourist season ramps up."

"I need specifics, Josh. I need to plan. I have a family."

"Of course," Josh said. "It's just that …"

"Don't give me that need-to-know crap, Josh. I need to know, and I'm betting you and Salazar already have this whole thing planned out. If you're going to move me around like a chess piece, I want dates and times. And money. Up front!"

"OK, I get it," he said. "Obviously, this is extremely confidential."

When he was finished, I sank back against the headrest trying to absorb the details. They were scant but the money sounded good. We talked about the terms of a contract, which would include a confidentiality clause. Finally, I heard myself agreeing.

"I'll FedEx the contract to you," he said.

The contract arrived the next day. I called Alisha and asked if she would go over it. When she's wearing her paralegal hat, I can count on her to spot anything out of the ordinary. She told me to fax it over.

I thought of Harlan. Something told me he could be part of this venture, too. I waited a day and then called. "Hey, I bet you don't know who this is, do you?"

"Margo, just thinking' of you. How the hell are ya?"

"Good! Did they call you?"

"Just this morning. I was getting' coffee at the truck stop and a text from Josh pops up. Looks like I'll be heading back your way."

"What does your wife say?"

"She says go for it. She's already dreaming up how we're gonna re-do the kitchen the way she always wanted it. Maybe take a cruise on top of that."

"Did they give you the details?"

"Just a taste. He didn't want to talk too much on the phone. He's ending me some papers to sign. Non-disclosure he called it. As long as it ain't against the law, I'm in."

Alisha emailed good news. "The contract looks pretty standard. No red flags that I can see," she wrote. "Just abide by the confidentiality clause and you'll be OK."

Things were moving at a fast pace. I got a message from Greg inviting me to dinner. My life was getting crazier, but part of me was loving it. My pride had taken a beating from Jack, and this felt like turnabout. It was my time for adventure, and it felt sweet. I called Greg and we set a date for the weekend.

Two days later, I got a call from the body shop. Our "new" Camry, recently purchased from a neighbor was ready to drive home. Now dent-free and sporting a new paint job, it looked mature but respectable. I hoped it would stay that way. The mechanic warned that even though it was more than ten years old, the model was still a favorite of car thieves. I thanked him for the advice, but it was hard to imagine it would be worth the effort to steal it. I slid behind the wheel. The interior was a little worn, but I liked it anyway. It felt good to have a car again.

The weekend found me driving it over the Ben Franklin Bridge to New Jersey. Shabby or not, the car felt solid. It gave me confidence, something I needed heading out to my first real date in close to twenty years.

Greg lived in Moorestown, small-town America on steroids. From my time in real estate, I knew that down the quiet, leafy streets and behind the smartly painted Victorian houses with period exteriors lived one of the most highly educated populations in New Jersey. The schools were top-notch and the residents had the tax bills to show for it.

Greg's house was a nineteenth-century twin not far from the main street. His freshly painted door and window trim were in soothing shades of sage and rust. He smiled a welcome at the door. His lips brushed my cheek. He settled me in a plant-filled living room comfortably furnished with a grey suede sectional. A photo of Carla and her kids on the mantel was hard to ignore.

"I love what you've done with the place. Is it yours?" I asked.

"You mean do I own it?"

"I'm sorry. That was rude but the real estate agent in me had to ask."

He laughed. "Yes, I bought the place three years ago. Height of the market, too. But the prices in this town haven't dropped much. I'll give you the grand tour in a minute."

Orchids blooming by the window were a surprise. "Looks like you have a green thumb."

"My buddy owns a nursery. He gives me his dying plants, and I nurse them back to life."

"Plants like you. I'm impressed."

We settled ourselves on the sectional. He offered Prosecco, and I was on my second glass almost before I realized it. I told myself to slow down. I wanted to stay clear-headed for as long as possible. Wine loosens my tongue, and I was dying to tell him about my latest deal with Josh. But there was that pesky confidentiality clause. I mentioned that I would be working in New Jersey for an upcoming gig and let it go at that.

"Let's drink to that," he said. He topped up my drink and we clinked glasses. He leaned in a little closer. "That shirt's a great color for you. It brings out your eyes."

I was wearing a green silk shirt and beige pants, but I couldn't forget that underneath was the matching black underwear. For the first time in ages, I felt bold. Single after twenty years, I'd spent what felt like hours primping. It seemed to be working. He admired my hair, shiny and freshly styled for the occasion. He laughed at my witty banter. I felt more alive than I had in a long time.

"Something smells good," I said. The dining room table was already set with a salad and crusty bread. We stopped and kissed on the way into the dining room. The buzzer on the oven sounded.

"Perfect timing," I said.

Dinner was roast chicken with lemon, garlic, and rosemary. When I asked for the recipe, Greg admitted he'd bought it at the local grocery and reheated. If there was dessert, we skipped it. I had more than my share of wine. My senses were heightened and my anxieties lowered. How was I going to negotiate the next few hours?

When was the last time I'd had sex? Right before Jack and I were forced to confront the cracks and fissures in our marriage. Until then our relationship was like that of many other couples who had been together a while, mostly a slam, bam, fast five minutes before we both dropped off to sleep after a long day.

Despite the mounting electricity between us, Greg was in no hurry. "Let's take it slow," he said. "I don't want to rush you."

It felt tentative at first, but things moved from the dining room to the bedroom. Greg loosened his shirt. His eyes asked for permission before he unbuttoned the top buttons of my blouse and slipped it over my head. Catching a glimpse of myself in black underwear in the bedroom mirror, I wondered what stars had aligned to bring me to this moment.

His hands felt warm, even a little rough. They were different from Jack's smooth, manicured touch. Jack had the hands of a salesman who rarely did more than pick up a pen or tap a keyboard. I didn't care. I wanted Greg to be as different from my husband as he possibly could be. I shook my head to clear those thoughts. Even with my eyes closed I felt Greg watching me. I told myself to relax.

"You OK?" he asked.

I met his gaze, his smiling eyes a deep grey blue. "You watching me?" I asked.

"I just wanted to see if you are enjoying this as much as I am."

I nodded, laughed, and closed my eyes. I willed my brain to turn itself off while Greg's kisses wiped the chatter from my head. I arched my back up to meet him. We tumbled over and let the moment happen.

13

One week later, I was sitting next to Josh in the front seat of the Prius as we made our way through Center City Philadelphia. Near the historical district, school buses waited while students on spring outings swarmed Independence Hall. I felt more than a little guilty knowing I would be missing some of Jamie's last weeks in high school, but I also knew she would be so busy that she'd hardly notice my absence.

We crossed the Ben Franklin Bridge into New Jersey and headed east toward the coast. It was all major highways until halfway across the state. Then the roads went from six lanes to four and then to two. Houses became smaller, businesses, what few there were, grew shabbier.

As we navigated a traffic circle onto Route 72, an image of a runaway truck flashed into my mind. Without thinking, I reached over and jerked the wheel to the right just as a tractor trailer piled high with junked cars rattled by in the opposite lane. It threw a bolt, and a chain flew off, just missing our windshield.

Josh went from rage to surprise and back to rage. The Prius skidded to a stop on the shoulder. "What the fuck!" He yelled.

In the rearview, the trucker hurtled on, oblivious to what had happened. We were shaken but unhurt "Sorry, Josh," I said.

"Don't apologize. You probably saved our lives. But there for a minute, I thought you'd lost your mind."

"I went with my gut."

"Glad you did. That could have been serious."

Without further incident, Josh and I arrived at our destination, Fork Creek, New Jersey. The village lies a few miles inland from Long Beach Island, but still close enough to smell the sea and hear the seagulls squawking. We were booked at an old Victorian inn, the Sea Drift Hotel. The place had nine guest rooms and a first-floor dining room. It was quaint. The lobby featured the only TV reception in the building. Since this was the off-off season, Josh claimed we would most likely be the only guests.

After dropping my things in the closet of my third-floor room, I called home to let my mother know I'd arrived safely. I gave her the hotel's name, address, and telephone number.

 Bored already, I slumped back down to the lobby, where Josh was finishing a call on his cell phone. He surprised me by asking if I wanted to go with him to meet the truck. I wasn't sure what truck he had in mind, but I agreed. Anything was preferable to sitting in the lobby or staring at the flowered wallpaper in my small hotel room.

The dirt road was bumpy. We followed hand-lettered signs to the Atlantic Cove Marina, tucked away on a spit of land jutting into the bay side.

"How did you find this place?" I asked him.

"Wasn't easy. We're keeping it on the down low. Salazar doesn't want the guys at the Coast Guard station to see what he's doing."

"What is he doing?"

Instead of telling me, Josh reiterated that Salazar wanted us to keep a low profile. He was glad our numbers were limited to what he called a few "key people."

Just then, a ten-wheeler with Florida plates pulled into the boatyard. Josh waved and hit the horn. When two brawny truckers climbed down from the cab, Josh grabbed the driver and moved away for a quick confab. The marina owner approached, and Josh brought him into the conversation. Uninvited, I inched closer.

"Ernie here will unload the sled, but we'll leave it crated until the guys from Aqua Assessment get here," I heard Josh say. We watched the truckers unload a crate.

Josh's cell phone sounded, and he stepped away to take the call.

"Why all the secrecy?" the marina owner asked.

I shrugged. It's what they do, I thought but didn't say it.

"Careful with that," Josh shouted at the man driving the forklift with the crate. He directed the driver into the boat hangar's dark interior, and once he was satisfied that all was intact, he covered the equipment with a tarp. He seemed relieved. He scribbled his signature on the truckers' paperwork, and they left.

It had been hours since breakfast, so Josh and I went for a late lunch. With few options, we settled for the drive-through window at a local fast food place. I couldn't resist grilling Josh for details.

"So, what was that equipment and what's the plan?"

"It's called an electromagnetic sled. EMS for short."

"What does it do?"

"Detects materials on the ocean floor. It was invented to find land mines left over from World War II. But we're using it to look for metals. Even though the old ships were made of wood, the EMS will detect any silver, gold, and brass on board."

"How?"

"It sends back signals and creates a diagram of the ocean floor."

"Signals—you mean like sonar?"

"Close enough."

"Sounds like it could take a while."

"It better not. We may be in competition with another bunch. But we have something they don't."

"Who are they?" I asked. He ignored the question, checking a message on his phone instead.

On our way back, a van sporting the Aqua Assessment logo pulled in ahead of us. Once Josh escorted them into the hangar, he was ready to drop me back at the hotel.

"Margo, I'll be tied up, so you'll be on your own for a while, probably until tomorrow."

I had brought a book to read. I'm not much of a reader — I don't usually have much time for reading—but my mother insisted on sticking a book in my bag when I was packing. It was a novel her book group had enjoyed, a mystery by a British author named Kate somebody or other. Now I was glad she talked me into it. Settling into the lobby, I opened to the first page of *Dressed to Kill* and let my mind become absorbed in it. I liked the female detective character. She reminded me that in another life I might have made a good cop. By midnight I'd finished the last page. Not a bad book, I thought, vowing to remember the author's name for future reference. Without the distraction, I might have gone crazy. The cabbage roses on the walls in my room were giving me the willies.

When the squawk of sea gulls woke me at six-thirty, I gave up on sleep, dressed, and staggered downstairs in search of coffee. The waitress offered a fresh pot from the kitchen. I thanked her, and she took pity, bringing a couple of sweet rolls to go with the coffee.

"How's your room?" she asked.

"It's OK, I guess, but it could stand a little freshening up."

"You didn't hear anything up there, did you?"

"Like what?"

"Some people say the third floor is haunted."

I laughed. "Haven't seen anything so far, but maybe I felt it. I thought it was just the wallpaper driving me crazy."

The early morning was gray and damp. I sipped my coffee on the hotel porch, watching the fog lift. A black pick-up truck of prodigious size rolled up. When I spotted Mississippi plates, a smile spread across my face. "Thank God," I said. "Somebody to talk to."

Harlan beeped and waved. "Margo, glad to see your friendly face."

"New?" I pointed to the truck.

He shrugged and looked sheepish. "Hey, if the money's good? Keep it coming', I say."

"Amen."

"How do you feel about ghosts?" I asked.

He laughed. "No problem. Why you ask?"

"They say the third floor is haunted, but so far I haven't noticed. Just letting you know."

Harlan laughed. "Any more of that coffee around?"

I went back inside and got him a cup of coffee. Once he parked the truck, we sat and gabbed. I led Harlan to the desk and he checked in.

Later, Josh appeared and drove us to a nearby strip mall. "Here it is," he said.

"Here" was a boxy storefront wedged between a defunct florist with a sign that read "Closed for Renovation" and a hair salon. Over the door, a freshly painted sign read "Key Investment Strategies." Josh unlocked the door to a front office housing two desks, a file cabinet, and a look meant to be beige and forgettable. The back room was a different story. A bank of computer monitors lined the wall, hard drives below. Two high-speed wide-body printers occupied a corner.

Two technicians were busy with cables. I had met them at Perception, but they'd barely spoken and didn't have much to say now. Josh huddled with the two, giving them instructions on the computer setup and ignoring Harlan and me. There was no place to sit, so we stood near the door, quietly watching. I didn't see how we fit into this setup, and I quickly got fed up with being ignored. "Josh what do you need us to do here?" I asked in a not-so-quiet voice.

Josh looked at me as if he'd forgotten I was there. "Oh. You two can go. We'll be setting up a work space for you at the hotel."

A second day wasted, I thought, but Harlan saw possibilities.

"What the hell," he boomed. "If we're getting paid to kick back, let's kick back." He whipped out his map, studied it for about two seconds, and pointed to Atlantic City, a wide grin creasing his face. "Woo-hoo! Blackjack!"

We walked the mile back to the hotel and climbed into his truck. The sun was out, and global warming was keeping the temperatures in the 50s. Atlantic City and its mix of sea air, boardwalk cuisine, and tourist kitsch was a welcome distraction from the high-tech world Josh was creating. I felt light-hearted and Harlan was tickled. He said the closest he'd been to the ocean was the Gulf of Mexico. I told him I didn't think that counted.

We took a walk on the beach. The tide was coming in, the waves gray green, their crests topped with foam. I told Harlan how I'd loved coming here summers as a kid.

"I never learned to swim. Guess I'm too old now. How about you?"

I nodded. "That's the one sport I was good at. But you can still learn."

"Yeah, I guess." Harlan picked up a shell and put it in his pocket.

At a casino entrance, we snagged some "dollars off" coupons at Wolfgang Puck's new restaurant. We took advantage, treating ourselves to an upscale lunch. Over steak for him and crab salad for me, Harlan lent a willing ear to my saga of family financial troubles. Harlan is not only a good talker but also a good listener, and his kind expression kept me pouring out my fears about my looming college financial burden. I went on and on about the kids needing this and the kids needing that. Every dollar I scraped together went to something for my kids, I groused. I should have been embarrassed, but I wasn't. It felt good to get it out of my system. Finally, I shut up.

Though he always gabbed about older relatives, I realized that he never mentioned kids of his own and I'd never asked. Now I asked. "What about you? You never said. Kids?"

"Margo, I'm afraid the Trebold name will end with me. We

prayed to have a family, but God didn't see fit to bless us with children."

I could have eaten my words. To cover my silence he said, "Let me show you my furry children." On his phone were photos of two poodles, one black, one white, cavorting in front of a sturdy brick rancher. "The black one's Pepper. She's the oldest. The white one we call Snow. Afraid we spoil them rotten." He scrolled through to a brown-haired woman with a sweet expression pointing to her roses. "And here's my wife, Lolly."

"She looks like a lovely person," I said.

"It's our twentieth anniversary next month. She's been hinting about it for weeks, so I better not forget."

"I could help you shop for something nice for her."

He nodded, liking the idea. To walk off lunch we made our way to Atlantic City's version of higher-end shops clustered near Pacific Avenue. We wandered through the chain stores with familiar brand names, but nothing resonated.

We headed back to the street. The sun held strong and we continued our ramble. An old-fashioned store with tinted windows drew us to it.

"What type of jewelry does she like?" I asked as we scanned the multitude of trinkets displayed in the show window.

"She always says she likes antiques," he said. "Like this stuff."

"Shall we, then?"

"Why not?" Harlan pushed the door open and we went inside.

As we browsed, I was drawn to a case that held several interesting pieces. One, a gold cross set with a cabochon emerald and two pearls, seemed to call out to me. I got Harlan's attention. "What about that?" I said, pointing at the cross.

"Emerald's her birthstone. She loves them."

The store owner's ears perked up. He hovered closer. "Anything I can show you folks?"

Harlan pointed to the cross.

"Lovely piece, isn't it?" The owner slipped the cross from under glass and unfurled a piece of black velvet on the countertop. He placed the cross on the velvet, smoothing the edges.

"We don't usually come across something this unique, but I bought it from one of the local families."

The piece had to cost a small fortune. Harlan hadn't mentioned a budget.

Harlan held the piece toward the window. The emerald sparkled in the afternoon sun. "It's beautiful. I think she'd love it. Margo, what do you think?"

"Want me to try it on?"

He fastened the clasp at my throat. A curious sensation overcame me. I felt myself falling into an abyss. It felt like another time, another place. Danger threatened from behind. I tried to draw a breath and heard a sickening rasp. Pain seared my throat as the chain tightened. Desperate, I tried to loosen it. I felt coarse fingers give the chain a final twist and rip it away. An oily smell filled my nostrils. I heard a gunshot, saw a flash. Everything went dark.

A voice called my name. "Margo, Margo."

My eyes blinked open. Harlan and the store owner were staring down at me.

"What happened?" I murmured.

Harlan knelt down and gently pulled me up into a sitting position. "You fainted."

The jeweled cross slipped to the floor. As though in a dream, I watched the store owner return it to the display case. He turned the lock with a quick flick of the wrist. The halo of suspicion emanating from the owner hit hard. I sensed his thoughts — a pair of thieves attempting a distraction robbery. He fingered a red security button. "Let me call 9-1-1," he said.

"No. Please don't bother."

The owner stopped fingering the red button. "Maybe you should take her to the emergency room," he said to Harlan.

He didn't want the police, he just wanted us out.

Harlan dragged over a chair and helped me into it. Embarrassed and confused, I tried to pull myself together. A pain in the back of my head thumped . "I'll be OK. Just a little light-headed."

"E.R.?" the owner said.

Harlan shot the guy a dirty look. "Let her sit for a minute. Then we'll get out of your hair." He offered me bottled water from his backpack.

I drank some water and made it to my feet. We left the store, me leaning on Harlan. I was thankful for his brawny strength.

"Margo, what the hell was that all about?" he asked after we stepped outside.

"The cross. I saw myself wearing that cross. It was me, but it wasn't me. I was somebody else. Does that make any sense? Then a hand snatched it off my neck. I saw a face in the rearview mirror. A gun went off, then everything went black."

We retraced our steps, found his truck, and drove back to the hotel. Harlan was quiet on the way. He seemed to be having a conversation with himself. "What do you think it costs?"

I gave him a look. Despite the vibes coming off the piece, Harlan was apparently still thinking about buying it. "That was a big emerald," I said. "I didn't have a chance to see the price tag, but I'll bet it's at least a couple thousand, maybe more."

That night before we went in to dinner, Harlan asked if he could tell the group what happened. There was nothing he loved more than a good story.

"Please don't," I told him.

Four of us sat around the table, Josh and Harlan to my right, and a new addition, Skitch Garson from the survey company Aqua Assessment, on my left. Skitch had piloted his boat, the Enigma up from Florida. Tall, blond, and outdoorsy, he was likeable and easy on the eyes.

Our table and one other were the only paying customers in the hotel dining room. The menu was limited, but I was happy with my choice of beef stew. Harlan had chicken, and Josh and Skitch both ordered shrimp. I thought it odd that Salazar hadn't arrived, and I thought about Nina, too, wondering if she would be with him.

The conversation grew animated over more beers and a couple of bottles of wine. I was glad to let the others prattle on, until Josh asked Harlan what he and I had done all day.

"Me and Margo had a walk on the beach in Atlantic City, a nice lunch at Wolfgang's Puck, and I almost bought a cross with a big honkin' emerald for my wife," Harlan said. I felt my muscles stiffen.

"Where was that?" Josh asked.

"Forget the name," Harlan replied. "Some little jewelry store with a lot of antique jewelry." I tapped his leg with my shoe, but apparently he'd had too much wine to feel it.

"Colombian emerald?" Skitch asked.

"Beats me," said Harlan. "It was a nice one, though. Margo here tried it on for me. But then things went a little funny."

I gave his leg a kick. He shut his mouth and looked down at the remains of his chicken.

"Funny how?" Josh asked.

Harlan shrugged in reply.

Josh looked at me. "Margo?"

I felt as if I had no choice but to finish the story. I tried to downplay the whole event, but I didn't succeed. Later that night, Josh knocked on my door. He wanted the name of the antique store. When I claimed forgetfulness, he pulled out a list and asked me to go over the names. Something told me to hold back, but I learned later that Harlan remembered the name and gave it to him.

We spent the next day waiting for Salazar to arrive, but he was behind schedule, and he didn't want us to start without him. We moved everything back a day. This marked the third day of hanging around with nothing to do but wait. I went for a walk, looking to explore a shortcut to the bay. While I was gone, Harlan drove Josh back to the store. Harlan went in alone and Josh waited in the truck.

Harlan told me about it later. "When I first went in, the owner tried to ignore me, but I wouldn't let him. Then he gave me the stink eye. When I asked about the cross, he got hostile, said it wasn't for sale no more."

Harlan pleaded, told him he wanted the cross as a gift for his wife. It was a no-go. The owner refused to say what happened to it. "He told me I better leave or he was calling the cops."

The next day Skitch was ready to take his boat, the Enigma, out on the water. Even though we weren't needed on board, Harlan and I begged Josh to let us go out with them. I hinted that I might have a technique that could be useful on the water. That was a crock, but Josh finally agreed, and we drove to the marina with him and Skitch and watched as the Enigma was prepared.

One of the workers readied a smaller boat to put into the water. Something about the way he moved, the look of his profile, the silvery hair, reminded me of my father. How he loved the ocean from his days in the Navy. Every year he counted down to his two-week vacation at the seashore. Some years, Mom begged for someplace different, the mountains perhaps, but come August we always found ourselves in a cramped rental apartment near the ocean. Usually the high point of every vacation was an all-day boat ride from Cape May to Ocean City and back again on the Pride of the Atlantic. A few times, Dad even caught a fish.

The year Bart turned twelve, Dad rented a twenty-two-footer from a dock in Margate. It was to be his big treat. Dad was determined to take his son out fishing. It would be just the two of them. But Bart wasn't interested. He claimed a stomach ache and stayed in bed. I could see the disappointment on my father's face, hear the hurt in his voice. So I asked if I could go with him. "I always wanted to drive a boat," I told him.

He looked surprised. Then his eyes lit up. He gave me a hug. "That's my girl."

That day, we spent hours puttering around the bay, casting

our rods. Dad even let me steer a little before we ventured out into the channel. We headed back to the dock, tired and sunburned with only one fish between us. It was one of the best days of my life.

As the gulls squawked overhead, I wondered what Dad would have to say about this expedition.

Business was still slow for the party-boat skippers who docked at the Atlantic Cove Marina. Their season had yet to begin, but they were puttering, cleaning, and gearing up. These men, raised on this water, were protective of their turf. It was like home to them. And they had plenty of time to speculate about what the hell we were up to. We were the entertainment, and we could hear their laughter as they sat around enjoying the show.

If Josh thought he'd been successful in concealing the reason for our operation, he was mistaken. He had been so worried about the Coast Guard finding out about our project that he'd given scant thought to the curiosity of the locals. When word spread that a group of treasure hunters was about to begin a search, the main reaction was mockery. I overheard stray bits of wit and sarcasm here and there. Now, as we prepared to set out, a couple of the marina workers snickered in our direction, laughing at the "bunch of crazies lookin' for gold."

The Enigma drew a lot of attention on her own. She was a powerful 90-footer with radar mounted on the cabin roof. Treasure hunters in other places, like the Caribbean and Florida, used such equipment. But, according to the marina manager, nothing like this had been seen in these parts. That wasn't all that was drawing attention. Fingers were pointing at a couple of mounted rifles in the cabin. Apparently, modern-day pirates were not unheard of in the Florida waters where the Enigma often sailed. But here at the Jersey Shore, the people were used to a little less drama.

As the men worked, Skitch filled us in on the most famous treasure hunters in recent history. In Florida, the adventures of Mel Fisher and his company were legendary. Over the last decades, they'd made the waters of the Caribbean their personal territory. Their biggest find was a Spanish galleon sunk off a string of islands, not far from Key West. After all those years, millions in Spanish gold was still there, and the Fisher family claimed it. They proved it was still possible to locate treasure, even a hoard that had spent several hundred years at the bottom of the ocean. Maybe this venture wasn't as crazy as it sounded.

As Skitch regaled us, I wondered if Fisher's story had inspired Salazar. Had he sent Josh out in search of somebody like Seiber and his seaman's diary? If so, why now? Was anyone else thinking about the treasure we sought?

Skitch finished the tale and shifted his focus back to the business at hand. As the sonar equipment came out of the crate, he told the marina workers to treat it with respect. The rest of the morning, we watched them wrestling with thick metal cables that attached the expensive equipment to the ship. After much sweating and many adjustments, the electromagnetic sled was in place on the water. By mid-afternoon we were on board, ready to cast off.

It was a beautiful warm afternoon, with a light breeze. Warm in my sweats, I breathed deeply, enjoying the salt air. I remember my dad always telling us that the ocean air had more oxygen. It really cleared out the cobwebs. Made you feel so much more alive.

Before we left, Ernie, the marina owner, reminded Skitch, "They're calling for rain later today. Just remember Barnegat Inlet is tricky. Some say it's one of the riskiest spots on the East Coast. Whether it's true or not, just be careful."

Skitch gave him a salute as the boat's engine roared to life. Josh surprised us when he whipped out a bottle of champagne and some plastic cups. We toasted success and left the marina. With its full complement of landlubbers on board, the Enigma pulled out of the dock and headed for open sea. Such a feeling of freedom. Off to the side, a gull swooped down and skimmed across the surface, emerging with a fish in his bill. The beauty of the bird's dive and the efficiency with which it secured the meal made me feel a little in awe. For a split second you could almost understand the allure of life on the ocean.

Harlan whispered in my ear, "Where's Salazar?"

I shrugged. "Looks like the party is starting without him."

Until now, I had only known the most basic details of the ship we'd be searching for. Now that we were under way, Josh loosened his tongue. He poured himself a second glass of warm champagne, and Harlan and I heard more of the legend of Captain Kidd and his treasure ships.

"Kidd was hired to get rid of pirates wherever he found them. Not only that he had permission to seize anything of value he found onboard any pirate ships," Josh said. "Unfortunately, he was slow out of the gate, and even after years at sea he had little to show for his efforts. The crew turned ugly and threatened mutiny. Kidd's reputation as a captain was in shreds. To return without profits for his employers meant his career would be over."

"Rotten luck," Harlan said. "Sounds like the poor bastard had pressure from all sides."

I had heard this much of the tale before and nodded knowingly.

"Finally, Kidd found some success on the Indian Ocean," Josh continued. "One lucky day, wealthy merchant ships crossed his path. They were filled with gold and gems, emeralds from the Mogul empire. After some fierce fighting, Kidd won the day. The booty was his. Now he and his men could sail back to the New World on ships loaded with gold and gems. He could give his backers their profits and keep the rest."

"Good for him," Harlan said, clearly mesmerized by the story.

"Not quite," said Josh. "Sailing up the New Jersey coast, Kidd heard trouble was waiting for him in New York. Meanwhile, a storm was brewing. So he buried the treasure from one ship along the New Jersey coast, but the second ship was lost in the storm."

"Bad luck, that," Harlan said.

"It gets worse," Josh said. "When Kidd finally returned home, he was arrested."

Harlan was transfixed, but I could see the wheels turning inside his head.

We cleared the inlet, gliding out past the buoys. For this early in the season, there was a fair amount of traffic on the water. Out on the horizon a barge inched along. Two commercial fishing boats headed in with their catch, a reminder that in this part of the state, the fishing industry was still alive.

Once Skitch found a location that suited Josh, we did a trial run with the equipment. Behind the boat, the electromagnetic sled was silently transmitting data back to the computers on dry land. Even while he steered, Skitch was on his satellite phone with the team back at the field office. I had to give Skitch credit. He knew his business. Trying to be as inconspicuous as possible, I sneaked a look at the laptop he'd propped on the ship's console. Glowing graphics revealed both the size and location of objects on the ocean floor, what Skitch referred to as the "real time visual analysis."

I got closer. Skitch spotted me, but he didn't seem to mind. Soon, Harlan was hovering nearby. Skitch told us about the electromagnetic technology and how it was first designed to search for unexploded bombs underground. After World War II, there were tons of explosives lying in coastal waters, and not just in Europe and Asia. "More than you might think is right where we are now," he said.

Harlan gestured toward the laptop screen. "What're we lookin' at?"

Skitch gave a snort. "Trash. Scrap. Debris."

I could see what he was talking about. Viewing the rubbish left behind on the ocean floor, it was hard not to feel shame at what our species had done to the watery habitat.

Before Josh chased us out, I heard him on the satellite phone spouting his own version of what was on screen. When he held the phone away from his ear, a familiar low-pitched voice barked orders from the other end. Salazar might not have been on board, but he was making his presence felt. I overheard discussion of an island, but there was no land to be seen anywhere, at least not yet.

For Harlan and me, the day was a mini-vacation. Too bad there wasn't more champagne. Wrapped in sweats, we lounged on the top deck, slathered our faces with sunscreen, and enjoyed the feel of the ocean spray as the Enigma skimmed over the waves.

Skitch tweaked the equipment, adjusting the quality of the transmission. Once the practice run was completed to his satisfaction, he began methodically criss-crossing the waves in sections Josh had laid out on a grid. Even though Josh hadn't verbalized his expectations, my guess was that Harlan and I were along to fine-tune the information. Harlan's dowsing, his ability to home in on metals, and my sixth sense, which allowed me to view them, would be part of the mix. I heard Skitch say that the equipment was powerful enough to transmit up to fifty miles offshore. But what we were looking for was much closer in, less than a mile out at the most.

Captain Kidd could hardly have picked a more fragile home for his treasure. Over time, barrier islands along the New Jersey coast had borne the brunt of storms, their beaches washed away for decades, even centuries. It had been more than three hundred years since Captain Kidd had voyaged up the coast. The coastline had changed since then.

I'd never given much thought to the history of the Jersey shoreline. My version of New Jersey history only went back to the time I could close my eyes and see my brother Bart with my dad just past the breakers, their heads bobbing up above the waves. Then it was just sea and sand and saltwater taffy. How many daytrippers and vacationers had any clue that there were World War II explosives off the Jersey coast? Now I realized the area had a past that was rich in lore and perhaps gore.

Since that one meeting with Seiber, I hadn't given much thought to the practical side of sailing on the wooden ships of Captain Kidd's day. Today, out beyond the sight of land, the vastness of the ocean fueled my imagination. What might it have been like on those tiny wooden ships, using only the captain's knowledge of the currents and the few simple maps to cross thousands of miles of water? I tried to imagine sailing from some distant foreign shore to where we were now, with only the stars and the most basic tools of navigation.

Up on deck, Harlan's complexion, always ruddy, was now lobster-like. I pulled my baseball cap low over my eyes and retreated to the shade of the overhang. Finally, we were on our way back in. I heard Skitch tell Josh that one of the challenges would be to take some of the onshore mapping equipment mobile. They were headed back to the so-called Key Investment Strategies office to meet with the tech team to make it happen.

Back at the marina, the group split. Josh and Skitch went to the operations office to check the transmissions and the print-outs. Harlan and I got dropped off at the hotel. That was fine with me. I was more than ready to sleep off the effects of too much sun. But on our way through the lobby, Harlan muttered, "Oh shit. The princess is here."

I followed his gaze to the dining room. There was Nina ensconced at the hotel's small mahogany bar, iced drink in front of her. Harlan wasn't Nina's biggest fan. No one had mentioned her arrival, but I figured she must have come in with Salazar.

Shooting Nina a quick hello, Harlan begged off. "I think I better see if there's anything I can do to doctor my poor skin. See y'all later."

Nina waved him away. "Margo, how great to see you!"

That was a switch, but she really did seem glad to see me. "Nina, good to see you."

I was happier to see her than I realized. "I was beginning to feel weird being the only woman in the group." When she surprised me with a hug, I wondered if maybe she felt the same.

"Let's walk into town and see if we can get ourselves a real drink," she said.

I longed for a warm shower and a nap on crisp sheets before dinner, but I had the feeling Nina wanted to talk. Her eyes were ringed with shadows, and her cheekbones were a little more prominent than I remembered. Something about the urgency of her manner made me believe that not going would be a missed opportunity. There was a different aura about her. Was it anxiety? For a few seconds I intuited danger.

We walked the few minutes to Fork River's main intersection. There wasn't much there. Just the post office, a hardware store, drug store, and the local watering hole, the Wreck Bar, aptly named. We pushed open the door. Inside, the dark-paneled décor tried for nautical. An oil painting featured a beached ship on its side with a masthead of a mermaid. We found seats. A fiftyish barmaid approached and said, "What'll you girls have?"

I ordered a white wine spritzer, and Nina ordered a vodka martini. When the drinks arrived, Nina took a long sip and leaned back with a sigh.

"How are you?" I asked. "Did you have some time off these last few weeks?"

Nina frowned. "No, we've been up in Manhattan talking to some money people. This venture has become bigger than Victor first envisioned."

So, now it was Victor. And they'd spent two weeks in New York together? When did Nina become part of the "we"? Wasn't Victor married? He wore a ring. Oh well, not my concern.

"How did it go?" I asked.

"It was tough. He needed to sell more shares to support a more long-term project."

I could imagine the cost of the EM equipment, the boat, setting up the office. All the technology was staggering. Then there were expenses for a project team that seemed to expand by the day.

Nina looked over her shoulder. "We've got a window of forty days. After that the competition could be heading up this way."

"Forty days? I had no intention of being away that long."

Nina's look turned to exasperation. "No, Margo, of course not. We won't need you that long. Once the site is identified and confirmed, you and Harlan will be finished. Then it will be up to the divers."

There was that "we" again. I relaxed into the moment and sipped my drink. "Did you do anything fun in New York, see any shows?"

"No, it was all meetings, connections."

At the word connections, I got a weird flash of Salazar in a dark warehouse exchanging briefcases with a shadowy character in a black leather jacket. Nina was there looking on. Maybe her place in the proceedings was becoming more central as time went on.

We made small talk, and I tried to explain how Skitch and Josh spent their day out in the boat, sharing as much as I knew about the sled and its workings. She gave only half an ear to what I was saying. "I don't need to know about the technical part of this venture, but I am interested in the emeralds."

The bump on the back of my head gave a twinge. "It's funny you mention emeralds," I said. "I saw an amazing piece in an antique store."

"Victor showed me a transcript of this old diary. Captain Kidd took some Asian emeralds off a ship. He brought them back to the New World but he was afraid to take them to New York. He buried them, thinking he could return later. He didn't know he'd be arrested in New York harbor."

So, Nina had seen the diary, too, at least some of it. I wasn't surprised. Now her imagination had been captured by legends of precious cargo lost forever, legends that had lured treasure hunters for hundreds of years and were still enticing the treasure hunters of today. It reminded me of the movies I'd watched at the Saturday matinees that Bart and I went to as kids. I tried a little fishing to see what she knew.

"Who owns the diary?" I asked.

"Some perennial student who said it belonged to his ancestor. He's this guy from Princeton who's spent years trying to solve the mystery of Kidd and the treasure. Come to think of it, he wasn't that old actually, but still. He found documents from the Admiralty office in London. Then there was some treasure map he found somewhere. And take a look at this."

She whipped out her cell phone, scrolling though her photos to a display of antique gems and jewelry. My eye was drawn to a piece that looked suspiciously like the emerald cross Harlan had considered buying for his wife.

I played dumb. "Do you remember his name?"

She thought for a minute and shook her head.

"Will you be out on the boat tomorrow?" I asked.

"Was it choppy today?"

"Not too bad, except for when Josh took the wheel. I don't think he's had a lot of experience. Otherwise, it was pretty smooth."

"I get seasick if the water gets rough." Nina's glass was empty. She looked around for the barmaid, hoping for a refill.

It was time to go. I drained my spritzer. The skin of my forehead had started to tighten from too much sun. "Time for my nap. You coming?"

"I guess so." Nina stood.

I made for the door, but something caught my eye, a framed photo of a man with a metal detector. Underneath, the caption read, "Local Man Finds Treasure on Beach." The story was dated October 10, 1978. I squinted at the small print. I nudged Nina and pointed.

The waitress filled in the details. "That's John Murphy, used to own this place. Crazy bastard. When he wasn't here behind the bar, he was down on the beach sifting through the sand with his metal detector. One day, after a storm, it paid off. He found five gold coins on the beach. Pretty amazing, huh?"

"Wow. What kind of coins were they?"

"I think some had foreign writing on them, but I can't remember what."

"Is Mr. Murphy still here? I'd love to talk to him."

"Sorry, John's been dead about ten years."

"What happened to the coins?"

"Might still have one of them at the Historical Society."

Nina gave the waitress money for our drinks. I thanked her and added the five I had in my pocket.

I climbed the steps to my third-floor hotel room. My phone buzzed a text. "Mom, call me. It's important! " My heart pounded as I dialed.

Jamie picked up. "I got it. The scholarship I applied for."

"Which one?"

"The Young Environmentalist Association! Two thousand dollars, no strings attached. I can use it for tuition, expenses, whatever. I'm thinking I should get the laptop and the little printer in Best Buy to take to school."

"Oh, honey, that's great. I'm so proud of you." A twinge of guilt stabbed. I should be there.

"That's part of the good news. But the other thing I have to tell you is that the letter from financial aid came in from Stanford, and there was another one, too."

"OK, let's hear." I grabbed the side of the chair.

"They offered me an eighteen-thousand-dollar grant for the first year. And loans for another ten thousand. What do you think?"

I did a quick calculation. "Oh, Jamie. It sounds like a lot of money, and don't get me wrong, it is. Still, when you do the math, it's not quite enough. I'd have to take out a second mortgage to pay for the room and board. And that's only the first year. You said there was a second letter. Who from?"

"Cornell."

"And?"

"The money was better. They offered twenty-six thousand and loans for another twelve."

"Oh God, honey. That's fabulous. It could work. Cornell's within driving distance. Less than three hundred miles away. So no plane fares. You could even come home some weekends if you needed to."

"I know."

"Remember last fall, we said whoever offered the best financial aid, that's where you would go."

"I remember." A teary edge built in her voice. Her California dream was dying hard. But die it must. It was time to get real.

"Most students would kill for that chance," I said.

"I know," she murmured.

"OK, Jamie, let's give it some serious thought. We'll have to make a judgment call soon. Agreed?"

"OK, Mom, I agree. But, wherever I go, the first down payment is due very soon."

"I'll take care of it, honey."

This was the future. The first in a long line of payments to be made—all on my own. Silently I cursed Jack, but no matter what, I was determined not to trash him to his kids.

"Mom, when are you coming home?"

"Soon. Why? What else is wrong?"

"Nothing. Gram is fine but she's just a little nervous about stuff. Whenever I go out to do this or that, she asks if I have your permission. It's my last few months before college, and I want everything to be smooth. Besides, what are you doing up there?"

"Believe it or not, your mother is on a treasure hunt, for real."

"Mom, this is so crazy. I know we need the money, but I miss you."

"Jamie, you know what's going on in the world. You know jobs are tight. Thank God we're not on food stamps and unemployment. Let's just hang tight for a couple of weeks. I should be home by then"

As I said those words, I hoped they were true.

The next day, Harlan and I had a full roster of work to do. Even though we worked at different locations, neither of us managed to catch more than a glimpse of the sun. I spent much of the day in the hotel, in a second-floor room with one small window. It was just Josh and me as he led me through session after session of remote viewing. Whenever I offered a piece of new information, it set him off on a new spate of questions, mostly centered on the physical composition of objects. I kept coming up with a bulky metal object. It didn't make sense. Until the twentieth century, most oceangoing ships were wood.

By the time we broke for lunch, I had done three twenty-minute sessions in a row with little to show for it. Josh tried to keep it light, but his eyes were serious and his voice had an edge. "At least we know where the treasure isn't."

In the afternoon things went better. My sessions produced some sketches of what could have been ship parts. But, instead of the moldering, softer wooden textures that would indicate ancient seafaring vessels, these objects seemed metallic. Looking at them later, Skitch surprised our group. "Bomb fragments," he said. "From Navy training sessions, most likely, World War II vintage."

Harlan found himself at the operations room tucked away behind the store front. The sophisticated electronics systems were up and running, ready to connect key components of the project. Out on the water, Skitch piloted the boat back and forth, transmitting signals from the ocean floor. Back on land, computer software gathered the data being generated miles away, translating the information into charts for Harlan to work with.

Harlan and I ran into each other on the hotel porch at sunset. "How'd it go?" I asked.

"Long day," he said. "I dowsed one image after another until my head was spinning,"

"Poor you."

"The walls were closing in. I was so desperate for a break, I kept asking the computer guys if they wanted coffee."

"Good move," I said.

"I finally escaped and walked down to the local Dunkin Donuts. It got real quiet when I walked in. The local folks don't know what's doing, but they know something's up."

"That's just how it is in a small town."

"Nah, it was more than that. When I paid the bill, the locals at the counter were askin' each other, "Who do you think they are, DEA, FBI, or Customs?"

DEA, FBI, or Customs? I didn't know whether to laugh or cry.

Meanwhile, little by little, all the data was being pieced together at the field office. Charts of the ocean floor were overlaid, placed one atop the other on a light table and aligned in register. The technicians were looking for what they called "hot targets," clustered together. That wasn't all. According to Josh, they were looking for a "consensus" from Harlan, Nina, and me.

I knew enough about remote viewing to know that the way Salazar wanted things done at this stage of the project was unorthodox. He knew it, too, but he kept pressing. To be most effective, remote viewing begins with a clean slate. The viewer should have no idea of the target. But we all knew what we were looking for. I kept my thoughts to myself.

But the boredom finally got to me, and I knew I couldn't take another hour penned up inside four walls trying to glean information about the ocean floor. I also knew I couldn't just tell Salazar that we were going at this thing all wrong — even though we were—I had to make my idea sound like a win-win. One night after dinner, I made my case to Salazar.

"How about if we go out on the boat? I can go up with Skitch and do a little psychic navigation."

Salazar scoffed, shook his head, and walked away. So much for win-wins, I thought, but half an hour later, I heard him telling Josh he wanted to try a different approach. He didn't mention my name.

After breakfast the next morning, Josh drove Nina, Harlan, and me to the marina. The plan was for Skitch to take each of us out separately.

Spring weather on the New Jersey coast can be changeable, but we caught a calm, sunny day. I was thankful for the fresh air. Skitch was working with the charts generated from the electronic signals, but he looked up when I stepped aboard. "Margo, welcome to the wheelhouse." He motioned me toward the controls. I focused on the sonar screen. It was a montage of spiking color. I crossed my fingers behind my back and tried to act like I knew what I was doing. Just like driving a car, I told myself. But this baby cost a million bucks at least. I figured that once we were out in open water, it wouldn't be so hard. Once we cleared the inlet, there would be nothing to run into.

"Ready to take the wheel?" His eyes crinkled in mild amusement, but something told me he thought this was an insane idea.

"You're going to be here with me, right"

"Oh, you bet."

Salazar's instructions were that I was to steer to the target locations, intuitively, without benefit of the chart. The old cliché "Be careful what you wish for" flashed through my mind, but I took a deep breath, sat down at the wheel, and gave Skitch a nod. Moments later, I was piloting a high-tech, million-dollar vessel into the Atlantic Ocean.

Later, as we pulled into the marina, I gave a jaunty wave to Harlan and Nina. My knees didn't buckle as I left the boat, and I marched off the dock feeling proud of myself. I gave Harlan a "thumbs up."

Harlan and Nina also took their turns on the bridge. Harlan dowsed the charts and directed Skitch that way. Nina claimed seasickness and insisted that they return to the dock immediately. Skitch called Salazar on his satellite phone, and moments later the boat turned and headed back to shore.

After a day of freedom and sea air, I was back in that beige room. Salazar left it up to Josh to wring the desired results from my psyche. That afternoon, he came in and drew up a chair. "Margo, we've only got so much time," he said. "I know you're tired but you know Victor. He expects results."

Josh placed three sealed brown envelopes face down on the table. "Before I give you a look at these, see what impressions you can get. Choose any means of sensing you want." He slid a tablet and a pen toward me. "I'll leave you to it."

He got up and left, closing the door behind him. His absence was a relief. For the next half hour, I did my best to focus on the envelopes, but I didn't get much. On the reveal, I saw just how little I had connected with what was under the waves. It was more than a little frustrating.

By evening, the general mood had lightened. Everyone except Nina gathered for dinner in the hotel's small dining room. Nina was still feeling the effects from her brief boat ride, but I figured she'd be fashionably late and that we'd all make a big fuss over her when she finally arrived. We knew better than to discuss our project in a public place, so Salazar took the opportunity to tell us about a conference he'd recently attended in Washington. He expounded on the paper he'd given and his follow-up article, soon to be published. Once Salazar wound down, Skitch and Harlan took over, regaling us with their personal "fish that got away" stories.

Josh was quiet, apparently not having any fish tales to share. Several times during the course of the meal, he scanned the room surreptitiously as if he was expecting something or someone.

Salazar's demeanor changed suddenly. His aura, usually yellow, now burned a jagged orange. I noticed his gaze riveted on a man in the corner. He leaned over and whispered something to Josh. Josh listened and then shook his head. He mouthed the word "no." I heard him say, "You're mistaken." Then the aura dimmed and Salazar calmed. He called the waitress over and ordered another bottle of the burgundy he loved.

I felt a sense of unease, and I wasn't sure where it was coming from. But intuition told me that once my contract was complete, I should put as much space between Dr. Salazar and Josh Bruckner and myself as I could. That was just as well, because at the end of the meal, Salazar made a surprising announcement.

He turned toward Harlan and me. "You'll be able to leave at the end of the day tomorrow or the day after, if you choose."

I was ecstatic. A weight lifted from my chest. The anxious lump at my core began to fade. I could go home, be with Jamie, who was feeling the push and pull of leaving home. Maybe I could even try to reconnect with thirteen-year-old Charlie.

Salazar reminded us that we'd still need to be on call, ready to return over the following weeks for the final evaluation. Then our work would be done. That worked for me, but I wondered about Harlan. I saw his face light up, then grow dark. For once, I couldn't quite sense what his feelings were. Too bad his fear of flying meant that if he left soon he'd still be on the hook. If Salazar called him back, he'd be obligated to make the long drive a second time. But, like me, he'd signed a contract. According to the terms, he and I were in thrall to the project for at least the next month. I wouldn't bring it up now, but later I would suggest to Salazar that I'd expect a retainer for the deal.

The second bottle of wine arrived. Salazar waited as the server uncorked it. I sensed that he was in no rush to leave the table. As the waitress cleared our empty plates, Salazar turned to me. "Margo, in case I forget, will you please remind me to have something for Nina sent up from the kitchen?"

So much for being fashionably late. "Is she ill?"

"Nothing serious. Just a headache."

"Perhaps something light would be best, a little soup? I don't think I want dessert anyway." I pushed my chair back from the table. "Let me go see what they have in the kitchen."

I followed the waitress to the kitchen and asked to have some soup and tea sent up to Nina on the top floor. When I went back to the table, I volunteered to check on her. "I'll make sure she's feeling OK and that she got something to eat."

I was anxious to call home and share the good news, so it was a good excuse to get away. Harlan stood and stretched. Claiming fatigue, he said he was ready to turn in. We headed for the stairs, and Harlan puffed his way to the second floor. I could sense his ambivalence about being sent home, but he didn't seem to want to talk about it.

I went to my room, called home, and talked to Mom. I told her I'd be home soon, sooner than expected, and that made her happy. Mom said she was fine staying with the kids for as long as I needed her to be there.

Jamie and Charlie were out enjoying the unseasonably warm weather. "They promised not to go far, and I told them I wanted them back in an hour." The good news was that she'd overheard Jamie telling a friend that she might go to Cornell instead of Stanford.

"Thanks, Mom. That's the best news ever!" I did a little dance of joy. "I'll sleep better tonight." I rung off.

I climbed the stairs to the top floor. The hallway felt cold. I knocked lightly on Nina's door. "Nina, it's Margo. I had some soup sent up for you. Do you want anything else?"

There was no response. I knocked again. The door swung wide. A stiff breeze hit me in the face. The tiny balcony door was open, and papers were scattered across the floor.

"Nina?"

No response. I stepped into the cold room and shivered. Nina hated the cold.

I found her face-down beside the bed. Blood pooled beneath her ear. I knelt down next to her, took her wrist, and felt for a pulse. A flutter under the skin told me she was still alive. I put my ear against her back and heard weak breathing.

The hallway outside was empty. I'd left my cell phone one floor down. The only help was downstairs. I ran.

Salazar and Skitch were still in the dining room. I grabbed Salazar, pulled his arm. "Come quick. It's Nina. She's hurt."

Salazar moved more swiftly than I'd ever seen him. We ran up the flights to the room. Salazar knelt, gently turning Nina. He checked her pulse. "She's alive." He patted his shirt pocket as though looking for his phone. Finally, he barked, "Call an ambulance."

I charged down to the lobby. The desk clerk was on the telephone. I grabbed the receiver out of his hand. "There's an emergency. One of our people is hurt bad. Call the police, call an ambulance."

He stared for a moment, then ended his call and dialed 9-1-1. "This is the Sea Drift Hotel. We have an injured guest." His tone was almost matter of fact. I grabbed the phone a second time and shouted into it, "This is an emergency. My colleague is barely alive."

A voice promised, "We're on our way."

Skitch and I paced outside. When the ambulance arrived, I pointed two paramedics to the top floor. How they negotiated Nina's stretcher down the narrow stairs and out the door with no mishap I don't know. Watching the ambulance retreat into darkness, I prayed that Nina would survive.

"Harlan, are you in there?"He opened the door, holding up his pants. "What's up?"

I ducked inside. "Nina," I stammered. "Nina's been hurt. Bad."

Harlan's eyes look puzzled.

"I'm not kidding. Didn't you hear the siren? I went to check on her. She was on the floor, barely breathing. I called an ambulance. You didn't hear all the commotion?"

He shook his head.

"The door to the balcony was open. Papers were flying everywhere. Salazar's laptop was missing and so was his briefcase."

"Oh, no. You predicted something like this."

"No, I didn't. I felt uneasy at dinner but I kept it to myself."

"I'm talking about when we were up at Perception. The day we were at Mystery Hill, the equinox, remember?"

"Yeah."

"You said Nina's in danger."

"So you say, but, to be honest, it's all a blank."

"They weren't after money, were they?" he asked.

"What money? But this does it, Harlan. I want to go home now. What about you?"

"This whole operation is losing some of its charm, but if I go home how, I'll only have to turn around and come back if he calls me. I'll sleep on it and see how I feel in the morning."

Next morning, Salazar was back to let us know that Nina was in critical but stable condition. Once I knew she was going to pull through, I started packing. Before I was finished, the local police arrived.

An earnest young detective herded all of us on the project into a hotel meeting room. Skitch, Josh, and Harlan waited while the police questioned me about what I'd found in the room, then they asked Salazar about his laptop, the briefcase, and his relationship with Nina. I could just imagine the married Salazar coming up with a story about Nina being his personal assistant and why they'd need to share connecting rooms purely for professional purposes.

While the police of Ocean County, New Jersey were familiar with drunk drivers, winter burglaries of summer homes, and the occasional three-car accident, this was new territory. They seemed skeptical about a motive. Salazar called it a robbery and made quite a big deal about the laptop and the documents that were stolen. Josh painted a very different picture for the local police. Josh tried to throw a smoke screen over the reason for our being there in the first place. He claimed we were a group of entrepreneurs looking for a quiet place to start a new environmental investment business. His version was that Nina was hurt by someone attempting a simple robbery, perhaps a drug addict, someone looking for something more valuable than papers. Would they buy it? If the police talked to the locals, they'd soon hear the conventional wisdom that our operation was very unusual.

One other thing worried me. It was my recent experience with the New Jersey police. Would that kind of thing show up next to my name in some sort of master record? If so, it would look bad. Here I was, only a little while later, in the middle of another crime. I told myself to keep my mouth shut. But that might seem dodgy. I just wanted to get home before my name surfaced in the police database of suspicious people.

Half the day was gone by the time they let us go back to our rooms. I looked for aspirin. Even though they told us we'd be required to stay for another day, I resumed packing. I wondered about Nina and thought of the conversation and the drinks we'd shared two days earlier. With so little sleep the night before, I thought I would just put my head down for a quick nap. I slept for hours and then remembered I'd told my mother I might be home by evening. I called her and tried to minimize what had happened, but I told her my plans had changed and that I would call again as soon as I knew more. Then I put my pillow over my head and fell back to sleep.

The sun's rays signaled the beginning of a new day. Before I could lift my head, I had the feeling that someone had been talking to me as I slept. I tried hard to remember the substance of the communication, but it had slipped away. One thing I knew for a certainty was that the treasure hunt was over for me. I already had earned the money, which was safely deposited in my account. I was willing to call that fair payment, shake hands, and walk away.

That morning found the local police replaced by state government agents. They rounded us up and drove us in a van to an anonymous two-story concrete structure on the mainland. Did they think this was a drug operation? Skitch, Harlan, and I made ourselves as comfortable as we could on three straight-back chairs in an airless room with fluorescent lights reflecting off gray walls. My heart fell when I heard what sounded like a lock being thrown. Chin in hand, I stared into space until a young fair-haired woman in a navy shirt and pants ducked in.

She asked for our identification. "Strictly routine. I'll just make photocopies in case we need to get in touch with you in the future."

She looked trustworthy, but at this point I was reluctant to give mine up. I asked if I could go with her. She didn't answer, but I tagged along. "I realize that we're not under arrest, but if we are asked to be here much longer, I'm going to request that I get in touch with my attorney," I told her. I didn't have an attorney. I just wanted to get the hell out of there.

Harlan and I were questioned separately for what felt like hours. At that point I wondered where Josh was. There was a lot of discussion about what my role was in the treasure hunt and how I became involved with Salazar and Josh. I realized that I never knew how Harlan had been recruited.

Skitch got lucky. He'd only met Nina briefly. Once his credentials checked out, I heard the young agent telling him he was free to go. I caught his eye on the way out, and he shrugged as if to say, "What the hell?"

Later Josh appeared. I wondered what kind of questions they'd asked him. When it was all over, we got into Josh's car. I got in the back, Harlan was in the front.

"Where's Salazar?" Harlan asked.

Josh looked over his shoulder as he backed out onto the road. "He went to check something out."

"Which hospital did they take Nina to?" I asked. "How is she doing? Has anyone seen her?"

"She's doing better," Josh said. He seemed to have little more to say.

Back at the hotel, Harlan and I met in his room. I talked about getting out of town, but Harlan made noises like he might want to stay a little longer. "You say your place is only an hour or so from here?" he asked.

"Maybe a little more, depending on traffic."

"Hell, I can do that at the drop of an eyelash and be back here before anybody even notices I'm gone," he said.

"I'd take you up on that offer, but there's something else I wanted to do."

"You sure?"

"If you just get me to where I can get a rental car that would be great. Then I can put this whole experience behind me."

I couldn't understand why he wasn't leaving, too. Did he really want the money that badly?

With a plan to meet in half an hour, I went to grab my bags.

14

All I needed was to get to a town of reasonable size. Harlan drove me five miles inland then jumped on the expressway heading north to Tom's River. We found the Hertz rental on Main Street where I happily plunked down my credit card and they rented me a red Chevy compact with only a few thousand miles on it. Throwing my gear in the trunk, I couldn't wait to get on the road. Money or no money, as far as I was concerned this expedition was over.

Harlan gave a final wave and then climbed into this truck. I watched him pull out of the lot. In two seconds I was right behind him, but I had one more stop before heading home. I needed to find Nina. Before I left, the hotel desk clerk told me she probably would have been taken to Ocean County Memorial. I got the number and called. They confirmed that Nina Pritchett was a patient and her condition was stable. She had recently been moved from the ICU. They put me through to her room, but no one answered.

Here she was, thousands of miles from home, in a small hospital in an out-of-the-way corner of the Pine Barrens in New Jersey. Did anyone in her part of the world know where she was? She hadn't mentioned much about family and friends in New

Zealand. She'd grown up on a sheep farm on New Zealand's South Island, near Christ Church. I had the sense that her parents were no longer alive, but there must be others who would want to know what was happening in her life.

She had said she'd been married and was now divorced. I remembered her telling me, "It's complicated." Her ex worked for an airline. They'd had no children. Nina worked in Wellington, teaching sociology at the University of Wellington. She'd done her dissertation on aboriginal people, was partially of that heritage herself. She'd met Salazar at an anthropology conference in Australia when he presented a paper. Apparently, that was the beginning of a relationship that had become more personal than professional.

I found my way to Ocean County Memorial, a blockish masonry structure surrounded by a stand of pines. A billboard announced a new wing opening in 2014. Nearby, a crane hoisted materials in the air above a yellow-helmeted construction crew clambering over exposed steel girders.

I parked my rental away from the site. Inside, a shift must have been changing. There was a bustle in the hospital lobby as men and women in blue and green scrubs moved through the doors with that happy quitting-time look on their faces.

I made my way to the information desk and gave Nina's name. The woman asked for ID, and I fished out a driver's license and handed it over. She keyed in the vitals, returned the card, and printed out a visitor pass. "Ms. Pritchett is on the third floor. They moved her from the ICU, so she's able to have visitors now. Elevator's to the right."

Hospitals are difficult places for me. The emotions that hit me at the door make me want to run in the opposite direction. I know other people feel that way, too, but for me it's way more intense. When I was eleven, my kid brother, Bart, broke his arm, and we took him to the emergency room. I got so upset and cried so much that my mother had to take me out to the car. Over time I realized that I had been feeling the worries and fears not only of the patients but also of their family members. Now I try hard to close off the part of me that receives the distressing emotions. I visualize a shield over my heart. It doesn't always work.

The elevator door opened to reveal an unfortunate man on a gurney escorted by an aide. I waved them on. I would wait. The second elevator deposited me on floor three. I got off and found a restroom. I was starting to feel panicked. I patted my face with cold water. My anxiety subsided, and I looked for Room 322.

It was a double room, but the other bed was empty. Nina's face was deathly pale. Her eyes were closed, and there were tubes and wires connecting her to a variety of devices. I wasn't sure how long my sensibilities would permit me to stay, but I wanted to hang in for her sake. I looked at my watch for the second time in as many minutes. Maybe I should just sit quietly and wait to see if her eyes would open. A nurse bustled in and checked her chart. Time passed. I waited. I went down to the gift shop and treated myself to candy and a tabloid. Another paperback caught my eye, *Ghosts of Long Beach Island*. On a whim, I bought it for Charlie.

Back in Room 322, I settled in with the magazine I'd bought to give to Nina. As I waded through tabloid photos of plastic surgery gone wrong, Nina's eyelids fluttered. I leaned closer. "Nina, it's me, Margo. Can you hear me?"

Again a flutter. The monitor blipped. Was that good or bad? Nina opened her eyes. She looked up at me. I took her hand and she gripped mine for a second and then let it drop. A single tear slid down her cheek. She opened her mouth to speak but no words came out.

"You're here in Ocean County Hospital. You're safe. No one can hurt you," I said.

For a crazy second, it occurred to me that Nina, living in a country that provided health insurance for all its citizens, might not have insurance here. I shook my head to clear that inconvenient thought away. I wondered if Josh or Salazar had thought of this. And speaking of Salazar, had he been here to check on her today?

Nina opened her eyes fully and tried to move up on the pillow. She took in the tubes affixed to her and a second tear followed the first.

"Do you want me to help you sit up?"

She nodded and I gently slid my arm under the pillow beneath her head. Then I remembered the bed controls. I found them and raised her head. We were closer to eye level now. "Can you tell me what happened?"

Her lips were chapped and dry. A pink plastic tumbler with its built-in straw was on a tray. I filled it with some water and held it toward her. She sipped a little, moistening her lips. "Looking for …"

"What? Who was looking?"

She shook her head to indicate she didn't know.

I remembered Salazar saying his laptop was gone. "Was it the laptop?"

She shook her head. The beeps on the monitor seemed to elevate.

A nurse poked her head in. "Do you need to use the bedpan?" Nina shook her head. Her eyes welled. The nurse drew the curtains anyway and told me visiting hours were over for the afternoon. "You can come back tonight at six or tomorrow morning."

I gathered my things. "I'll be back," I said to Nina. "I promise."

I wrote my name and a slew of phone numbers on the back of an old business card from my real estate days. I begged some tape at the nurses' station. Back in Room 322, the curtains were still drawn. "Nina, I wrote my number on a business card. I'm taping it to the magazine." There was a muffled response, but I couldn't make out what she said. I left everything on top of the bed tray where I hoped she couldn't miss it. "I'll call you tomorrow."

Then it hit me. I might not be able to get back any time soon, and for sure, not tomorrow. Still, for Nina's sake, I promised myself that even if I didn't come back I would try to get in touch with the people on the other side of the world who cared about her. In the meantime, I could use the Internet to try to connect with her colleagues at the University in Wellington. A hospital brochure in the lobby provided the correct name, address, and phone number for future reference.

Time to go. I opened the bottled water I'd bought and splashed a little on my face and wrists to bring me back to the here and now. I left the room and headed for the elevator. I ate the last of the candy bar from the gift shop, then left the hospital and made for home. It was the tag end of the afternoon by the time I found my way to the Garden State Parkway. Thirty miles punctuated by annoying toll-booths made for slow going. I switched to back roads, ones without tolls or traffic lights that would take me west toward Pennsylvania. By six-thirty, the lights on the Ben Franklin Bridge were a welcome sight.

I was looking forward to seeing my kids. The lovely deposits in my bank account were at an end, but I knew there were more important things to think about. The kids weren't as excited to see me as I was to see them, but Mom was relieved. She wasn't used to being on call all hours of the day and night. While I'd asked Jamie and Charlie to be mindful that their grandmother wasn't used to the comings, goings, and drama of adolescence, they probably wondered, "What drama?"

Mom and I shared a drink before dinner. It was great to be home. I gave her the abbreviated version of the recent happenings. I downplayed the Nina situation and some of the other events. Overhead, I heard a groan, then a laugh. Thirteen-year-old Charlie was lurking at the top of the stairs.

"Charlie, what's so funny?"

"Mom, you're killing me." He tromped downstairs to the living room. "Pirate treasure?"

"Carry on all you want. I figured you'd be the one person to think it was neat."

"Neat?"

I thought about the book I'd bought him in the gift shop. Fat chance he was getting it now. His adolescent snark was starting to piss me off. "It put money in the bank, and it helped me make the mortgage payment. And don't forget some of it went toward the two weeks of science camp you begged me for this summer. I can always cancel, if you want."

Mom had made one of my favorites for dinner, her chicken pot pie. The aroma was comforting. The faces of my family calmed me. For the moment, it was a peaceable kingdom. Fatigue faded and I was grateful. We made fast work of the pot pie.

"That was beyond delicious, Mom," I told her. "Thank you for dinner, and for everything else." The kids chimed in. They loved their grandmother's cooking almost as much as I did.

Once the plates were empty, my mother started with the questions. I owed it to her to be honest. Reluctant to acknowledge the bizarre nature of the venture, I'd done my best to make our trip sound like the scientific expedition I hoped it would be.

"Margo, don't get me wrong. You had an opportunity and you took it. It didn't turn out, and you did the right thing, leaving when you did. "

Even at this stage, I wasn't so sure. "I guess I wanted to believe this was a legitimate project. There was a Dr. Seiber, a young Ph.D. Josh introduced me to. We met him at a museum for heaven's sake. His research was scholarly. There was a sense of history to it."

Mom still wasn't convinced. "Yes, it sounds fascinating, but I'm just wondering. Why did everything have to be so secretive? What were they hiding?"

"They said there was competition but I don't know who it was."

"Still, I'm wondering. Why did you get in so deep?"

"That's a good question." I poured myself a little wine. "Jamie, you remember those articles you found for me on the Internet, the ones where the scientists used remote viewing for those archeology sites in the Mediterranean?"

"Yeah, Mom."

"Maybe it was the archeology. Strange as it sounds, the people in charge of the project hoped we could find a way to go back in time. That's why they brought in people like me and Harlan and used us to remote view and dowse. They hypnotized Nina to see if she could see into the past. If it had worked, it could have been groundbreaking. I just got caught up in the adventure."

We cleared the table. Charlie rolled his eyes, said good night, and drifted away. Jamie claimed homework.

"Who would this treasure belong to if you found it?" Mom asked.

"I'm not sure. In some states its finders' keepers. I don't know what laws New Jersey has on the books. This is not your everyday project. There's a lot of gray area where the average person wouldn't have a clue as to what's legal and what's not."

"Margo, what if somebody comes after you?"

"Why would they? I don't have anything anybody would want."

"Maybe it's not what you have. Maybe it's what you know." My mother still had some worry around the eyes.

"What do I know?" I spun out the tale of long ago. "My God, Captain Kidd roamed the seas over three hundred years ago. But a lot has changed since then. Even I know that. Think about the Atlantic coast. Every ten years or so major storms blow through and wipe out the beaches. A lot can change. Landmarks disappear."

"What about poor Nina?" my mother asked.

"She works at a university in New Zealand, but, like me, she came on board because of other talents. She's easily hypnotized. Like I said, she goes backward and forward in time."

"They tried to hypnotize me at a party once, but it didn't take," my mother said, smiling at the memory. "I guess I'm more of the 'believe it when I see it' persuasion."

My mother has always been accepting of my abilities, especially as I got older. They were beyond her frame of reference, but she never belittled their reality in my life. She patted my hand. "Oh, Margo. How did I ever have a daughter like you?"

"Mom, you act like I'm the only one in the family who's wired this way. What about your son, Bart? He's sees things like I do, he just doesn't talk about it. And your sister, Ruby? She's had her own stories to tell."

"Yes, but Ruby didn't take it too seriously. She just says she has a guardian angel that helps her out sometimes."

It took a while for Bart to become comfortable with his gift, but after he did, he used to joke that he'd been beamed down from the mother ship at birth. As kids, one of our favorite games was to hide at the top of the stairs when our parents had company. From our perch, we would read the auras of the grown-ups who came to visit. Of course, we didn't know they were called auras. We called them colors. Afterwards we would write down the colors and decide who we didn't like.

We told my mom about the game and said we liked her color best of all. It was always green. She gave us a funny look, like she didn't get what we were saying. Bart decided we shouldn't tell other people what we could do. It was our secret. He swore us both to secrecy. He poked our fingers with a pin, and we signed an oath in blood. He was eight and I was almost ten.

I burrowed between cotton sheets in my own bed and waited for sleep. Mental pictures of a forlorn Nina tethered to a hospital bed weighed on my mind. Was Harlan right? Had I predicted the danger that would stalk her? I didn't remember saying those words. But in my mind, that prediction somehow made Nina my responsibility. Before drifting off, I made a silent promise to her that I would try to get in touch with her people in New Zealand.

I don't know if Mom slept as well as I did. Over morning coffee, she told me there was still one thing troubling her. "What about the money they paid you? If they've done anything illegal, doesn't that make you part of the crime?"

I tried to allay her fears. "I was being paid for my information, my services. Think of it this way," I said. "If they paid me for computer services, would I be guilty? No. What if they hired me as a cook, would I be guilty? Again, no."

Mom nodded but her eyes were skeptical.

"It's not like they would give me a share of anything they found. Even if it was worth millions."

Pretending finally to be satisfied, she was ready to pack up and go home. She kissed the kids, dug out her car keys and promised to call later. Once the kids left for school, I settled in at the computer.

In one of our early discussions, Nina told me she was an instructor on a sabbatical from the sociology department at the University of Wellington. I searched the Internet and found Nina's work address, telephone number, and email. I phoned her department, but the time difference separating the Eastern United States and the Pacific Rim worked against me. Instead, I settled for email. Her colleagues were listed on the university website.

Greetings,

I'm getting in touch with you in the interest of your colleague Nina Pritchett. We've been working together here in the U. S. Nina was recently injured. She's being treated at the Ocean County Memorial Hospital in New Jersey. The phone number to her room is 856-994-1208. She is under care and is on the way to recovery. If you could provide contact information for her next of kin, I would much appreciate your help.

Sincerely, Margo Fellshur

With all the hoaxes swirling across the Internet, I hoped this wouldn't be taken for one more scam. With no request for money, I legitimized myself by providing name, address, email, and phone number in hopes the request would be seen as genuine.

I didn't stop there. There were only a few Pritchetts listed near Christ Church, Nina's hometown. I printed out names, addresses, and telephone numbers for people who might be relatives and spent the morning leaving messages, asking if they knew who might be her closest kin.

After that, I called Alisha and filled her in. In the five minutes she had left of her break, I told her as much as I could. Since our March meeting she'd been kicking herself about losing out on what she called "the big money." But now, hearing that it had gone sour, she congratulated herself. "I guess it was for the best," she said.

"Alisha, I'm just glad you were spared this mess. Otherwise I'd feel so guilty."

"If my boss hadn't refused to give me the time off, trust me, I'd have been right there with you. You know me, I always go for the drama."

We promised to meet for lunch soon, and I continued making calls. One of them was to Jerry. "I'm back. How's business?"

From the sound of his voice, he was in a great mood. "The market's picking up. I just submitted an offer for nine hundred and fifty on that Dunsmore property in the suburbs. You remember the one that's been on the market for almost a year."

"Do you think the owner will take it?"

"He better, it's the best he's going to get."

I crossed my fingers. "Do you need help?"

"Let's talk after the weekend," he said. "I've had some other calls. Maybe things are looking up."

Next, I called Ocean County Memorial and asked for Nina. I was put through to her room twice and heard the phone ringing. No one picked up. Maybe a good sign? Was she well enough to be up and about? I guessed she was still there. I called again several hours later. That time the operator informed me that she had been discharged.

Obligations fulfilled, I turned off my cell phone and stayed away from the computer. I was in cocoon mode. The next two days segued by. I did my best to be in the here and now. I grounded myself with a daily session of yoga, made an appointment to get a haircut, and enjoyed a pedicure. I even treated myself to a massage.

Jamie screened the house phone with instructions not to tell me of any calls that were not of immediate urgency and certainly to take no calls from anyone outside our circle of family, friends, neighbors, and employers. Slowly the anxiety began to lessen.

While I was away, Jamie struggled to make peace with her future. For one thing, Stanford was a dream we couldn't afford. But that wasn't all. An inner voice told me there was a purely selfish reason for wanting her to stay on our side of the country. I wasn't ready to see her gone so soon from my life. "You'll be able to come home more often," I had told her. "If you were stuck out in California, we probably wouldn't see you except at Christmas and over the summer. And even that might be iffy."

The letter confirming the generous freshman year financial aid package had pride of place on the mantel. When it came time to applying for aid, less was definitely more. Looking back over the year gone by, the real estate market had done the Fellshur family a favor. Between my low sales commissions and her father's lack of gainful employment, our household income level boosted her into the grants and scholarships category. There would be some loans, but the free money was a relief.

I was grateful when the school guidance counselor dug up a recent Cornell alum for Jamie to meet, a newly minted grad who had snagged a good job at a local consulting firm. Once she met the young woman for coffee, my daughter came away with a new perspective. Her new friend must have painted quite a picture of what the Ithaca campus had to offer. Now Jamie was sold on the benefits of life at Cornell. With the transformation almost complete, I sent the first down payment.

Once things began to feel a little calmer, I allowed myself to check my email. There were two replies from Nina's colleagues expressing concern and promising to try to find her next of kin.

There was also a message from Harlan. The subject line read, "Money be damned!" He'd planned on hanging tough in New Jersey but bailed the day after I did. He shared what he could about Nina. She'd suffered a concussion but was in no danger. Her vision was fine and her faculties were returning, but she hadn't been able to provide details about the assault or what the attacker looked like. True to his word, Salazar gave Harlan the green light to take off, with the caveat that he would return when called on.

Everything was looking up, but even so, I was finding it difficult to free myself from the whole mess, especially since Jerry wasn't ready for me to come back. I know myself well enough to know that I'm happiest when I am busy. But now I had one of my most dreaded monsters to contend with, "time to kill."

❧❧❧❧

15

An Internet search found a copy of Seiber's dissertation in the University of Pennsylvania's online library catalog. What a break! The university campus is only a few blocks from my house, and "community members" were allowed access to the collection during the week. I decided to go.

The May morning, sunny and cool, was perfect for a walk. I headed east toward the university. The campus is wealthy little enclave, an economic growth engine spreading over the urban landscape. Glossy science labs, classrooms, and dorms merge with high-end stores, banks, hotels, movie theatres, and food trucks that service an affluent student body.

Early May is the tail end of spring semester. Still, Penn students came and went dressed in a mix of jeans, saris, and everything in between. Walking through the leafy enclave, nostalgia for long-gone student days gave me a twinge. I envied my kids the college years waiting for them.

Penn's Van Pelt Library sprawled over half a city block. At the door, a guard gave my driver's license a quick glance and waved me through. The interior, mixing tradition with technology, still held on to a bit of museum feeling. I registered the faces of the students moving in and out, some in a rush to absorb knowledge, others looking for a place to avoid it.

Where to begin? The catalog number scrawled on a piece of paper would get me only so far. From his perch at the reference desk, the librarian took a look. "Fourth floor, history stacks" was his verdict.

Off the elevator, I wandered the open stack, enjoying the smell of books and paper. It took me back. After browsing a while I found Seiber's treatise on a bottom shelf. Nearby students huddled around a glowing tablet, a digital reminder, if I needed one, that things were different now. But the bound volume in my hand was real. An empty study carrel beckoned.

I scanned the table of contents. Albert had allotted sizable real estate for nautical history. His account of the New World left no doubt about the role of the high seas as the main trade route. Small wooden ships, less than two hundred feet long, were the only way to move goods and riches back and forth between the colonies and Europe. In that perilous, watery world, merchant ships were the prey. The wealth of nations depended on the ability to protect the vessels.

Peter Prosser, Albert's seagoing ancestor, was part of the safety net for these merchant ships. He signed on with William Kidd, who was sworn to guard Her Majesty's ships, shielding them from pirates and other enemies. The captain was charged with protecting wealth. But that wasn't Kidd's only assignment. Acquiring wealth for his employers by raiding enemy ships wasn't just tolerated, it was encouraged.

The seaman's diary contained snippets of days spent on board a two-masted sailing ship, views of the weather that held sway over both officers and crew, and the trials of daily life at sea. The verbatim quotes were like a letter from the past. I read all I could find, fascinated at how the language changed over the years. Fortunately Albert made needed the modifications that left the document more decipherable.

Peter Prosser's Journal

September 29

At sea, having been out from the port of New York one week, this day. Aboard the Adventure as boatswain's mate with Captain Wm. Kidd who has received commission by the crown to protect ships and trade of the East India company. Captain Kidd said by many to be on the whole a gentlemanly and clever man. I fancy myself fortunate to be under one of the best and soberest captain at sea.

November 4

Forty days out and we sprung a leak and got as much of our cargo on deck as we could, expecting to get to the leak but finding it in vaine, we put the cargo below again. The men worked with a will and did not much complaine. Yet I have some concern of the crew - in particular three ruffians who I like not.

December 7

Some part of the passage we had good wind and fine weather and I am most thankful that I have not been sea sicke. Never being so long from home before, many the hour of a long night watch I walked the deck crying and fretting from the loss of my parents.

December 26

Yesterday being Christmas I had a fond remembrance of plum pudding at my family table. Onboard the crew did celebrate the occasion by a fish dinner and some small beer. Later Mr. Kidd was cheered by sailors who danced a hornpipe to music I played on my pennywhistle.

April 19

I fell ill for three days and the Boatswain, Mr. Greely has become angered being short of help. Though not fully recovered I vowed that I would do my duty as such or he would flog me.

May 9

One hundred eighty-six days out and perishing for want of bread. Our men being very fatigued what with the poor, wormy food and stifling quarters. We have naught to show for our voyage and the men grow mutinous. Mr. Kidd is desperate.

Prosser's descriptions of his hardships at sea mixed with a young man's longing for home and family were touching but not what I was hoping for. There were no details of Kidd's captured bounty, no clues to its final resting spot, no map.

I wanted to talk to Seiber, but how? Home once again, I turned back to the Internet, but the Princeton University directory didn't yield any email address for Seiber. The Rosenbach was within walking distance of the campus. I went there that afternoon, hoping someone might know where he was. Surprisingly, the young woman at the door remembered me. Even more amazing was her openness. I learned that Dr. Seiber was spending a good bit of his time in Philadelphia, much of it at the museum. I left a note with my contact information, and she promised to pass it along.

I didn't hear back for days. During that time, I told myself to back off. I tried to pretend that I was no longer involved in what was going on at the New Jersey coast. Once Seiber got in touch, I gave up all pretense of disinterest.

"Albert, I hope you remember me. Josh introduced us," I said.

"Yes, Margo, I remember you. How are you?"

"Fine, thanks. Would you have a few minutes to get together with me?"

"What is it you have in mind?" he asked.

"Please believe me when I tell you that I have no interest in the treasure. But I wanted you to know what's going on. Do you know that your transcripts and notes were stolen?"

"I heard that someone got hurt. That was upsetting to say the least."

"Is there any way we could meet?"

Seiber was agreeable and we made plans to meet at the museum. I waited for him in the downstairs waiting room. When he showed up, he ushered me to the workroom. From his briefcase, he produced a handful of printed pages, transcriptions from the diary. He handed them to me. The dates were spread out over a year.

"See if this tells you what you're looking for," he said.

Yeare Two

January 4

After a long voyage to the Indian Ocean we put in at St. Mary's Island for provisions and took on small beer, coffee and sugar which cheered the men somewhat. Mr. Briggs, the first mate says our ship is very leaky and rotten. Under the letters of commission we may intend to take for our use the first good ship we meet with under enemy sails. I doubt not a grievous worry.

March 19

The Cara Merchant a ship of Moorish origin showed no colours. But she rode low with cargo. Kidd fired five times on the Moor's ship and took fourteen men on board. They let the officers off at a deserted island and threw the crew into the sea to swim for it. We took all the riches of the ship as our own. Setting a crew of elevene on board hur we ran up our colours and made off with the cargo of gold, pieces of 8, bullion, gemstones and other precious goodes.

June 22

"There upon our arrival in the Greate Egg Harbor Bay we put in for repaire, the Moorish ship listing mightily. One James Gillam put ashore with several chests from Captain Kidd's sloop, the bounty belonging to his superiors in New Yorke. Six days hence we sailed north to Barnegat Inlet. I know not the magnitude nor what was put on shore at any island near Barnegat save only two guns of weight of fifty stone apeace. Yet I vow Kidd will hold his treasure as ransom for barter against his accusers who sully his name.

"The language has changed, but I can still read it," I said.

"You'd have a hard time with the original. Even though Prosser was an educated man by the standards of that day, there were many changes to the spelling just to make it readable. And the handwriting ...don't ask."

The pages disappeared back into his briefcase. I would have loved to read more, but this was all I would see that day.

"Here's something else I thought you might want to see." Seiber produced a small plastic envelope and emptied the contents into his palm. It was a small gold piece, a coin worn thin at the edges and lumpy in the middle, yet the metal still maintained its allure. He let me hold it.

The coin felt alive in my hand. "Would I be able to borrow this for one night?" I asked.

He looked as though I'd asked him to cut off an ear. "No, I don't think so. Why would you want to borrow it?"

I told him about the Mediums Guild. It had occurred to me that we might once again try our hand at psychometry.

"What the hell is that?"

"Have you ever heard the term psychic anthropology?"

"Can't say that I have."

"Dr. Salazar showed us a video about it when we were at Perception Studies Institute in New York. In a documented experiment at a Florida university, a local medium performed blind readings of Mayan artifacts and objects whose uses and origin were already known."

"How?"

"The medium did a cold reading. She just sat quietly, held the objects and reported any impressions that came to her."

He looked skeptical.

"Even with no prior knowledge of the objects, she really clicked. Not only did she see how the items were used, she had impressions of who used them, going so far as to describe physical characteristics.

"Are you sure? I've never heard of anything like that."

"Crazy as it sounds, the information she provided could be verified by alternative sources. And if you'd allow us to try it with the coin, it might be interesting to see what pops up."

Seiber gave it a moment's thought and then nodded. "I'll let you do it on one condition—I want to be there. What about tomorrow?"

And that is how Dr. Albert Seiber became an honorary member of the Mediums Guild.

Asking my fellow Guild members to donate their precious leisure time on such short notice was a tough sell, even with promises of a delicious spread complete with dessert and drinks afterwards. I was only able to convince Alisha, Zara, and Paula. With Albert, we would be a group of five.

I was hopeful as I assembled a salad, made a dipping sauce to go with the shrimp cocktail, and unwrapped a cake from the bakery. Everything went into the refrigerator next to the wine and soft drinks. In the living room, I arranged fresh cut flowers in honor of spring. With daylight savings time we had another hour before dark, but I put out candles to invoke a quiet mood. I turned off the phone. Just before 6:30, my colleagues began straggling in. I thanked them for coming. We would use the same techniques as on that November evening with Carla's belongings, but decided to spend more time warming up.

Everyone was prepped and ready by the time our guest arrived. Albert looked shy at first, but he warmed up quickly. He was fascinated by the group, asking how we'd become aware of our abilities. Alisha told about learning to read tea leaves from her grandmother as a child. Zara took part in ESP experiments in college, where she shocked the professors and surprised herself by testing off the charts. As a youngster, Paula learned palm reading from her next door neighbor, a Romanian seamstress.

Finally, it was time to start. Was it just six months ago that we'd sat in a circle in this very room? I could almost look back on that experience with wonder at the innocence of it. What were my motives now? Remorse? Regret? The taint of money?

Clouds rolled in and the room turned gloomy. Outside a siren blared. Albert jumped a little.

"Street noise, the bane of city living." I pulled the drapes and hoped they would shut out some of the noise.

Tension hovered over the table. "Why don't we close our eyes and concentrate on our breathing for a few minutes," I said. Even with my eyes closed, I felt Albert's questioning presence. Was he thinking of this as some sort of bizarre experiment? Perhaps he was alert for another reason. After all, the glowing coin in easy reach was tempting. It called out to me.

I began a guided meditation that has helped others to go inward. We visualized a light hovering above our heads. I suggested that we count slowly down from ten to one while allowing the light to enter our consciousness. Finally, I sensed a calm descend over the table.

"Shall I go first?" I asked. I reached out for the coin. It felt warm, almost alive. I placed it in the palm of my left hand and rubbed my right hand over it in a circular motion. Its energies stirred, the coin turned hot, so hot I almost dropped it. Part of a face, a toothless mouth, appeared, a cruel twist to the lips. Another visage flew into my mind, then another and another. In my head a voice croaked, "My share. My share." Another whispered the words, "Gold, gold."

I passed the coin to Alisha and wrote down my visions. How would she raise the energies of the coin? Would others whose hands held the coin be conjured up? She looked at it for a minute or so. She placed it in her right hand, lightly stroking it with her fingers. Then she placed it on the palm of her left hand, breathing slowly and deeply. I looked up to see her eyelids flutter as she went deeper into a trance.

After several minutes, Alisha's eyes fluttered open. She passed the coin to Zara before she began to write. Zara and Paula followed suit. Finally, Paula passed the coin back to Albert. He blushed as all eyes turned to him. After sitting in silence for several minutes, he placed the coin back on the table. He stared it almost as though he had never seen it before. Later, he would say he saw what he could only describe as waves of a fiery energy emanating from it surface.

The coin was calling out. I wanted to know its secrets. As though reading my thoughts, Albert held the coin tightly between his outstretched palms. Then he placed it between the fingertips of both hands. With a sigh, he opened his eyes, looking around as though he'd just woken from sleep. He picked up a pen, but instead of writing a sentence or two like the rest of us, he drew a claw shape. When he was finished, he looked around and blinked sheepishly at the group. "Can I have a glass of water, please?" he asked.

I went to the kitchen and returned with several bottles of water for the thirsty. It was almost dark, so I lit a few more candles.

"Shall I start?" I asked. Murmurs of agreement. I described my vision of the faces and the words I'd heard. We went around the room to Zara, who saw the coin as one of many being stamped out in a dark, smoky workspace. Once formed, the newly minted coins were dropped into a leather bucket of murky water. Alisha saw only hands shaking the coins out of a leather pouch. Paula's coins were stacked on a table. Then it was Albert's turn. Albert saw many coins, in a small chest. He didn't mention the drawing he made.

I wondered if it might be a map. Slipping a scrap of paper into my lap, I scribbled a quick copy of Albert's sketch. He still seemed somewhat dumbstruck. He blinked, shook himself, and gulped some water. We passed our findings to him, all except my sketch. I slipped that into my pocket.

Once the activity was complete, I offered food and drink. Albert devoured several shrimp and gulped a glass of wine before he had to run to his appointment. I thanked him for coming and wondered how he might feel about the events once he'd thought it over. Once everyone left, I removed the scrap of paper from my pocket. I looked again at the rough outline. Was it important or just a snippet of a dream?

Next morning, Greg popped up at my door. His face made a bright spot in my day. I had missed that knowing look of his, the sound of his voice. During odd moments when I was away, I found myself mooning over him, like a teenager. Back home I'd trolled the Internet looking for his photo, but the business portrait on his company website showed him with stiff, slicked-back hair, not like him at all, I thought.

"How did you know where I live?"

"You're in the phone book, you know. Remember that ancient bit of technology?" His lips brushed my cheek. He smelled good. "Can I come in?"

"Looks like you already did. Cup of coffee?"

"Sounds great!"

He followed me to the kitchen. "What year was this house built?" he asked.

He ran a finger over the chair rail in the dining room. Too funny, I thought. Hadn't I given his place the same scrutiny?

"Probably around the same time as yours, end of the 1870s or so."

Please, God, don't let him ask for a tour. The messy rooms on the second floor wouldn't do much for my image. I poured two coffees from the morning pot. I sipped mine but Greg's disappeared fast.

"Did I catch you in the middle of something?" he asked.

"Just paying some bills. Why?"

"How'd you like to make me some lunch?"

"My calendar's free. If you're willing to take pot luck, I can scramble something together."

I was dying to spill my guts about what had gone on in New Jersey. Until now, I'd been careful not to discuss the what and where with anyone except family. The story buzzed in my brain, fighting to get out. Could Josh still sue me for breach of contract if I talked about it now? I started out slow and told him a little something of what had happened on my expedition. I focused more on Nina's injury.

Greg's eyes never left my face. He held up his hand. "Margo, do you trust me?" he asked.

I nodded.

"I feel like you're not leveling with me. You still haven't given much information. Why were you there?"

Too late now. I was on a slippery slope, and it was a short ride down. Once I got started, I described the treasure hunt, Captain Kidd's lost treasure, and how I came to leave the project. There's something about sitting at a kitchen table that encourages truth-telling. He listened carefully, asking questions about the technology.

Finally I ran out of steam. "Are you hungry?" I asked, hoping to change the subject.

"Always."

I scoped out the kitchen cabinets. The breadbox held only crumbs. The pantry yielded up canned tuna. I added mayo, celery, and onion and arranged some lettuce, cucumber, and tomato around it. And voila! We sat down to a lunch of tuna salad. It wasn't gourmet, but somehow I didn't think he was there for the food.

Up in my bedroom, we propped ourselves against the pillows on my bed. Our clothing spilled across the floor. I played Mata Hari, surprising myself by peering up at him through a bejeweled scarf I sometimes wore for Mediums Guild events. He retrieved my shirt from under the blankets and wrapped it turban-like around his head. "How do I look?" he asked.

I gave him a playful punch and we wrestled like a couple of teenagers. We kissed again, this time long and slow.

Later Greg checked his watch.

"I guess you better get going soon."

"Why?"

I pointed to a photo of Jamie and Charlie on my night table.

"They look like great kids."

"They are."

"I'd really like to meet them. But maybe not today. What time do they get home?"

"Maybe another hour or so." They wouldn't show up until after four, but I'd need some time to readjust, switch gears. This single life was all new to me. It felt weird, but with Greg to help me along, it might feel more comfortable.

A little while later, as Greg stood at the door, ready to leave, he asked me a question. "What are you doing tomorrow?"

"Just the usual. Looking for work, I guess. Why?"

"I want to visit Steve's mother. Follow up on a few details. Want to go with me?"

It was one year and counting since the deadly disappearance, with no resolution in sight. Anniversaries can be difficult, this one especially so. The thought of the grieving woman was painful, but I wanted to support Greg in his quest for answers.

Next day, I parked my car in Greg's drive and climbed into his SUV. It took less than half an hour to reach our destination, the Kovacs residence in Mount Holly, New Jersey. It was a two-story single on a quiet small-town street. It needed a coat of paint and a weed-whacker to remove ragtag greenery between the sidewalk cracks. I put aside my real estate persona and tried to focus on the task at hand.

Steve's mother, in her fifties, with black hair and a full figure, looked younger than I expected. Her eyes were tired but they lit up at the sight of Greg. He seemed to have that effect on women.

"Thanks for letting us stop by, Mrs. Kovacs," I said.

"Call me Delores," she said.

"And I'm Margo."

On the mantel was a snapshot of Steve on a boat, holding a dark-haired toddler. Next to it, a teenage Steve struck a pose in his high school football uniform. In the center, a young mother and father smiled happily at three young children.

Greg nodded toward the family portrait. "I haven't seen Cindy since high school. What a beautiful family she has. How's she doing?"

"They're doing really good," Delores said. "They live about an hour away, almost to Delaware. Her husband works for that big pharmaceutical company down there, in sales. I go down to babysit sometimes, so my daughter can go with him on business meetings. They have them in places like Florida, Mexico, always nice vacation spots."

She asked if we wanted coffee. Greg said no thanks.

"I know it's hard to think about, but would you mind telling Margo and me what you remember from that night that Steve's trailer got broken into?"

"It was the same night Steve disappeared. A neighbor heard it, I didn't. He called the cops."

"Did he see anybody?'

"Saw somebody run across the yard and out the back."

"They get in a car?"

"If they did, he didn't see it."

"Did he hear a car starting or anything like that?"

She shook her head. "The police thought it was kids that did it, but I didn't think so. Would you?"

"No. What do you think they were looking for?" Greg asked.

"Gear off his boat, maybe? Diving equipment and such, but I didn't know all of what Steve kept in there."

Greg kept going. "What about fingerprints? Cops check for those?"

"You won't believe it. Months later. After they found the bodies." She looked drained.

I felt bad. Were the questions wearing her down?

"Then the state police come back. By that time, it was too late. We'd moved the stuff out of the trailer into the garage."

"What did Steve plan to do with the equipment?"

"He for sure wasn't going to sell it. He had this idea to get back in business. His plan for the summer was to start small, go down the shore, and rent a boat."

"You still have his stuff?"

She nodded. "Sure."

Greg gave me the eye. I knew what he was thinking. This would be my chance to touch some of the objects and maybe see if there was any emotional residue in the air.

Delores led us through to the back, down the steps and across her tiny backyard. She unlocked the one-car garage, a pack rat's paradise. The diving equipment and nautical gear was stacked floor to ceiling. There was barely enough room to wiggle through, even sideways. Greg bumped his shin on the corner of a protruding box and stifled a curse.

"Sorry," Delores said. "I'm not usually such a hoarder. I just wasn't ready to let any of this go. It's mostly Steve's stuff." She looked at me. "You're a mother, right?"

I gave her a hug. "I totally understand. And by the way, thanks for showing this to us. I know it's not easy."

She dabbed at her eyes. I gave Greg a look that translated, "Lighten up."

She patted her pocket, finding the key to a green metal cupboard. "See that? She pointed to where a smallish wooden cabinet rested on a shelf. It measured about 24 inches wide and about eighteen inches high. Its ancient brass fittings were corroded and dark.

"I could swear I've seen this before," Greg said, cautiously fingering the lid. "Could we open it?"

Delores nodded. "Just be careful."

I squinted hard at the surface. It was battered and stained, but in places a patina was still visible. My hand brushed the top of the box. It held a strange yet somehow familiar energy. An image of Albert's gold coin flitted into my mind.

Sliding my fingers over the surface, a mix of emotions hit. Images followed. There was the dizzy pitch of a wave, a sail swelling in the wind. There was the high-pitched sound of a pipe. A voice called out, "Aye, mate."

Delores switched on an electric lantern. The visions flickered and were gone.

We gave Greg as much space as we could as he worked the lid up. The ancient hinges gave way but the chest was empty. Greg got a funny look on his face.

"A few weeks after Steve came back from Florida, he showed me a piece of jewelry," Delores said. "It was an emerald with pearls. He was going to give it to your sister. Do you know if he ever did?"

"There was a photo of her and Steve together. I think she was wearing it. A cross, right?"

"Right." Her voice broke. "I'm glad. At least he gave it to her."

"And she got to wear it," Greg said, his voice close to breaking as well.

We thanked Mrs. Kovacs for her trouble, and Greg said to give his best to her daughter, Cindy. Her eyes were still red when we left.

Back in the car, Greg told me where he'd seen the chest.

"A few years back, I looked Steve up. He took me fishing out in the Keys. While we're out there he brings up this crazy story, tells me about sunken treasure. I asked him if there was something in the water in Florida that encouraged pipe dreams.

"I meant it as a joke, but he got pissed. 'No, you're wrong,' he says. Next thing, we're docking in Key West. Steve insists that we visit Mel Fisher's Treasure Museum. Don't get me wrong, the Fisher family made a fortune finding sunken treasure, but it's like winning the lottery. Chances are about a hundred million to one.

"After that we went to Steve's house for dinner. I met his wife, the ex-beauty queen, who I'd heard about for years. OK, she was gorgeous but with a mouth on her and mean eyes, like a tiger ready to pounce.

"Steve told me about his next door neighbor, Pops Coleman, a retired merchant seaman. The guy lived alone, no family. As he grew older, Pops' world shrank to Steve and Steve's little boy, Brett. Steve bought him groceries, arranged for help to come in to cook and clean. Basically, Steve helped Pops stay in his home. But Pops was failing. He told Steve he planned to leave his home to the Seamen's Recue Organization, but there was one thing he wanted Steve to have."

"The cherry-wood box in Delores's garage," I blurted.

Greg stared at me for a moment and then nodded. "Pops pressed Steve to take it then and there and made him promise to hide it."

"But it's empty," I said.

"Steve showed me a secret compartment with a catch, a tiny drawer on the back that held an old map. The map was in tatters, but someone made a copy. It was a spit of land somewhere. Pops told Steve it was a location where treasure had been off-loaded centuries before. Soon after, the old guy passed away."

"Did Steve tell anyone else about it?" I asked.

"I don't think so. He said he hadn't even told his wife, but he needed to tell someone, and he trusted me. He made me promise to keep his secret, and I did."

"Did he ever show you the necklace?" I thought back to the antique shop.

"No. He said he had it tucked away in a safe place."

"Until he gave it to Carla?"

Greg nodded.

"When Steve came back to New Jersey after the break-up, he talked about searching for the mythical treasure. I told him not to let his imagination get the best of him, but Steve was convinced the treasure might be off the Atlantic coast."

"It's a long coast," I said.

"Steve said legally if anything is found in coastal waters it belongs belong to the state. He didn't know, but he said there were ways to keep it quiet."

"What did he mean?" I asked.

"I never did find out," Greg said.

16

It was mid-May, almost a month since I'd seen a pale and distressed Nina hooked up to a hospital respirator, and I had often wondered about her. I was thinking of her when the phone rang. The caller ID showed a crazy-looking number, but something told me to pick up.

"Margo, it's me." Hearing her voice sounding stronger and healthier lifted a weight from my chest.

"Oh, Nina, I'm so glad you're all right. Where are you? Do you need anything?"

"Thanks, Margo, I'm fine. I've been what you might call incommunicado. It's only been in the last couple of weeks that I rejoined the human race. I've been staying with a friend in Connecticut."

"I'm surprised the hospital discharged you so soon."

"They didn't," she said after a moment's hesitation. "We left against the doctor's recommendation. Salazar tried to tell me it had something to do with my not having insurance, but I don't think I buy that."

"No," I said.

"Anyway, I heard from my cousin Michael and several people at the university, and I want to thank you for contacting them. You did what nobody else did, Margo. I would have called sooner, but I only just found your number. It was all the way at the bottom of one of the messages you sent."

"You're welcome," I said, thinking it was odd that she'd heard from so few people. "What about your injuries? You could have been killed."

"Yeah, that first week just seemed to drift by. My thinking was muddled. I was very weak, still suffering from dizzy spells."

"Were you at Salazar's place?" I asked, knowing it was none of my business but not caring.

"Yes," she replied. "As I started to get stronger, it all finally sank in. I waited until Salazar was away on business, then I packed my bags and told Maria I was going to meet him in Manhattan. She drove me to the bus station in Saratoga Springs. From there I took the bus to White Plains. My friend in Connecticut came and picked me up."

"Do you remember me visiting you in the hospital?"

"I have a vague recollection, but that was the other thing — I almost felt like I couldn't remember."

"Nina, I hate to sound like a nanny, but you need to get yourself back home."

"I have a flight booked for tomorrow, out of Newark. I'm staying at the Marriot next to the airport. My friend drove me."

"That's great news."

"I know. But before I leave, I have something I want to show you. A picture."

"What picture?" I asked. I could feel my heart beginning to pound.

"Please, Margo, can you come to Newark?"

"Nina, if there's something going on, if you have evidence of something dodgy, maybe you should take it to the police."

"Which police?"

"The robbery happened near Toms River, New Jersey. They

have cops. There's also the county sheriff's office and the state police. And people from a federal agency showed up, too."

"That's my point, Margo. It's too complicated, too confusing. I don't know enough about your country to figure out where to begin."

And I didn't know what to tell her.

"I won't put myself back into a situation where Salazar is involved," she said. "Please, Margo, can you come? My flight leaves tomorrow morning at ten."

I looked at the clock. If the traffic gods permitted, I could make it there and back before dark. And I wasn't scheduled to work in Jerry's office that day. I felt the fates conspiring. "What's your room number?" I asked.

The traffic gods were kind. Two hours after speaking with Nina, I was in the Marriott's parking lot, calling her cell phone number. She met me in the lobby, and we hugged. It was fascinating how our relationship had changed. Once Salazar's energy was removed from the equation, we could almost call ourselves friends.

Up close, she looked drained. There were blue smudges under her eyes, as if she hadn't slept. We went to a nearby Mexican restaurant I had spotted on the way in. The outdoor patio was filled with people enjoying the mild weather, but there were still a few tables available, and we asked for one. We both ordered Margaritas, but Nina asked the waiter to make hers a "virgin." Things really have changed, I thought.

I had a million questions, but Nina insisted on showing me the photograph first. She dug a folder out of her handbag and opened it. Inside were copies of newspaper clippings. She found a quarter-page article from a Florida newspaper under a picture of two men standing together, the late Steve Kovacs and his business partner, Bo Alvarado. The headline read, "Classmates Grow Business from Hobby."

The story that followed told about two high school buds from small-town New Jersey who had spent their summers as lifeguards on the Jersey Shore and who both loved to dive. To be near the water, Steve went to college in Florida and stayed on after graduation. Bo followed him soon after. Together they set up a tourist business, taking out day-trippers and would-be divers. Eventually, their business did well enough for them to buy a second boat.

After scanning the story, I looked at Nina. "Steve Kovacs is dead. I know people who knew him. And now I'm wondering why you would have this stuff."

"These were in a binder in Salazar's office. Something told me to take it."

A buzzing sensation filled my head. I fanned myself with the menu. "Something told you?"

Nina looked down at the table. She seemed to be having an argument with herself. After a moment, she looked up again. "Margo, I never had this experience before. Maybe it was the concussion. I don't know." She tapped her forehead. "Maybe it opened up something in here."

"Tell me about it."

"After I left the hospital, I was still out of it. I spent most of the first week in bed, drowsing, drifting in and out of consciousness. One day, I heard a voice call my name. A woman appeared in front of me. I sat up in bed. I knew she was an apparition, but I wasn't afraid. She floated down the hallway to Salazar's office, and I followed her. At the doorway, she faded. His office door was closed, but he wasn't there. I went in. A folder was open on his desk. The papers began to rustle like there was a breeze, but the window was closed."

"Go on."

"I made copies and hid them in my room. Salazar never found out."

Nina pulled another news clipping from the folder. It showed a photo of a smiling Bo Alvarado on a Florida dock, with Steve on a boat behind him. In the forefront was a tall brunette. The caption read, "Former Miss Florida Sonja Kovacs Christens Jersey Guys II." Sonja Kovacs was Steve's wife at the time. I got a funny feeling about Sonja. I made a mental note to Google her.

Nina tapped the image of Alvarado with a finger. "Did you ever see this guy hanging around anywhere?"

I squinted at the face—dark eyes, broad brows, chin ringed with a beard. I shook my head. "I never saw him, but I heard about him being Steve Kovacs's business partner in Florida. What I heard was that Steve sold his half of the business to the partner and came back home to New Jersey. Months later, Steve's body was found with the body of his girlfriend, Carla. I had some involvement with the case. It got a lot press. That's how Josh found out about me."

I'd shared a little of the history of my brief rise to "psychic super-stardom," minus names and details, during a few wine-fueled chats at Perception in New York. I told Nina the rest of the story now, including the theft at Steve's mother's house.

"What do you make of it all, Margo?"

"Maybe Alvarado stole Steve's map and sold it to Salazar."

"He wouldn't have told Salazar that Steve was dead, would he? I'd like to believe Salazar doesn't know about that."

"No reason he would have," I said. "Lots of reasons he wouldn't have."

Nina seemed relieved, but then she took a breath and looked at me. "There's one more thing, Margo. My friend in Connecticut is a therapist. She does hypnosis. She regressed me. When she did, I saw the face of the man who attacked me." She pointed to the picture of Alvarado. "It was him. He didn't have the beard, but I know those eyes."

I looked at the picture, stared at Alvarado's eyes. Seeing them now took me back to the antique shop, the emerald necklace around my throat. Were those dark eyes the ones that had stared back at me in my vision? Had I seen them in another dimension?

Nina pulled one more page from the folder and slid it to me. "Last one," she said. It wasn't a news story. It was a photocopy of a drawing showing the outline of a small claw-shaped island. It was the same shape Albert Seiber had drawn at my house.

"Pirates," I murmured.

"What?"

"These guys—they remind me of pirates."

"I'll be glad to put several thousand miles between myself and this mess." Nina said.

"Think you'll see Salazar again?"

"No," she replied quickly. "Never." She handed me a slip of paper. "Margo, here. That's my email address. You already have my phone. If you ever call and I don't pick up, just leave a message. I'll call you back."

"OK, I'll stay in touch," I said.

"What will you do?" she asked.

"First, I'll need to make copies of these documents, if you don't mind. Then I plan to call Carla's brother as soon as I get home."

"There's a business center at my hotel. We can make copies there."

On the drive back, I thought about Carla. The case hadn't been about her at all. She was just with the wrong person at the wrong time. The police hadn't looked beyond the end of their noses. They had locked onto Carla's husband as the most likely suspect early on and never let go. Meanwhile, the state police had brought me in for questioning. They never did call me a suspect, but they asked how I knew where to look for the bodies. Now the case seemed to be in limbo. Steve had lived in one town, Carla in another. The bodies were found in a third. Who had primary responsibility? Seemed like no one did.

I called Greg that evening.

"Hey, Margo." His voice felt therapeutic. "I've been thinking about you."

That was good news.

"I've been thinking about you, too." I gave him an abridged

version of the Salazar treasure hunt, up to and including Nina's encounter with the man she came to recognize as Alvarado. I didn't tell him about the emerald necklace and the effect it had on me.

"Did you tell the police about the relationship between Steve and Alvarado?" I asked.

"Sure. They said they'd get in touch with the authorities in Florida."

"How well do you know him?"

"Pretty well. He's younger than me, went to different schools. But sometimes we bumped into each other."

"Did you ever suspect him?"

"Not really. What would his motive be?"

"To get his hands on Steve's map, maybe?"

Greg snorted. "Two people killed for an old seaman's pipe dream?"

"He attacked Nina and stole Salazar's laptop."

"So she says."

"I'll scan the articles and send them to you."

I went to bed that night wondering where Alvarado was. According to Nina, Salazar and company were still roaming the waterways of the Mid-Atlantic coastline. Before Memorial Day, the Jersey coast was still in quiet mode, but that was changing day by day. By the middle of the summer, the seaside would be overrun with visitors. How would they be able to maintain their secrecy in the midst of a crowd?

Harlan and I tried to connect every few days. I updated him on Nina's findings and what that might mean. He was back in Mississippi but still on call, still in the game. With his big rig in the shop for repairs, he couldn't return to the road without the thirteen thousand he still owed the garage. He spent time at home dowsing remotely, using maps that Salazar FedExed him.

"Now they want me to come back up. Lolly wants to kill me, but I guess I'm headed back north."

It's funny how being financially strapped can cloud your

judgment. I should know. "You sure you want to do that?"

He laughed. "Maybe I'm one of them."

"One of what?"

"One of them treasure hunters."

He had a point. His family had a history of looking for water, oil, minerals. He was a treasure hunter, for sure.

Was it the power of suggestion? I couldn't say, but that night I dreamt of Alvarado, cutlass in hand, chasing me through a swampy marsh. I stumbled and fell, but instead of using the cutlass to chop off my head, Alvarado dropped to his knees and used it to dig. He kept on digging. I woke in a sweat.

The clock read 4:25. I lay awake, trying to remember the dream. As soon as it was light, I padded downstairs. I brewed a pot of strong coffee to wake my brain. I spread everything on the case, last year's news articles on the disappearance

17

Jamie's graduation drew closer. It was one of those dates that loom on the horizon, a rite of passage that parents both welcome and dread. My own high school memories drifted into my mind, the dizzy mix of "get out of jail" freedom mingled with "Oh God! What do I do now?" doubt. Did my graduate feel that way, too?

Maybe one day Jamie and I would have a chance to talk it over, but not now. Running in and out, grabbing meals as she went, my daughter was a denim-clad blur. Her days were filled with rehearsals, class picnics, and cap and gown pick-up. At night there were parties, some with parents' blessing, others that parents didn't even know about. I pretended not to notice when she came tiptoeing up the stairs, banging into the bathroom door or falling to the floor in a fit of giggles.

The big day, June 14, arrived. It was warm, muggy, and threatening rain. Families streamed up the school steps in high spirits, calling out greetings. It felt good to be part of this close-knit community built through years of PTA, team sports, and holiday bazaars. With a twinge, it hit me. This might be the last time I'd share space with this group. I'd miss the jumble of races, languages, and backgrounds that made the school such a rich slice of city life.

The crowd inside the auditorium fidgeted on wooden seats, fanning themselves while they waited for the graduates to appear. With only four hundred seats to go around, students were limited to four tickets each. The Fellshur third-row contingent was just Charlie, Mom, and me. Bart, Jamie's uncle, would have loved to be there with us, but his job didn't allow him the time off. Instead, he'd sent a dozen red roses that arrived the day before. Even so, when a classmate begged Jamie for her spare ticket, she refused to give it up. Some part of her still hoped her father would magically appear. It was her dream, one I didn't share, but my heart ached just the same.

In the row in front of us, the parents of Raj Singh, the class valedictorian, radiated a sense of pride. I tapped Raj's father on the shoulder and congratulated him on their son's accomplishment.

"Thank you. Congratulations to you as well. Cornell, I heard!" He shot me a thumbs up. The valedictorian's mother chimed in. "Raj will be pre-med at Harvard."

"I heard. Congrats on that, too. I'm sure he'll do very well," I said.

Raj and Jamie had been friends since sixth grade. I had a feeling that Raj always hoped their friendship would turn into something more, but it never did. Maybe they were too much alike, both high achievers and both idealists. Junior year, Raj and Jamie stirred up school politics when they put on an anti-prom with handmade decorations, homemade refreshments, and music by a student d-jay. Jamie's homeroom teacher, the official prom's faculty sponsor, was not pleased with the competition. She gave me a call, annoyed that so many juniors, and a fair number of seniors, had opted out of the school's official event. While I expressed my apologies, I was more than a little proud of my daughter's dissenting anti-consumer streak.

All at once, chatter died down. There was movement down front. Tapping his stand, the music teacher called band members to attention. The auditorium grew quiet as strains of "Hamilton

Forever," the school song, filled the hall. A string of wrong notes from a clarinet gave Charlie the giggles. Before I could shush him, shuffling at the rear got everyone's attention. We stood, applauding the seniors as they made their way down the aisle and onto the stage, all ninety-seven of them.

Mr. Meeks, the principal, came to the microphone. "Please join me in welcoming the Hamilton Academy's Class of 2012." After the clapping and whistling trailed away, Principal Meeks asked us to refrain from using flashbulbs during the ceremony, but he could have saved his breath. There were few cameras in evidence. Smartphone technology made picture taking as easy as breathing. While he rambled on, I studied the program insert listing college destinations for the graduates. It cataloged a fair number of private colleges, a slew of state universities, and a respectable number of Ivies. I was glad to see that Stanford was not on the list.

The guest speaker, a local news anchor, encouraged the students to "Aim for the Stars." Charlie piped up with, "As if." This time his grandmother shot him a look.

After Raj gave his address, it was time for the main event. One by one, the students came forward to collect their diplomas. As the F's got closer, I dug for a tissue. Jamie's name brought cheers around the room. She blushed and Mom and I dabbed our eyes. Once the class threw their caps in the air, giddy confusion took over. I was ready to take more photos, but Jamie had already shucked off her gown backstage. We made for the exit, managing to get a few shots amid the pandemonium on the school steps. After hugs, kisses, and tears, it was time for lunch at the Ritz Hotel, Mom's treat.

Back home there was a package waiting by a flower pot next to the front step. Charlie spotted it first and handed it over to his sister. Jamie looked puzzled. Then she opened it, broke into tears, and charged up the steps to her room. The box, left behind, held a ceramic angel and a card that read, "Fly High. Love you, Dad."

I wanted to throw it at the wall, but I put it in the closet instead. Once she was out of the house and with her friends, I scrutinized the packaging. It bore Canadian postage stamps and a blurred Canadian postmark. Some Internet detective work tracked the source of the gift, a Canadian department store chain. A call to their main office offered little help. The customer service manager was sorry but she couldn't give me any information on the sender.

I called Alisha, told her about the Canadian postmark, and asked her if she had any thoughts about how I could discover Jack's whereabouts. She told me her law firm used a skip tracer, Dan Bryce, when they were looking for deadbeats.

"They don't get more deadbeat than Jack Fellshur," I said.

"You're right. What's worse than cleaning out your kids' college fund? Do you want Bryce's phone number?"

Before I called him, I went back through our family records, pulling out Jack's Social Security number, old credit card bills, a copy of his birth certificate, his last known address, and anything else Bryce might ask for. Then it occurred to me to talk to Jack's landlady.

18

Summer wore on, with possibilities for some, but apparently not for me. I was bored. Jamie was working her usual summer job at the snack bar, and Charlie was off to science camp for two weeks. I worked for Jerry doing office work, usually only one day a week. Some Sundays I helped stage the occasional open house.

Greg was in the midst of his busy season, doing aerial survey photography for a mapping company that took him to distant places. We saw each other when we could. He made a rule that unless we had something new to share, we would avoid talking about what he called "the case." Instead, we would talk about our lives and ourselves and spend more time getting to know each other.

"Like two normal people," I said, loving the idea. But letting "it" go was no easy matter for me. It wasn't simple for him, either.

One sunny Tuesday morning in July, he called to say he was taking a vacation day at the Jersey Shore. "I'm revisiting my youth, seeing some old faces from back in the day. Come with me?"

"As long as you're not heading back to the quarry, I'm in."

"Throw some sunscreen in your bag and I'll pick you up in an hour. We won't have any beach time, but we can still enjoy the day."

I didn't ask what it was about, but some small part of me knew.

Greg showed up right on schedule. He tapped his horn, and I breezed out in T-shirt and shorts, my hair in a ponytail. No matter what, a chance to escape the heat of the city was a treat. We crossed the bridge into New Jersey and got on a highway heading east. Greg kept the conversation light, telling witty stories about some of his more colorful clients.

We had driven this way before, and a sign for the New Jersey Pinelands Reserve gave me chills. Our last time there, it was winter. The place looked different in the summer sunshine, but it still triggered thoughts of winter. Greg seemed to be handling it fine. If not, he wasn't saying. I was glad when the pines grew sparse and we turned southeast toward the ocean.

Traffic on the causeway to Long Beach Island moved slowly, but we were in no hurry. Gulls swooped and squawked overhead. I rolled down the window and sucked in the salty air. "Can you smell that? My dad always said sea air is the best therapy there is."

"It's easier to relax here, for sure."

"Promise me one thing," I said.

"What's that?"

"If we run into Salazar and company, we hide."

Greg laughed. "This island is over twenty miles long. Chances of seeing them are slim to none. But on the off chance we do, don't worry. I'll protect you."

I gave his shoulder a playful punch. "Even you might not be able to protect me from that much bad juju."

Summer at the seashore was in full swing. Kids on bikes and skateboards weaved in and out of the crawling traffic, and groups of spandex-clad joggers jostled each other on the sidewalks. Every few blocks we stopped for family groups hauling chairs, umbrellas, and boogie boards across the road toward the beach.

We turned off the main drag and made for the bay. "You hungry?' Greg asked. Without waiting for an answer, he pulled up at Dave's Clam Bar. The place looked like the perfect summer spot, an open-air eatery with views of the bay. We found a couple of seats and grabbed a menu. The waitress greeted Greg like an old friend. "Long time no see."

Greg laughed. "You know I couldn't stay away. Give me the usual."

He passed me the menu and I passed it back. "I'll have what he's having."

By the time we finished the clam chowder and a bucket of steamers, it was mid-afternoon. The July sun was still strong when Greg and I parked at the marina. He took my hand. Together we strolled along the weathered boardwalk. The breeze blew fresh and strong, the temperature at least ten degrees cooler than the city temperatures I'd left behind.

He pointed to the horizon, where commercial fishing vessels were heading back in. "See those boats out there?"

"Yes, very cool."

"More than cool." Greg said. "Don't you city slickers ever wonder where your fish comes from?"

It was easy to forget the fishermen who go out before dawn and spend the day spreading nets, pulling them up, and bringing the catch back to shore. "Is there more about commercial fishing that I should know?" I asked.

"I was just pulling your chain. Right now, there's someone I want you to meet. My buddy Art is the captain of the Lucinda. He's a great guy. You'll like him."

"How do you two know each other?"

"Summers in college I worked for him, keeping his engines in shape."

"That beats my summer jobs by a mile."

"What did you do?"

"Waitressing, mostly. One year in a department store. Stuff like that. Except sophomore year, I got lucky, worked on an archeology dig."

"Must have been fun."

"It was. I even daydreamed about being an archeologist, until my dad talked me out of it and convinced me to get a real job."

Greg smiled but he seemed distracted.

I wondered why we were here.

Greg read my thoughts. "I wanted to check on my investment."

"Your investment?"

"Yeah. I loved the old tub so much, I bought a fifteen percent share of the Lucinda. Wait until you see her."

"What is it with you Jersey guys and the ocean?"

He swatted my ponytail. "What about you and your tarot cards? Same thing."

"Not."

He shrugged. "It's in our blood. Besides, I want to talk to Art, see if he's heard anything. You know -- the local grapevine. Art is a trusted man around here. If anybody knows what's going on, it'll be him."

One by one, fishing boats slid into the docks, each one a little enterprise unto itself. I watched as first one crew and then another tied up, weighed the catch, iced it down, and hosed the decks. Then it was quitting time. Happy to be back on dry land, they headed to the parking lot in high spirits. They looked satisfied, I thought.

Greg called out to one of the guys. "You see the Lucinda today?"

"Saw her go out, but she's not back yet."

We grabbed a coffee at the local convenience store. Waiting while Greg paid, a twinge of anxiety clutched my middle. Last time I heard from Harlan, he, Salazar, and Josh were still in the area, maybe only a few miles up the coast. I looked over my shoulder, pulled my baseball cap over my eyes and dug a pair of wrap-around sunglasses from my bag. The odds of bumping into them were scant, but not impossible.

Unfinished business dogged Greg's thoughts, too. Despite promises not to let "the case" interfere, Greg had brought the articles about Steve and his ex-business partner to show his friend. Since my meeting with Nina, we'd come up with a clearer photo of Alvarado, one Greg found in an old yearbook.

Greg pointed to a battered green tub of a ship riding thirty feet high. "There she is."

The Lucinda slid into the pier, and we watched the crew go through their paces. After they left, a rugged, ruddy forty-something guy stepped off the boat. Greg called out, "Hey, Captain. How's the catch?"

His friend shot him a wide grin. "Greg, what the hell are you doing here?"

"I came to buy you a beer."

The smile got bigger. "Now you're talkin'."

The captain and I swapped names. Instinctively, I extended a hand, but Art chuckled. "No offense, Margo, but I don't think you'd want to shake this paw right now." He was right. There was a pungent scent of fish, salt, and sweat in the air.

Art turned to Greg. "What was that about a beer?"

Art led us to The Barnacle, a favorite with the crews. Greg bought the beers and we found seats away from the noisy bar.

"How are the fish treating us this season?" Greg asked.

"No worries. We'll have a good return this year. Let me tell you something. Those Japanese traders are paying beaucoup bucks for the big ones. Just last week, I saw a guy sell a huge tuna right off the docks. They paid over three thousand bucks."

Greg gave a low whistle. "We need to get a piece of that."

"I would, but, unfortunately, there are laws. The bluefin's getting scarce. Not that these guys care. Now they come in, lookin' for the schools with spotter planes. This time next year, we'll be lucky if these waters aren't fished out. It's a crime."

"You still fishing your special spot out by the old wreck?"

Art looked pained. "Hey, keep it down."

"Sorry."

Art glanced around before saying in a low voice, "Got an even better one, closer in. We don't have to use as much fuel to get there and back. I'll tell you where later."

Art winked at me. "Sorry, the walls have ears."

While Art went to the head, Greg filled me in. "Each captain guards his special fishing ground like gold." He chuckled. "They also go to great lengths to find each other's secrets."

When Art returned with a second round of beers, we toasted the Lucinda. There was a lull in the conversation, which Art finally broke. "Greg, you guys aren't here to talk about fishing, are you? What's up?"

Greg glanced at me, and I pulled the photo of Alvarado from my bag and handed it to Art.

"Have you seen this guy?" Greg asked.

Art took a pair of cheaters out of his shirt pocket and gazed at the photograph. "Maybe. He looks kind of familiar. But the guy I'm thinking of looks older."

"This was taken maybe ten, twelve years ago," Greg said. "In high school."

Art looked up from the picture and nodded. "He was around not too long ago."

"You saw him at the docks?"

"At a bar. He was jaw-jacking about gold coins. I thought he was drunk or crazy. Somebody told him to go buy a metal detector. What's the story?"

"It has to do with Carla and her friend Steve. I want to talk to him."

"I'll see what I can find out. Can I keep the photo?"

Greg said he could.

"Don't you worry, not much happens around here that the locals miss."

I knew that was true.

"Let me know if he turns up again," Greg said.

"Will do," Art said. He finished his beer and stood up. "The wife warned me to be home on time."

Greg snorted. "Yeah, right."

Art shrugged. "Or at least not too late."

❧❧❧

19

Good news came in mid-July, when Alisha helped me get some work at her law firm. It was temporary, filling in for a receptionist on maternity leave. The work was easy. I answered phones, smiled at visitors, and helped with the filing. I was grateful and the pay wasn't bad. I began to reevaluate my options, thinking I could get used to this law firm thing. The office was plush and the people mostly civilized. The bad news was that it would last only six weeks. Then it would be time to get a real job. I even thought about becoming a paralegal. Alisha said that the paralegal certificate, together with my real estate experience, could be a good fit. I made a mental note to check out the program at community college. Who knows, maybe I could even get a grant.

I met the law firm's skip tracer in the office and gave him a down payment for his services. He explained that the credit bureaus and other tracking companies would check and cross-check the information I provided. Courtesy of Jack's landlady, I had learned the full name of my husband's girlfriend. Audre McArthur. Her last known address before she arrived in Philadelphia was Brooklyn, New York.

On weekends I volunteered at a food bank and collected donations for underprivileged kids. Was I trying to throw off some bad karma? If so, it didn't feel like enough. Even though the work I had done for Josh and Salazar wasn't illegal, I was guilty of bad judgment. Without saying it outright, some of my Mediums Guild colleagues let me know they thought I had been using my skills for the wrong reasons. I wondered how Uri Geller felt.

Harlan checked in whenever he could. During one telephone conversation, he told me Salazar and Josh were focused on a particular latitude and longitude, based on the sonar mapping Skitch did back in May. He wanted to send me copies of some printouts Skitch left behind and have me look at them and tell him what I thought.

"There's a copy of an old map, a funny old drawing of a piece of land shaped like a claw," he said. "I must have dowsed the area fourteen or fifteen times over the last two days. And guess what?"

"What?"

"My brain was fried and my arm was like a noodle, but I always settled on the one spot."

"That must be significant," I said.

"Forget about it. It's not there."

"What do you mean, not there?"

"According to this old journal, the spot was called Potters Island. But the latest geographic survey says it doesn't exist."

When he told me that, I knew I had done the right thing by bailing out, but I didn't say so. "What's next?"

"They're gonna dive anyway."

"Who's diving? Don't say Josh."

"They have a couple of local guys lined up. Josh wanted experienced divers who know the water. "

"What happened to the other crew, the ones we started with?"

"Skitch and them? Long gone. Salazar scared them off weeks ago."

"What are you using for a boat?"

"A boat called the Corsair. Salazar rented it out of the North

Star Marina. Says he doesn't need anybody but the two guys he hired and us. If it wasn't so crazy, I'd laugh."

"What do you think of all this?"

"I try not to think. Just trying to go along to get along while I'm still on the payroll."

I was glad not to be in his shoes. I understood his situation all too well. There were debts to pay, and I knew Lolly's part-time job didn't pay much. It was all on him.

When August rolled around, my focus was on Jamie. We knew we were at the end of one chapter, yet not quite ready to begin another. She said her farewells to life at home in fits and starts. She felt antsy, eager to move on to the next stage of her life, yet still afflicted with separation anxiety.

Our day-to-day conversations were easier when we focused on material considerations. We became obsessed with shopping for all the college must-haves. Jamie and her roommate had been in touch, texting about who would bring what, things like toaster ovens and coffee makers that could be shared.

The guest room became her staging area, where she evaluated items for her dorm, adding some, rejecting others, in an ongoing process that meant carrying dusty boxes down from the attic, buying odd bits of used furniture and kitschy decorations at yard sales, purchasing sheets and towels from Target, and then exchanging them for different ones. As the month progressed and the clutter built, I threatened to hold a sidewalk sale if she didn't get it sorted out.

Charlie kept out of her way, and out of mine, too, for the most part. He spent most of his time out of the house, hanging out at the pizza parlor or trolling the city streets and parks with his buddies, looking for the perfect ramp or railing to practice the latest skateboarding tricks. I tried not to think about it, except to pray for no broken bones.

⋙⋘⋙⋘

20

Summer was wetter than usual, with record levels of rainfall in August. Storms coming up the coast from Florida spoiled many vacation plans. Hurricane season on the East Coast is a given, but that year it got off to an early start. Local TV stations worked themselves into a frenzy over tropical storm Daisy, the latest storm set to hit the eastern seaboard at hurricane status — on the same day Jamie was scheduled to move into her dorm room at Cornell.

Jamie's last day at home broke gray and warm. I heard her moving around in her room when I woke at six. I knocked on her door and stuck my head in. She was already showered and dressed.

"What time did you get up?

"Five o'clock? Maybe earlier."

"It's not like you to be such an early bird."

"I know, but this feels like the first day of high school on steroids."

I gave her a hug. "Cornell is lucky to have you. Don't forget, you were in the top ten percent of your class."

"So was everybody else there. I'm not special."

She sat down at her dressing table. Our eyes met in the mirror and I blew her a kiss. "I can use some coffee. How about you?"

"Guess so." She began to brush her hair hard, something she did when she got nervous.

I could only guess what was in her heart. In the cold light of morning, a flash of anger ripped across my heart. I made for the stairs, determined that she wouldn't see me cry. Jack, wherever you are, you should be ashamed of yourself.

How he could walk away without a backward glance was hard for me to fathom. Jamie had been his angel. He called her his little pumpkin. Now she was the child of a single parent. But she bore it all silently and never once spoke against him. His face appeared before me and I willed it away. Twenty years of that life faded away—no, faded wasn't strong enough. It burned to the ground.

A rented van, filled with Jamie's new life, sat in the driveway. I'd never driven anything that big before, but I told myself the route would be easy once we got off the Northeast Extension of the Pennsylvania Turnpike. According to MapQuest, it was a five-hour drive from Philadelphia to Ithaca, New York. Routine pit stops and traffic setbacks might add another hour. Jamie and I reminded each other that we were leaving by 8:30 a.m. at the latest. According to the most recent communication from the Cornell Office of Student Living, freshmen were to arrive at their dorms no later than 3 p.m. on August 28.

We were in the van and on the road before nine o'clock, hurricanes be damned. Rush hour be damned as well. We inched west along the infamous Schuylkill Expressway, and it was close to ten o'clock by the time we pulled onto the Northeast Extension. The wind picked up. Hurricanes be damned! I thought again, but I got in the right lane and stayed there.

Jamie didn't have much to say. It felt as if my daughter had already made some sort of emotional transition into the future. Whatever that entailed, she wasn't sharing. Charlie sat in the back, passing the time with video games.

With both my passengers silently engaged in personal pursuits, I had only the English-accented voice of my GPS for company. I call her Fiona. Even when I answer her back, the conversations feel a little one-sided. As the highway stretched ahead straight and long, Fiona, too, fell silent.

The voice in my head took over. I was driving my daughter to a new world, a world I wouldn't be a part of. From now on, it would just be me and Charlie rattling around in our big old house in the city. His hormones were getting the best of him, I knew that.

I made a decision—I would try to find a new way to connect with my son. He needed space to explore the world on his own terms and grow into a young adult, but, within that space, I hoped we could learn a better way of communicating with each other.

Would it be a good time to let Charlie meet Greg? I daydreamed about inviting Greg over for a casual meal, maybe a Sunday barbecue once school started. Could the two of them be friends? Greg had a lot in his favor. When I mentioned having a friend who worked as a pilot, Charlie was not only surprised but also interested.

At Scranton, we left the turnpike for Route 81, and an hour later we were in New York State. I promised the kids we would stop for lunch in Binghamton. Though they claimed starvation, we agreed to bypass a sign that advertised buffalo burgers. We settled for pizza instead. Back on the road, traffic was light, and we made good time. The landscape spread out around us. Towns were fewer, separated by fields and farms, and livestock was plentiful.

We began to see signs for Ithaca, and I felt my pulse quicken. Soon we were there. The gates to the university were imposing. Inside, Cornell's array of buildings was daunting. Jamie used the campus map she had picked up a month earlier at freshman orientation to guide us to her dorm, Douglas Hall. Just as we parked, the clouds broke and rain pounded the van. We sat and waited for the rain to stop until a helpful parent gave us some trash bags to cover our stuff. We began to unload and make runs into the building, one person pushing the hand truck while another held the umbrella. The dorm lobby was a madhouse of freshmen and parents waiting for elevators. Frantic residence assistants were helping the newbies settle in before the upperclassmen arrived.

Jamie's dorm room was small but adequately furnished. Did she notice that her roommate had already laid claim to the room's choicest pieces of real estate? The bed nearest the window and more than half the closet space were already spoken for. She and Jamie hugged hello, but I sensed a battle for territory looming. I reminded myself that it wasn't my fight. They'd work it out one way or another.

Once we were done unloading, I perched on my daughter's bed. "What should we do now?" I asked.

Jamie shrugged.

Charlie, already squirming, nudged me in the back. "Mom, c'mon."

I tried to prolong the moment. "How about we go find a grocery store and get you some snacks?"

"I'll be OK, Mom. Really."

There was no ambivalence in my daughter's voice. At least she didn't roll her eyes. But one thing was clear—she wanted us to go. After hugs and kisses all around and a quick "Love you, Mom," it was over. Charlie grabbed my arm and led me out to the elevator.

Outside, the rain had slackened. We hadn't seen much of the grounds on the way in, so Charlie and I drove around campus to satisfy our curiosity. Even wet, the place was beautiful. Fall came early in Ithaca. It wasn't yet September, but some trees were already turning. It looked the very essence of the American college ideal.

There was a break in the clouds, and the sun peeked out as we drove near Cayuga Lake and parked. Charlie pointed to a historic marker that read, "Homestead of Joseph Cornell, founder of Cornell University." Charlie and I strolled through the botanical gardens, wandering in silence among the beautifully sculpted beds. He had grown plants for his science fair project, and I wondered if he was still interested in botany.

"Note to self. Next year I'd love to grow something more ambitious than petunias in the backyard. What do you think?"

"Good idea. Can we get out of here? I'm starved."

"Charlie, do you think Jamie might want to go to dinner with us?"

"No, Mom." He looked like he felt sorry for me. "I don't think so."

"OK, I get it."

We grabbed a burger at the first joint we could agree on. The food revived us a little, but I was glad I'd thought ahead to book us a room at a local motel. Exhausted, we checked in and settled down to watch some television. I woke in the middle of the night and threw a blanket over Charlie. Before I turned off the TV, the ticker at the bottom of the screen announced that the full force of Hurricane Daisy had turned at the Outer Banks and headed out to sea. That was good news for Pennsylvania, New Jersey, and Delaware, which were spared the worst of it.

Next morning, I checked my phone for messages. There were two, neither from my daughter. I fought off the urge to call her, texting instead to let her know we would be on our way home soon. I hoped her first night went well, wished her a good weekend, and invited her to call whenever the mood hit.

I listened to the first message, from my mother. She wondered if Jamie had gotten settled in OK. That was an easy one. I called her back and got her voice mail. "Everything is great, Mom. We're on our way back, I'll fill you in tonight."

The other message, left the night before, was from Harlan's wife, Lolly. "Have you heard from Harlan? I keep watching the Weather Channel. That storm moving up the coast has me scared. And with him out on the water? He's not the best swimmer.

Please, please call me."

I gave her an early call and explained that Daisy had gone out to sea and the worst was over. In the meantime, she'd heard from Harlan. They'd stayed off the water during the storm, he said. Even so, she was still glued to the Weather Channel, worrying now about a cold front heading south from Newfoundland.

"Right now, I'm close to two hundred miles from the Jersey shore, but if I hear anything I'll get in touch," I told her.

Outside, the sun was shining, but the air had an electric feel. We stopped to gas up, and Charlie and I went inside for snacks. TV screens above the counter were filled with images of floods and property damage along the Florida coast.

I got a short text message from Greg. *Hi Margo, hope your trip to Ithaca went well. Call me ASAP.*

While Charlie considered the snacks on offer, I called Greg. He was with Art. They were checking out the Lucinda.

"How is it at the shore?"

"Could have been worse. Some of the smaller boats that stayed in the water took a hit. But the Lucinda's a strong old tub. She's OK."

"Anything else?"

"Some debris washed up and there was beach erosion in some spots."

"Doesn't sound too bad." I told him about the call from Harlan's wife. "Have you heard anything about Salazar and Josh?"

"No, but Art saw our friend a day before the storm hit."

"What did he say?"

I heard muffled sounds, as if he had put his hand over the phone. He came back on. "Something may be up. Whatever it is, I want to go check it out. What about you?"

"What about me?"

"I bet you could use a break. Do you want to come down here?"

"You know it. See you tomorrow."

Hearing from Greg did it. I wanted to be there. I checked the time. It was close to noon, but if I could get back to Philadelphia before five, I could drop off the van and avoid paying for an extra day.

Mom's townhouse complex wasn't too far from the turnpike exit. She'd been angling for Charlie to come out and spend a day or two with her before school started. They had a good relationship, and, truth be told, he was her favorite. I decided now was the time to take her up on her offer.

Charlie didn't go for the idea, even though I bribed him with the newest version of his favorite video game, Call of Duty. "I love Gram but there's nothing to do there."

"Her pool is still open. You can swim."

"Yeah, but it's no fun sitting around there by myself."

"Maybe you'll meet somebody your own age."

"Doubt it."

"Too bad. You'll survive."

School didn't start until after Labor Day, and that was more than a week away. With Jamie at college and Charlie now a full-fledged inhabitant of Teen Planet, I had come to a realization. It was time for me to start building more of a life for myself. I made a judgment call and dropped him off for a few days with his grandmother.

Giddy with freedom, I dropped the van at the rental place just as it was about to close. I took a taxi home, grabbed a shower, and fell into bed, trying not to notice the emptiness of the house. Next morning, I was in such a hurry to leave that I almost didn't see the blinking message light on the house phone.

It was from Nina. She had called from New Zealand. She'd had a dream about Harlan. "I'm on a boat. Out on the water, it's foggy, gray, and ugly. There's a loud noise, and I see Harlan in the water. I call out to him but he doesn't answer. Then I woke up."

I tried to call her, but it went to voicemail. There was nothing to do about it, so I got in my car and headed east, toward the bridge and Long Beach Island, where Greg waited at the marina.

Stuck in the usual traffic on the causeway to the island, I flipped on the radio. The weather was the news story of the hour. Even with a weakened Daisy blowing out to sea, more than four inches of rain had fallen overnight. The local jock was busy with shout-outs to the Coast Guard and the local rescue and fire companies.

Storms in that area are no joke. After the rain stops, there's the storm surge to worry about. Long Beach Island is so narrow in some places that you could almost throw a rock from the bay-side and hit the ocean. It takes a beating from water on both sides. There was still plenty to clean up. Coming over the cause-way, I could see tangled mounds of debris washed up in the marshes.

At the marina, too, there was plenty of work to be done. Crews checked fishing boats at anchor for leaks and damage. According to Greg, it could have been much worse. But not everyone thought so. One captain complained to Art that his day-tripper business was hurting big time. "This has got to be my worst summer in ten years, and now we got more weather up the ass. Damn cold front moving down from Canada."

Before Daisy blew through, Art heard the locals snickering about the crazies diving out past the inlet. Inside my head, I re-visited Harlan telling me, "Josh and Salazar were going low tech with a couple of divers and a local charter boat captain."

"What's the name of the boat they're on?" Greg asked.

"Harlan said it's called the Corsair."

"I know the Corsair," Art growled. "Decent size, forty-footer. Guy named Richter owns it. Not much of a captain, in my book."

I remembered the Enigma, the ninety-foot techno craft riding sleek in the water while Harlan and I sunned ourselves on deck. Back then, only a few months before, everything was done by the book. But Skitch, the Enigma's captain, had pulled out of the project, taking his boat, his computers, and the electromagnetic sled with him. According to Nina, some of the backers had pulled out, too.

Things had changed, but one thing stayed the same—Salazar's obsession was still in high gear. Standard operating procedure was history. Harlan said they were winging it now, trying to find whatever they could before time ran out. Art had pals at the North Star Marina, including the owner. He called and asked for the boss. "Is the Corsair still in dock?"

"Nope. Richter took her out today."

"He should know better," Art said. "Even under the best conditions, Barnegat Inlet has some of the worst water on the Jersey coast."

Even so, Greg was game, ready to go out and take a look. "If the airfield wasn't so far from here, I'd take my Cessna up and buzz 'em. That would drive them crazy, wouldn't it?"

"Why do you want to go after them?" Art asked, dumbfounded. "Why do you care?"

"Just a feeling, that's all."

Art stared at him.

"OK, buddy? Tell me we can do this one."

Art shrugged. "I guess we can make it. "

"What about you, Margo?" Greg asked. "You want to do this?"

I checked in with my instincts, then with my gut. I visualized the calendar, focusing on a date two days from now, September 1. In that glimpse of the future, the clouds parted, and a ray of sun fell across the hull of the Lucinda. She was riding high. If she was still in one piece by then, chances were good we would be, too. It was madness, but whatever we were doing, it felt almost destined to happen. I nodded. "I want to see what they're doing out there as much as you do."

At the marina, most of the fishing boats were still at anchor, in no hurry to go back out. Art persuaded a couple of his guys, Pete and Mike, to come with us. He was the kind of boss people liked to say yes to. Within minutes, we were under way.

The Lucinda's outsides were scruffy, but up on the bridge she was state of the art. Her captain was happy to show her off. "I can't take all the credit," Art said. "Some of this is Greg's doing. He convinced me."

"You've got to have the latest equipment out here," I said.

"Right. Fishing's not the safest job in the world."

That was an understatement.

"Greg, show Margo what we've got."

Greg explained the binnacle. Art moved on to the electronic navigation display, with autopilot remote. "These are sensors for wind, depth, and speed." He ran his palm over the glossy wooden steering wheel. "My wife says I'm more at ease here at the wheel than home in my own bed."

I nodded as if I knew what I was seeing. Landlubber, I scolded myself. You don't know the difference between port and starboard. I could have used marine flash cards. But it wasn't completely foreign. I pointed to a half-empty bottle of Jack Daniels tucked in a corner. "For emergencies?"

Art laughed. "You never know."

The lesson continued when Art switched the radio to Channel 16. "This is what we call the universal line. I check in on this channel every so often just to see what's shaking," Art said. "But especially on a day like today. Boats need to make contact if there's a problem. Otherwise I stay on Channel 8 or Channel 9."

We pulled out into Barnegat Bay, heading to the inlet. Three boats moved toward us, making their way back in. The lead boat blew its horn. One short blast, then two long, a warning. On the second boat, a captain grabbed a bullhorn and called out, "More fog's rolling in."

Art tooted his horn and waved.

The water was choppy and the rocks on either side looked ominous. We passed through the inlet moving north toward the lighthouse.

"You said something back there that caught my notice," I said.

"What's that?" Art replied.

"That Barnegat Inlet is one of the riskiest spots on the East Coast. That true?"

Art laughed. "That's just to scare off the newbies."

Fingers crossed, I hoped he was telling the truth. If not, it had scared this newbie pretty good.

Art steered the Lucinda north, through a curtain of fog.

"Where's this coming from?" I asked.

"You can blame Canada," Art said. "When the water's warm and the air blows in cool, you've got perfect fog conditions."

Boats were still taking licks from the weather, and radio chatter was unceasing. Art listened and kept going.

I couldn't find my sea legs. Between the rocking boat, the heavy fog, and the gray water, I was getting dizzy.

Art saw the color of my face. "Sorry, kid. Never said going to sea was easy."

The Lucinda rose with a wave, lurched, and fell. Greg gave me a life jacket, and I strapped it tight. "Margo, don't worry," he said. "You're in good hands with Art. He's got salt in his blood."

After a trip to the head, my stomach had nothing left to heave. Greg passed me a Dramamine. I slumped on a bench outside the wheelhouse and dozed off. By the time I woke up, the Dramamine had started to take effect.

I remembered something Art needed to see. Some weeks earlier, Harlan got his hands on computer printouts from Salazar's project, prime target locations encoded with latitude and longitude. This was where Salazar and Josh decided to focus their dive. After all the work he and I had done searching for the treasure, Harlan wanted confirmation, so he sent them to me with a note asking me to "view" them. I never had the heart to do it, but I'd kept the copies just the same. Right or wrong, I felt some ownership. Maybe they would come in handy now for a different reason. I gave them to Art.

He took a passing look. "That's not far from where I was heading. We're in sync. Heard talk of some action up that way, near the reef."

The radio crackled to life. "This is Captain Don Richter on the Corsair. This is a Mayday, Mayday, Mayday. We need help. I repeat, this is Corsair. Our Call sign is D9146-5."

Art grabbed the microphone, but before he could respond, we heard someone else. "Corsair, this is the Coast Guard Atlantic

City Boat Rescue. What's your position?"

"Our position is 74'06 by 39'46. But we're drifting at one knot. Over."

"Roger, Corsair. Visibility is low. Due to weather conditions, we may be more than a half hour away. We'll direct any boats in the vicinity to come to your aid."

Art got on the radio. "This is the Lucinda; we're close by and can assist Corsair. Atlantic City Boat Rescue, come back."

"Lucinda, thanks for the assist. We will get someone en route, but the situation is poor and we have another rescue in progress."

Art acknowledged the transmission. The Coast Guard signed off, but he stayed on the channel, trying to raise the Corsair again and again until he got through. "Corsair, this is Captain Art Flannigan on the Lucinda. Give your location again. Over."

"Roger, Lucinda. We're one point five miles north of the lighthouse. At 39'47 off Island Beach.

"Corsair, can you shoot off a flare?" Art yelled.

The answer was muffled.

"Say again, Corsair," Art said, but there was no response.

Greg checked the radar. "They're north of where they were supposed to be. But something's weird." There were two green blips on the radar screen where I expected to see one. The first remained static. "That's the Corsair," Greg said. "I don't know what that other one is." The second blip was moving around the first one.

"Another boat's circling them," Art said.

Above the clamor, the Corsair's captain yelled, "We're taking on water."

"Captain, how many do you have on board?" Art asked.

"We got seven, two divers, three passengers, and me and my son."

"Roger, seven on board."

"Lucinda, the other boat is kicking up a wake. We're being swamped."

"Corsair, I repeat, can you shoot off a flare?" Art yelled.

Greg kept watch on the radar. "Art, what do you make of this?" The two blips on the screen merged.

"Oh, Christ. I don't like it."

Another voice filled the airwaves, a different voice, a panicked voice, a familiar voice. "Close the hatch. Keep him out of here."

"Could it be Salazar?" I asked the air.

Through the static, we heard a shot, then shouts and curses and another shot. It sounded like chaos. We heard a grinding sound, and then the Corsair's radio fell silent.

Art radioed the Coast Guard. "This is the Lucinda. Calling in a Mayday on the Corsair. Possible gunshots fired. Vessel with injured on board. North of Barnegat Lighthouse off Island Beach. We are en route to assist. Please acknowledge."

"This is the Atlantic City Coast Guard Station. Lucinda, what are your RDF coordinates?"

Art gave them our location and followed up with the Corsair's call sign and her last known latitude and longitude. Greg took the wheel while Art stayed with the radio, trying to raise the Corsair.

Up on deck, I squinted through binoculars, searching for a red flare, but nothing broke the monotony of sky and water. We moved north and east until the drone of an engine buzzed through the murk. The noise grew more distinct. "Can you see anything?"

"I hear it but I can't see it," Pete shouted.

We waved toward the sound, jumping and yelling as loud as we could, but we were as invisible to them as they were to us. The sound passed on, moving away, growing fainter. Only then could we see the glimmering orange tail lights of the Coast Guard helicopter heading south, toward Atlantic City.

Art raised the Boat Rescue station again for an update, but they were overloaded. "We have two boats heading out now," the dispatcher said. "We're waiting for the other two to come back. Over."

Art grimaced. "I know you're stretched thin, but can you send us some help?"

"Can't confirm a time, but you are next on the list. Over and out."

The rain subsided. The sky lightened as the storm moved out to sea. The Lucinda rolled with the waves. There was no word from the Corsair. We listened, alert for the thrum of a helicopter or the splash of a Coast Guard cutter. But there was only the sound of the waves slapping the sides of the boat.

Out on the horizon, a pale speck bobbed in the water. Pete saw it, too. He pointed at it, and the Lucinda headed that way. I held my breath, willing whatever it was to come closer. I watched it ride up a swell and then down. The Lucinda closed the gap. The speck grew larger and materialized into a raft, with something or someone attached. Two hands clutched the edge while a face bobbed above a red life vest.

"Man in the water," Mike yelled.

It was Harlan, barely holding on to the raft. Lolly's words echoed in my brain. He's not much of a swimmer.

Pete threw a line. It fell short.

Greg yelled out, "Art, we got a man in the water, off the starboard. Pull her around."

"Can't. Not enough room. It might send him under the rudder."

Greg threw a rope ladder over the side. Without a word, Pete clambered down. There was a thud and a groan as he slammed against the side of the boat.

On deck, Greg tied off another line and tossed out a life preserver. For once, the wind cooperated. It carried the line in the right direction, close enough for Harlan to grab. He gripped it and held on. Slowly and agonizingly, he pulled himself toward the Lucinda.

Greg lowered another line with a loop at the end. He grabbed the bullhorn. "Try to put this around your middle."

Harlan wrestled the line over his head, but his stamina was gone. It was up to us to pull him in. From somewhere, I found more strength than I ever knew I had. Little by little, Greg, Mike, and I pulled Harlan close enough so that Pete could draw him up and away from the swirling water.

Finally he was up and over and on the deck, sputtering and gasping. Harlan's lips were blue and he was shaking wildly.

"Get him something to drink," Pete yelled. "He's dehydrated."

I scrambled for water and held a bottle to his lips. He gulped it, then choked and sputtered, coughing up water and phlegm. I tucked a towel under his head.

Greg found a blanket and wrapped it around a shivering Harlan. He coughed again, spitting out more water, his chest heaving. After a few more moments, he started breathing more evenly. Exhausted, his eyes drooped and then closed, and then he was out. Several minutes later, his eyes opened, and he looked around, dazed.

"How long were you in the water?" Greg asked.

Harlan stared at Greg as if he were speaking a foreign language.

"He's in shock," Greg said. "Let's get him below."

Greg and Mike half dragged, half carried the shivering man below. Tucked into a bunk, Harlan conked out again.

"Maybe he shouldn't sleep," I said. "He may have a concussion."

We looked at each other, not sure what to do next. Greg slipped out and came back with the bottle of Jack Daniels. "Harlan, drink this," Greg said.

Harlan lifted his head. He spied the whiskey and opened wide. Greg dribbled some into his mouth. Harlan let out a sigh and sank back down.

Pete went in search of food, banging the hatch behind him.

At the sound, Harlan jerked upright, his eyes wild. "Josh," he yelled. "Watch out. He's got a gun!"

"Who?" Greg asked.

"He's shootin' up the boat."

"Who? Who's shooting?" I asked.

Not sure where he was, Harlan looked around. "Call Lolly. Where is she?"

I took his hand. "I'll call her. Don't worry."

Over the intercom, Art called Greg back to the bridge. Before he went, he handed me the bottle of Jack Daniels. I strongly considered taking a slug.

Off in the distance, there was a whirring sound. A break in the fog brought a welcome sight, an orange and gray helicopter working its way northward.

I left Harlan to his rest and went topside.

The radio crackled, and then I heard the chopper pilot say, "We have Corsair on radar. We have a basket ready. As soon as we make visual contact with survivors, a rescue swimmer will go into the water."

Art told the pilot we had one survivor onboard.

Greg called out, "Pete, keep your eyes peeled for anybody else in the water."

"Any location on the others?" the pilot asked.

"Negative," Art said.

The chopper moved off toward the horizon. Several minutes later, the pilot came back on. "We have a visual on another raft in the water."

The raft came into view. In it were two men, one with dark hair plastered to a pale forehead. He held another man with blood on his shirt. The helicopter circled around. It hovered -rescue basket at the ready. Wind blew the basket like it was made of paper. We watched transfixed as the rescue swimmer jumped into the water. With no motion wasted, he pulled the basket down and connected it with the raft. He and the other man hoisted the injured survivor into the basket. The swimmer gave the signal and the basket rose out of the water, swaying and spinning as it was pulled into the waiting chopper. The basket went down a second time, and the other man climbed in.

Once the two were safe, Greg continued to scan the radar for signs of the Corsair. The rest of us kept our eyes on the water. On the bridge, the chopper pilot's voice came through. "Lucinda, we've got Corsair in view. Will take over any other rescue from here. Return to dock. We'll have EMTs standing by. Where should they meet you?"

That sounded like an order.

Art gave our destination, Barnegat Marina. He turned Lucinda around, and we headed back in.

As promised, paramedics waited at the marina. No sooner did Art tie up the Lucinda than they were up the gangplank. One of the EMTs who carried Nina out of the hotel a few months earlier helped get Harlan off the boat. For these guys, human catastrophe is all in a day's work.

I clambered into the ambulance with Harlan, and Greg promised to follow in the car. Siren blaring, we headed off the island. Soon we pulled up to the emergency entrance of Ocean County Memorial, the same hospital where Nina was treated. With the emergency room all but empty, the doctor attended Harlan right away. His vitals checked out pretty well, but they started an IV and decided to keep him overnight for observation. The patient didn't object.

Once he was settled in, Harlan borrowed my phone to call Lolly. I went into the hall to give him some privacy. From the tone of his voice I could hear his concern for her. She must have felt the same. By the end of the conversation, it was settled. She would be on the next flight north to take care of her man and make sure he got home safe. Harlan was just finishing up some broth and crackers when Greg showed up. He told us that Art had contacted the Coast Guard and found out that the captain of the Corsair was going to be all right. Harlan begged us to stay with him until visiting hours were over. We would have stayed anyway, since we wanted to know what happened on the Corsair. And Harlan wanted to talk.

"The day started out bad. Josh and Salazar were at each other's throats. That's nothing new. Been like that since Skitch and them left. But today was different.

"Even with the weather so bad, Salazar wanted to go out. He

said we could dive and nobody would see us because of the fog. Josh said that was crazy. When the divers showed up, there was some tension. I didn't feel real good about them. I said so, but Salazar told me it was none of my business. The divers balked about the conditions, but Salazar doubled his offer and they agreed.

"So we go out. The fog gets thicker. Don, he's the captain, he's locked in on the coordinates we gathered from my dowsing and the remote viewing you did, Margo. Luckily, where they planned to dive, the water wasn't so deep. But even with the special lights, it must have been pitch-dark down there. How they could see anything, I'll never know. I'll give them this, though—the way they hit the water, they were pros. They're down there maybe thirty minutes before they signal Salazar to let him know they found something. Topside, the one pulls out a few gold coins he's got tucked up inside his suit. He gives them to Salazar. The other one brings up something in a net."

"What was it?" I asked.

Harlan shook his head. "Salazar wouldn't let me anywhere near it, but next thing I know, he's real excited, like a crazy man. He's crouched over this thing, working at it, scraping at the muck and getting nowhere. Then he yells, "Give me your knife.""

I pictured Harlan's big Bowie knife.

"So I hand it over. That's when I get close enough to see what he's got. It looks like a brick, but a brick covered in barnacles, maybe fifteen inches wide, twelve inches deep. Splinters of rotten wood are sticking out from bands of corroded metal. The whole thing is held together by bronze corner pieces."

"Was it a chest?" Greg asks.

Harlan shrugged. "Salazar takes the knife, starts chipping away at it. A piece broke off and fell to the deck. When I go to reach for it, he yells at me not to touch it. Too late, I picked it up anyway."

"Where was Josh?"

"Josh was holding the flashlight for Salazar. He grabs the broken piece out of my hand, holds it to the light and puts it in a bag. I could have swore it glittered green right then."

An emerald?

"Next thing we know, we hear this boat circling around. When it comes in closer, we see it's one of them fancy speedboats like on TV, a cigarette boat. It pulls up alongside the Corsair. One of our divers gives the other boat a signal, and all hell breaks loose. Out of nowhere, a guy jumps on our boat."

"Who was he?"

"Damn if I know. Dark beard, bushy eyebrows. From the sound of it, he knew Salazar. He knew him pretty good. He says, 'You stole my map. You stole the gold.'"

"Salazar still has my knife, and he waves it at the guy. 'Your map?' he says. 'How is it yours? I paid you for it. We did the work. We found the spot. Your map was worthless. It was nothing!"

"The other guy pulls out a gun and points it at Salazar. The gun goes off, Salazar ducks and the bullet goes through the window and hits the captain. Richter loses control of the boat. I drop out of sight and keep my head down. When it got quiet, I peeked around. The guy starts shooting up the equipment. A bullet hits the radio. We were knocked out."

"Where was Josh?"

"Hiding out below. Don't get me wrong, I hid out, too."

I shook my head, hardly believing what I was hearing.

"The boat took on water. Her generator failed. After that, the guy reloaded and started in shooting again. The only thing to do was jump."

"What about the others?"

"The divers got out of there fast. I think they swam to the other boat. I had a life jacket on and went over the side. Somebody threw more rescue gear into the water. A raft banged me in the head and I grabbed for it."

"What about Josh and Salazar?" I asked.

"Last I saw of Josh he was hanging onto a cooler, floating out to sea."

"What about the guy with the gun?" Greg asked. "You sure you didn't hear a name?"

Harlan scrunched up his forehead. "I think Salazar called him something like Alvarez."

"Alvarado," Greg yelled. He smashed his fist into the plastic bed stand. Glasses and utensils spilled to the floor. "I knew it."

A nurse came running. She looked in and shushed us. "Sorry," I said to her. "Just got a little excited. We're OK."

Greg got up. "I gotta call Flynn, right now." He went out into the corridor.

I quizzed Harlan about Alvarado. "Did he mention anybody named Steve?"

"Not that I recall. He just threatened Salazar. Said he'd cheated him out of the gold."

"Did you ever see an old map?"

"More times than I wanted to. Give me some paper."

I found paper and a pen. Harlan scribbled out a claw-shaped isle off the coast of a larger land mass. "Too bad this is what they were fightin' over."

It looked like the one Albert drew at my house that night. "Was it Kidd's map?"

"It might have been Kidd's map or maybe it wasn't. Who knows? It doesn't really matter now. The joke was on us. We chased our tails until we found out where it used to be."

"What do you mean used to be?"

Harlan winced like it hurt him to say it. "That island has been underwater since 1962, when a hurricane swamped her."

"Poor you," I said, patting Harlan's shoulder. "That was some bad day you had!"

"Poor stupid me! Out in that damn water, I started thinking about who would come to my funeral. Then I felt bad that Lolly'd have to do all that work by herself." Harlan slumped back on the bed, exhausted. "One thing's for certain, I'll never complain about a bad day for the rest of my life."

Harlan drifted off and I kept watch. I must have dozed, too. A voice calling my name woke me. I looked up to see Greg at the door. "Margo," he whispered. "Come quick."

On a television screen near the nurses' station, a reporter promised breaking news just ahead. And there it was. First, we heard the captain's son being interviewed about his harrowing ordeal onboard the Corsair and the heroic rescue of him and his father by the Coast Guard. That was followed by footage of a battered and handcuffed Alvarado being marched out of the Atlantic City Coast Guard station by New Jersey State Police. In the background, I thought I saw someone familiar. "Isn't that Flynn?" I asked.

Right before they switched to the weather, the screen flashed photos of Josh Bruckner and Dr. Victor Salazar. Above their heads, the word "Missing" stood out in bold yellow letters.

Greg called Detective Flynn for the second time and left another message. He told him we had another eyewitness here at the hospital.

Detective Flynn returned Greg's call. That's when we heard the rest of the story. After the Coast Guard got the survivors out of the water, they took control of the Corsair. Alvarado tried to escape in the cigarette boat, but it ran out of fuel. When they caught him it was dead in the water. The Coast Guard put Alvarado in restraints and towed both boats to shore.

Early the next morning, Josh's body washed ashore south of Harvey's Cedars. I was surprised by how bad I felt. Salazar's whereabouts remained a mystery. Perhaps he was a strong swimmer and made it back to shore. Perhaps not.

I was eager to know what they found on the Corsair. Art used his connections to the local police, and we found out that whatever the divers had brought up from the ocean floor was missing. The gold coins and the strange encrusted brick were gone.

21

A couple of weeks later, Alisha and I faced each other across my kitchen table. I'd asked her to come over to read my cards.

"I will if you want me to, but take a look at this first." She dug out the chart she'd cast for me on my last birthday. "Last night, I took another look at it."

"That's so nice of you."

The chart had new information she'd added in green ink. "Look at this. You're at some sort of turning point. I think you knew that."

"I'm trying to take this all in stride, like a grown-up."

"Margo, don't be so philosophical. This is important. I see a moon in your return chart. Before you can move on, it's important to see where you've been. The good news is that Mercury is retrograde until the end of October. There's still a chance to step back and review. Until you do, making any new plans will make as much sense as combing your hair in a wind storm."

At the mention of weather, I tried to smile. But part of me wanted to cry. Thinking back to the previous October, I remembered the moon, full and bright, the night Greg and I met. I wanted to understand what this whole year had been about. It felt like the dream that evaporates just as you wake up.

That night I sat up late at my desk, rereading old news stories on the computer, piecing things together. The house was quiet. Charlie was in bed. A breeze wafted through an open window. Outside, a stray cat yowled. Another answered and together they began a raucous duet that only ended when a neighbor threw water at them.

I dozed. When I awoke, it felt as if someone had given me friendly advice as I slept. It was a good feeling, as if I wasn't alone. When I got up to close the back window, I felt a hand on my shoulder. For a split second, I sensed my father there with me, his presence fleeting but real. A voice in my ear whispered, "Go on."

OK, Dad, go on. But where?

Mom suggested that I talk to a career counselor. "Margo, nowadays there's no shame in starting over," she told me. "People go back to school, get retrained all the time. I heard that being a court reporter pays pretty well. If you need a loan for the tuition, I'd be happy to help."

"Thanks, Mom. I'll give it some thought."

The Halloween season was once again looming large on the Mediums Guild calendar. That meant paying work, but I didn't feel ready to dive back into that. Part of me was ready to move ahead, yet my thoughts were still on pine forests and darkened beaches. Something was drawing me back to the mysteries of Long Beach Island.

The full moon would rise on October 28th. Something told me that was when I needed to be there, but I didn't want to go alone. Greg seemed like the most obvious companion. I called to ask him but he had a big job lined up in West Virginia that week and would be out of town.

When I hung up the phone, I saw Charlie standing there, looking at me. What he did next floored me. "I'll go with you, Mom," he said.

I wanted to come around the table and give him a huge hug.

But I played it cool. We were in new territory. At thirteen and a half, Charlie was sprouting hairy evidence of adolescence. I told myself I shouldn't let it scare me. On the inside, he might still be the same, even if the outside changed from one day to the next. Maybe it didn't matter. Now that it was just the two of us, the important thing was having a chance to connect in a new way. "Thanks, Charlie," I said, barely containing the tears that wanted to flow. "I really appreciate it."

October 28th fell on a Thursday. As luck—or fate—would have it, the following day, Friday, was a school in-service day, a day off for the students. As soon as Charlie came home from school that Thursday, I hustled him into the car and we drove across the bridge into New Jersey, heading toward the ocean. There wasn't much traffic going in that direction, and we arrived at our destination in just over an hour.

Without summer people, the island was quiet. Some of the stores were dark, but we strolled around until we found a surf shop still open for business. Together we spent a pleasant hour checking out the surfing gear and skateboards. Not surprisingly, Charlie found the board of his dreams. Maybe I was feeling grateful for the company. Whatever the reason, Charlie walked out with the new skateboard tucked under his arm. It would have been fun to take him to Dave's Clam Bar over on the bay, but it was closed for the season. We found a seafood restaurant in Surf City called Neptune's Table and enjoyed a meal of fried shrimp instead.

It was almost dark by the time we finished dinner. The evening breeze still held some of summer's softness. We found the car and drove away from the stores and tourist hotels. Except for the occasional jogger, the streets were empty.

"Mom, where to now?"

"There's someone I want you to meet."

We parked near the Barnegat Marina and got out. I breathed in a pungent fragrance, a rich mix of seaweed, rank bait, and wet wood that Art called the "perfume of the sea." Charlie was having a good time looking at all the sport boats parked side by side. He read out some of their whimsical names, and we laughed at a few of the sillier ones. Moving out on the pier to where the commercial fishing boats were docked together, I looked for the familiar green hull of the Lucinda. I spotted her name on the bow in big white letters. "There she is. There's the Lucinda!"

I blew her a kiss. "Never knew I could learn to love a boat," I said. "Your grandfather would have loved to take a ride on her, wouldn't he?"

"So would I," Charlie said. "That would be awesome."

"We can't do it now, but I bet we could make it happen soon. Her captain loves nothing better than to show off his boat."

The next thing I knew, Charlie was wandering away.

"Where are you going?"

He was walking slow, eyes on the ground, picking up stones as he went, saving some, rejecting others, until both his hands were full. I trailed behind as he headed toward open space at the far end of the pier. Once he found the right spot, he planted his feet firmly and got to work, skipping stones, one by one, across the bay with an expression on his face that was pure seven-year-old.

What the hell. I found a few skimmers of my own. It brought back old times as we stood side by side in a silent challenge match to see whose stone could skip furthest. Once our supplies were exhausted, Charlie declared it too close to call. Fair enough. His stones skipped the most times, but one of mine skipped the furthest. We laughed and gave each other a high five.

Across the open water, lights twinkled on the mainland. The moon came up, bathing the bay in a rich, mellow light, and I remembered why we were there. "That's what you call a full moon," I said.

"Cool! It looks so close you could touch it. Wish I had a telescope."

"Tonight I don't think you need one," I said. We stood transfixed until a barking dog broke the spell.

It was getting late. "Come on," I said. "There's one more spot I want to visit."

We moved toward the end of the island. We were on the ocean side now. With Barnegat Lighthouse in view, we made our way up the path to the beach. Charlie kicked off his sneakers, enjoying the feel of the cool sand between his toes. I had brought a blanket and spread it out between the dunes and the sea. As we sank down on it, Charlie stifled a yawn.

"Are you tired?"

"No, I'm fine, Mom. Look over there." He pointed at a passing craft.

The lights on the vessel wavered back and forth on the water as though in communication with the shore. Behind the dunes, a whistle piped three times. The hairs on the back of my neck stood up. I turned toward the sound but there was nothing there. I grabbed Charlie's arm. "Did you hear that?"

"Probably just some kids pranking us."

The tide came in. A gull skimmed the surf and flew off with a small prize. The wind picked up. I zipped my sweatshirt higher and pulled up the hood.

We sat quietly, taking in the moon, the ocean, and the stars. Near the water's edge, a swirl of sand blew up, spiraling into a column illuminated with an eerie greenish glow. I looked at Charlie. He gripped the blanket, his eyes like saucers. The moon shone down and the essence became brighter, pulsing before our eyes. Like in a dream where you try to run and can't, we were unable to move. While we watched, a figure materialized, and the high, bright sound of the whistle piped again. Then silence. The spirit vanished with the tide.

Charlie jumped to his feet. I grabbed the blanket, and we high-tailed it back to the car. I was ready to go home, feeling like I had some answers even if I didn't know exactly what the questions were.

In silence, we crossed the causeway that would take us off the island. Soon Charlie was dozing. I turned on the radio for company until the Philadelphia skyline came into view. When I dug in my handbag for money for the bridge toll, Charlie woke. He turned to me. "That was real wasn't it, Mom?"

"Yes, I think so. Were you scared?"

"No. Well, maybe just a little. I don't know if I'll tell my friends about it."

"That's up to you, Charlie. I'm just glad you were there to see it with me."

"Me too."

❧❧❧❧

22

After months in the cold case file, the murders of Steve and Carla moved to the top of the police agenda. Detective Flynn became a dervish of activity. He went back to the Evidence Room. Shell casings found on the Corsair matched up with the one they'd found in Steve's car. Other evidence turned up. Phone records and credit card bills put Alvarado in New Jersey at the time the couple disappeared. After the state crime lab matched Alvarado's thumbprint to one found on the rear view mirror in Steve's car, he was charged with homicide and held without bail as a flight risk. The trial might be held within the coming year.

Greg and his family could finally begin the process of healing. Grief counselors offered their services, and Carla's ex-husband allows their children to spend plenty of time with Greg's family.

And where am I? It turns out I didn't need the skip tracer to track down Jack after all. He realized that if he wanted to marry Audre McArthur, artist, girlfriend, and mother of his third child, Dayton Jacob Fellshur, born September 29, he would also need a divorce from the wife he already had. These developments came to light two weeks after Halloween, in an interesting phone call from Vancouver.

"Jack, divorce is fine with me," I told him. "But first you need to repay the money you took from your kids. Then we'll talk. There's also the little matter of child support, which is in arrears."

I was proud of my composure. I had kept the conversation businesslike, almost cordial. Meanwhile, I realized that divorce was not only acceptable to me but, just maybe, it was the jolt I needed to get me unstuck.

By the end of the week, a check drawn on a Canadian bank arrived via FedEx. The amount, five thousand dollars, is only the first installment on the twenty-three thousand he made off with. The check was cosigned by a David McArthur of McArthur Insurance of Vancouver, British Columbia. Something tells me Audre's mother and father would like their grandchild to be the son of legally married parents before he's old enough for pre-school.

Considering everything that's happened, things are the same and yet different. I still check in with Jerry and show the odd townhouse or condo when he needs me to. But my heart isn't in it.

Greg and I continue to see each other. He and Charlie have become good friends. Recently, Greg, Art, and company took Charlie out for a jaunt on the Lucinda. The water was choppy that day, so I stayed on shore, but Charlie had a blast.

Jamie is due home for Thanksgiving break, and I can't wait to see her. She is all but through her first semester at Cornell and doing well. She says it's easier than she expected.

I have a surprise for her, too. I can't wait tell my daughter that one of us ended up at community college after all. Starting in January, I'll be teaching a course in tarot reading, palmistry, and a variety of other techniques as part of the school's popular adult continuing education program.

Come spring, I'm booked to work a weeklong cruise to Mexico as part of the entertainment. I got the gig as a result of one of my TV appearances. The De Mateo sisters, the two New Jersey psychics I met last February, called out of the blue. They asked me to join them for something billed as "A Cruise into the Unknown." I'll be lecturing on remote viewing and the realm of the intuitive and perhaps doing a demonstration or two. It sounds like fun, but one issue did give me pause. When I mentioned it, they swore that nobody gets seasick on those big cruise ships, but I've already laid in a supply of Dramamine, just in case.

THE END

Lee Fishman arrived in Philadelphia as a college student and fell in love with city living. After spending several years as a librarian at the Free Library of Philadelphia's Central Library, she found her true calling, writing. With a passion for unraveling mysteries, she'd love to be a detective in her next life.

Mediums Guild is her second novel. Her first, *Edge of a Dream* depicts challenges newly arrived immigrants face in adjusting to a new life in America.

For more information visit her website
www.leefishman.net